The -30- Press Quarterly:
Issue 3

Cover artwork by Ashley Franz Holzmann. Follow him over at asforclass.com *or on Instagram* @AsForClass.

Interior design by Ashley Franz Holzmann

Edited by Kristopher J. Patten

30press.com

You're beautiful readers. Keep reading. We'll never stop writing.

Table of Contents

Introduction From The Editors   1

Life is Beta   5

The Tale of Roly Poly   9

A Tunnel In Vietnam   17

A Man In My Backyard   57

EMERGENCY ALERT   83

Patient 314   119

The Black Library   201

Mister Pleasant's House For Broken Children   219

I Was Almost Involved In A School Shooting   239

Torn Apart By A Serial Killer   245

About The Creators   267

Introduction From The Editor

─────────

I started putting the NoSleep eBook together almost exactly five years ago. The first few were not great; I had taken on a project I really knew nothing about and had given myself the extra difficult task of coming up with cover art for the damn thing. If you look back in the archives on nosleepebook.com, you can get an idea of my troubles; PDF files that display in almost 50 point font, a version of the NoSleep logo that has been edited in MS Paint for a cover, and an interior format that is inconsistent from one story to the next. Over the next few years, I taught myself more about ebook development and relied on the NoSleep community for cover art. This is when the NoSleep eBook really started taking off. Instead of a few interested Redditors, we began to reach new audiences from different corners of the internet. I also started taking the ebook more seriously as a way to celebrate authors and help their careers as professional writers.

One step we've taken to that end is by making the NoSleep eBook into a legitimate publication as the -30- Press Quarterly. While the ebook version will remain free forever on nosleepebook.com and other book sites, physical copy sales of the Quarterlies go right back into the NoSleep writing community. From paying for professional editors and layout designers to providing free books and monetary prizes for the monthly NoSleep writing contest, we're making that happen.

Things are certainly different than when I started this back in 2012, but the community aspect remains a staple. This book wouldn't be successful without the amazing authors who pour their psychic energy into their stories or the readers who consume that nightmare fuel. Together, we can dump our weird brew of NoSleep horror into the mainstream. As of this writing, there are a few projects in the works to do just that. So let's get freaky.

Thank you for your support over the last 5 years. Here's to 5 more!

Kristopher J. Patten
Chief Science Officer
-30- Press
November 19, 2017
30Press.com

January
—2017—

Strange Experiences With An App Called Life is Beta

By Ha-Yong Bak

I woke up to the sight of my 2 year old son tapping away on my cell phone. I put out my hand and, after a couple of whines and tears, he handed the phone back to me. I checked my phone to make sure he didn't make any phone calls or texts. He hadn't made any embarrassing faux pas for me but I did see an app called *Life is Beta* on my home screen. The icon was just a circle inside of a solid blue square.

I put my phone in my pocket and got ready for work. After I ate my breakfast, I kissed my wife and son goodbye and walked to the subway station. The ride to work usually took around 40 minutes so I turned my phone on and clicked on the new app.

The first thing that threw me off was the fact that there wasn't a loading screen or anything. It just automatically jumped to a character floating in the middle of the screen.

Even stranger was the fact that the character looked just like me in every way. Even the face was exactly like mine, right down to the two pimples I found on my forehead that morning. Feeling a bit curious, I tapped on the screen and he started to walk towards the right. The screen turned black for a second and, when it bounced to the next screen, I almost dropped my phone. He was sitting in a subway car and playing on his cell phone.

After a couple of seconds, the subway in the phone stopped and a handful of people entered and exited. Right as a lady in a yellow coat started to get on the subway, my character started to flash and the scene froze. I tapped on the character and he got up and bolted out of the subway. I tried to tap outside the subway but the screen wouldn't pan. The lady that boarded the subway started to pace around the subway, but no one really paid her any notice.

After she walked around three times, she started to shake and drew two guns from her purse. The subway filled with the chaos of blood and running passengers as she emptied both magazines. When she ran out of bullets, she took a large knife out of her purse and stabbed herself in the chest.

The screen on my phone went dark and I felt the subway come to a stop. I looked up and saw a woman in a yellow coat board the subway. Without a second thought, I ran out of the subway and caught a cab.

As soon as the flag dropped, I started searching the news to see if there were any recent shootings in my area. After a while I started to relax and, by the time I got to work, I was laughing to myself about how dumb I was for listening to a stupid game. My phone rang the moment I sat down. My wife.

"Please, please, please, just answer the phone."

"Hello?" I answered. I could hear her breathe a sigh of relief.

She told me that she was watching the news when she heard about a lady shooting up the subway I usually rode to work. I couldn't respond. I felt my hand start to shake and my throat close up. I managed to croak out an "I love you" and an "I'll call you back" before hanging up.

I turned on the app again and saw that my character was floating in the middle of the screen. I kept tapping at him, but the screen would not change. I clicked the home button to my phone and tried deleting the app, but my phone did not give a delete option. Frustrated and scared shitless, I just shoved my phone back into my pocket and tried to forget about what happened this morning.

I didn't check the app again until around 2pm. I felt my phone vibrating so I checked it and saw a notification from *Life is Beta*. It said "New Experience" next to the logo; I didn't want to but I clicked on the box in case it was trying to warn me again.

When I opened up the app, I saw an animated version of my manager typing on his laptop. The view shifted to where I was looking at my manager's laptop.

On his screen was a lady holding up a man by his hair. I could see what my manager was typing out: "Use your fingers to dig his eyeballs out."

The woman held up 3 fingers on her other hand and my manager went back to typing. "300 hundred for that? You're fucking nuts. $200 and we have a deal."

She nodded her head and using her index finger and thumb started to dig out the man's left eyeball.

I clicked on the home button before I saw anything else, but once I closed out of the app I got another notification. It simply said, "Call 911."

I ran to the restroom where I dialed 911 and explained my manager's extra-corporate affairs to the dispatcher. I requested that I stay anonymous and hung up the phone.

Fifteen minutes later, my manager was taken out of his office by two police officers. He was pleading with them, telling them it was all a misunderstanding, but we could hear the sounds of a man screaming in pain from our manager's laptop.

That was the last notification I received today but I will let you know if I receive anymore.

Stay safe everyone, and be careful with who you trust.

The rest of Ha-Yong Bak's *Life is Beta* saga is available in his forthcoming short story compilation. You can find it and help fund its creation on Indiegogo at https://www.indiegogo.com/projects/life-is-beta-books-horror#/

If You Find A Book Called The Tale of Roly Poly, Don't Open It, Don't Read It!
By J.M. Flynn

The book doesn't look particularly creepy. There are no ominous images on the cover, no words of foreboding. There is only plain red canvas with gold letters that read: *The Tale of Roly Poly.*

I had never seen the book until Ginny pulled it from her collection on the shelf. It may have been left by the previous owners; we had only moved to this neighborhood a month ago.

Ginny was already snuggled under the covers when I opened the book. At six, she was starting to read and never needed to be coaxed to bed if I promised her a story. Well, almost never. Princesses were her new obsession and we'd covered most of the classics like *Sleeping Beauty* and *Cinderella. The Tale of Roly Poly* was a departure from the usual set list.

"Are you sure you want this one, Pumpkin?"

Ginny yawned, "Yes, Daddy."

I shrugged and began to read.

There were two boys,
two children like you.
One was called Jack,
the other was Hugh.
The boys sat in their room

for there was nothing to do.

They were so bored,

a common bugaboo.

The book contained a simple illustration of two boys in a bedroom decorated with baseball-themed wallpaper.

They thought and they thought,

they huffed and they puffed,

until Hugh said, "Phew!

Enough is enough!

Let's play a game!

We'll upend this loose end."

"I know!" said Jack.

"I'll call on my friend."

I groaned internally and hoped that Ginny would fall asleep soon. This wasn't exactly Dr. Seuss.

Jack took the book

and said the words written down:

"Come out, come out,

you silly old clown."

With a whish and a whoosh,

and fizzle and pop,

Roly Poly arrived

with a great big plop.

There was an enormous figure that dwarfed the two boys next to him. The man was dressed as a traditional pantomime clown, complete with a ruff, white make-up, and garish red lips.

"How do?" said the clown. "I've come to play."

"You?" said Hugh. "Oh dear, holy moley!"

"Don't be scared," declared Jack.
"It's just Roly Poly."
"What shall we do?" said Hugh, all a flutter
as he pulled out his toys from the bedroom clutter.
There were many games of various names,
all wires and megawatts,
a singing machine, a trampoline.
There were even two robots.
"Oh, no!" said the clown.
"This will not do!
Let's play some real games.
Ditch this techno voodoo.
Come with me and you'll see
my home is quite grand.
You'll have all that you need
in Topsy-Turvy Land."
The two boys nodded,
their hearts filled with glee.
They took the clown's hand
and counted three Mississippi!
Hugh and Jack closed their eyes
as the world twirled and twirled.
They whooped with joy
as a new land was unfurled.
The clown's home was quite splendid,
full of candies and treats. The fun never ended;
no parents, no chores, no bedtime or rules,
no horrible homework from boring old schools.

The boys played and played and all three were glad

until one fateful day when the clown became sad.

"What's wrong, Roly Poly?

Is there something we can do?"

the boys asked and asked

but their worry still grew.

"Oh, dear," the clown mumbled.

"My apologies, most humbled.

I'm just very hungry,"

as his large tummy rumbled.

"Would you like chocolate or chips or gooey cream cake?"

"We have hot dogs and ice-cream and every milkshake."

But the clown shook his head

for his belly did ache.

Then he grabbed little Hugh,

"A fine meal you will make!"

My stomach flipped when I saw the illustration on the next page. I shut the book immediately.

"Let's call it a night, Princess."

Ginny tried to protest but her eyelids were heavy with sleep.

"What happened to the boy, Daddy?"

"I'll tell you tomorrow."

I kissed Ginny on the forehead and turned out the light.

I went downstairs and poured a large glass of wine before reopening the book. On the page, the clown held one of the boys above his head and had bitten into the child's left side. His teeth tore away chunks of pink flesh as blood trickled down his ruby-stained lips. The boy's eyes were shut, his tear-streaked face frozen in an agonized expression. Spurred on by morbid curiosity, I continued to read.

Roly Poly grabbed the boy and held him aloft.

He took a big bite—sweet Hugh was so soft.

He gnashed and he gnawed, he chewed and he slurped,

and when nothing was left, the clown loudly burped.

He looked around; there was no Jack to be found.

The boy had run; the chase had begun.

Jack ducked and he darted, he ran and he ran.

Roly Poly just chuckled, "Come back here, young man!

This place is large; indeed, it does sprawl!

There is no way out; no way at all."

The clown was quite right for, try as he might,

Jack rushed to escape but there was no exit in sight.

The boy grew tired, his breath became weary.

Roly Poly caught up, sounding quite cheery,

"You're tougher than most—you, I will cook."

And he hung the boy up on an old meat hook.

The child screamed and he shouted, "You great fat liar!"

The clown licked his lips as he stoked the big fire.

I turned to the last page. The boy dangled from a hook over a gaping fire pit. Parts of his skin were cracked and blackened as the flames licked his small frame. The clown prodded the fire with a stick in one hand. The other hand waved to the reader as a maniacal smile revealed two rows of long, sharp teeth.

The clown was so happy, this sweet meat was a treat.

Hail to the chef—Bon appétit!

The book ended there. I felt the bile rise in the back of my throat. What kind of twisted individual wrote something like this? It was probably a desperate hack writer looking for some notoriety. Whatever it was, it left a bad taste in my mouth. I finished my wine and threw the book in the trash.

I woke up early the next morning and took the paper lying on the doorstep. It was Sunday but I never liked sleeping in. I put on a pot of coffee and glanced at the headline on the countertop. My heart froze.

Fifth Anniversary of Local Boys' Disappearance

Hundreds have taken part in a remembrance rally to mark the fifth anniversary of the disappearance of brothers Hugh and Jack Healy. The brothers, aged eight and six, were abducted from their home on January 07, 2012. Police have issued a fresh appeal for information this weekend [story continued on page 3].

I ran outside and removed the cover of the trash can. Perhaps whoever wrote that book knew something about the boys' disappearance. At the very least, I needed to report this sick material to the police. My stomach lurched as I regarded the contents of the can. The book was gone.

A primal panic rose in my chest as I dashed upstairs to Ginny's bedroom. A single piece of paper lay atop the crumpled sheets of her empty bed.

Ginny picked a good book,
a true tale to excite,
but Dad did not like it;
he thought it was trite.
He stopped the story at the moment of glory,
"Oh no, not for you! This part is unfit!"
The clown did not like that,
not one little bit.
So Roly Poly told Ginny,

who was ever so skinny,
"Let's have some fun!
We'll show that old ninny."
And now Ginny plays
in the land Topsy-Turvy.
Full of sugar and spice
And all things that are girly.
While the princess holds court
in dresses of satin,
the clown simply smiles,
"She'll do; she'll fatten."

It's been one week since Ginny went missing. I've given the page to the cops but they're as baffled as I am. Every hellish verse of that awful book is seared into my skull. I can't sleep. I can't eat. I'm typing this as both an appeal and a warning. If you find this book, don't open it, don't read it. Call the police. A child's life may depend on it.

I Saw Some Strange Stuff In A Tunnel In Vietnam
By Conor Murray

———————

I've kept my mouth shut for almost 50 years; why the hell would I start talkin' now? Well, friends, terminal cancer will do that to you. Shit you thought you'd take to the grave suddenly becomes shit you desperately wanna tell someone... anyone. I won't bore you with a long lament about my time in Vietnam. It was shitty. It was shitty for everyone involved, but it was particularly shitty for me as I was 5'3.

If you don't know what being particularly short during the Vietnam war entailed, let me fill you in. You arrive in country and a senior officer points at you and says, "You'd be a good fit for the tunnel commandos, wanna join?" Now, technically, it's a question as service in those platoons was voluntary. But it sure as shit didn't feel like a question... it felt like an order.

And so that was my burden for the war, to be a "tunnel rat", climbing down into deep, dank, dangerous tunnels filled with people and animals who wanted to kill me. Usually, we operated in the huge Cu Chi tunnel complex near Saigon, but not on that day; on that day we were ordered to investigate a tunnel complex way up north, west of Da Nang. Two of us were sent into the tunnel, myself and Benoit. Now, usually, black guys managed to avoid becoming tunnel rats on account of them being so tall but Benoit was burdened with the double misfortune of being short and

17

black during the Vietnam war, a curse I wouldn't wish on my worst enemy.

I was first into the hole and Benoit followed, we both had our Model 39's, some C4, our wits, and not much else. If you're wondering why we carried the small caliber Model 39's, go fire a Colt .45 in a narrow tunnel and come back to me. The last guy who tried that got a ticket home with blood pouring out of his ears.

We crawled for what felt like an age. The tunnel was a tight fit, which meant it was probably freshly dug. It also stank something foul. That usually meant either spoiled food or some poor VC bastard died down there and was left to rot.

After about 40 minutes of crawling in total silence, I saw the tunnel ahead open into a room. I tapped Benoit on the head with my foot and heard him ready his pistol. I climbed down into the open chamber, pointing my pistol at the shadows. The room was dimly lit by a small oil lamp. It was also deserted.

We took a moment to adjust. It was the longest single tunnel segment either of us had ever crawled through. It also had no traps, which was unusual. Where was everyone who dug the damn thing? Save for the lamp hanging from the roof and a canvas tarp on the opposite wall, the room was empty.

I approached the tarp and used my pistol to move it aside. Behind the tarp was a stone staircase leading down.

"A stone staircase this far underground?" I whispered to Benoit.

"VC didn't build this. This is old, very old, older than America old," Benoit whispered back with fear in his voice."

"We've come this far, we have to keep going," I replied.

We both walked slowly down the narrow staircase. Our flashlights had red lenses and I swear the illuminated staircase looked like we were descending into hell. The staircase was almost as deep as the tunnel was long. Finally, I saw the staircase blocked by another tarp, light coming from the other side. I moved aside the tarp with my pistol, my finger trembled on the trigger. My eyes lit up, my heart raced, I almost pulled the trigger… but I didn't. Something made me pause. The room had at least 10 people in it, none of them armed.

I pointed my pistol at the group and illuminated them with my flashlight. They didn't respond, just stood there rocking gently forward and back.

"Benoit, don't shoot. There's people in here, but there's… something wrong with them."

I stepped into the tiny room, lit only by small candles, and Benoit followed. We both shined our flashlights at the people. They paid no attention, just continued to rock gently forward and back.

I shined my light in one of their faces, clicked my fingers; she didn't respond. Her clothes told me she was VC. They were all VC. Three women and seven men, all gently rocking forward and back, not a care in the fucking world. Their eyes were a solid color, which color I can't really say as I could only illuminate them with my red flashlight.

Benoit motioned with his flashlight to the corner where their rifles all sat in a pile… badly rusted.

"Jesus Christ, Benoit, how long have these poor fuckers been down here?"

"I don't think Jesus Christ frequents this establishment," came Benoit's terrified response in his thick Cajun accent.

I cast my light to the front of the room, toward where the VC were staring, and found a small altar. Walking toward it, I could see a gold statue resting atop a simple stone plinth and illuminated by several candles. The statue was an ornately crafted, very beautiful naked woman. The top half, anyway; the bottom half was something like an octopus. Dozens of tiny gold tentacles had been meticulously crafted to the woman's torso instead of legs. The statue had some writing at its base, a writing I didn't recognize. I reached out to pick the statue up and take a better look but Benoit shouted "Stop, don't touch it!"

I retracted my hand about an inch from the statue.

"We need to leave this place… quickly," Benoit said as he put his hand on my shoulder.

"Are we just gonna leave them like this?" I asked as I shone my light in their eyes.

"We'll plant the C4 charges and put them on a 90 minute timer," he said, already removing the C4 from a pouch on his belt.

"They're unarmed…," I implored, turning to Benoit.

"These people are dead, maybe worse than dead. I saw something like this once before, at home in the Bayou."

I didn't argue any longer. We planted the C4 charges in a rush, set the timers for 90 minutes, and ran up the stone staircase as fast as we could. It felt like a lifetime until we reached the small room with the lamp. I climbed into the tunnel and Benoit followed. Suddenly, we could hear a woman's voice faintly calling from far behind us.

"Ignore it, keep moving!" Benoit shouted from behind me.

I didn't need to be told, I wasn't going back.

It was the longest crawl of my life. I saw daylight and kept crawling even though my hands were raw and bloodied. I emerged into the light of day and gasped for fresh air, Benoit followed. We warned the others about the C4 charges but told them nothing else. Benoit and I sat in total silence away from the tunnel entrance… Waiting… praying.

The ground shook with a dull thud and a spray of dirt emerged from the tunnel. We both breathed a sigh of relief. It is only after an experience like that, that you ask yourself the small questions. To this day I still ask myself, "Who the fuck was keeping the candles lit in that damn room?"

***

I told you already I wouldn't bore you with most of the details of my time in Vietnam. I also won't ever refer to it as 'Nam. As I found after returning home, it's the rear echelon assholes who spent the war pencil pushing who most like to put on a husky voice and say 'Nam, in some deep and mournful way.

The short story is, after the incident in the tunnels west of Da Nang, Benoit and I were a little messed up. We were useless for tunnel work. Both of us were transferred into two separate regular platoons in the mechanized infantry. About a month after that, I was on a search and destroy mission when a rookie stepped over a VC tripwire, the tripwire was connected to one of our own captured claymores. The claymore blew the rookie's legs off and lodged a bunch of metal and bone fragments in the side of my torso.

I survived and, for my trouble, I got a ticket home. Well, I say home but I really I got a ticket to a military hospital called "Camp Zama" in Japan. They managed to pull most of the bits of shrapnel out of my torso over two operations. The hospital was dangerously overcrowded. At night, the screaming of the other patients was horrendous and the stench reminded me of that fucking tunnel.

I was actually happy when, due to overcrowding I was transferred to a much older building in the complex. It was some type of disused asylum ward, a total wreck with only about 15 patients. Mostly guys with minor injuries. But I didn't care; it was far enough away from the main buildings that I didn't have to hear the poor bastards screaming for their mothers every night.

I was on the mend, which was a blessing and a curse. My tour wasn't up and, if I was declared fit to serve, I might be sent back to Vietnam. And I was not going back. Not after what I saw in that tunnel. Two American military doctors and a female Japanese nurse arrived to assess my situation late one evening.

"Your injuries seem to be healing quite well," said one stern-faced doctor.

"Physically, at least," said the second doctor who wore narrow glasses. The first doctor gave him a look that could cut glass.

The doctor wearing the glasses was clearly the psychiatrist. He would be my ticket home if I could convince him I had lost my mind, but I couldn't overplay my hand. The nurse just stood behind them, diligently taking notes.

"How is your emotional state? Have you had any troubling thoughts? I understand you were a tunnel commando," probed the psychiatrist.

"Yes, I… I sometimes have nightmares about the things I saw in the tunnels. I… sometimes think about… harming myself." I put a quiver into my voice to add to the effect, but neither of them were buying it; I've never been a good liar. How fucked up a situation was this? After the shit I saw, I needed to fake being mentally unstable just to get a ticket home. I was despondent and I dropped the act. Much as I wanted to go home, I couldn't tell them about what happened in the tunnels. I wanted to go home but not to be thrown in a mental asylum.

"What kind of things did you see in the tunnels?" the psychiatrist asked calmly.

"Doc, near Da Nang I went down into the deepest, darkest tunnel you can imagine and, if I told you what I saw in that tunnel, you wouldn't believe me anyway, so just write whatever you need to on your clipboards and leave me be."

The stern-faced doctor was unimpressed with my tone but, as I was speaking, the Japanese nurse stopped taking notes. Her face went deathly pale and she stared at me with a look of terror on her face.

"Well, we'll check on you again tomorrow. Try to get some rest," said the psychiatrist who had a curious look on his face and, with that, they all shuffled off. The nurse stared back at me as they went, her face still pale with fear. I went to sleep that night knowing that soon they would send me back to Vietnam.

I awoke late that night to the whispering voice of a woman, I couldn't hear where it was coming from. I got out of bed and walked uneasily, rolling my drip along with me. The woman's voice was coming from the next corridor. I thought it must be that nurse, but the voice sounded all too familiar.

I wasn't going to walk the halls without a weapon, so I searched the unmanned nurse's station. I found a scalpel in one of the drawers; it would have to do. I shuffled through the large wooden doors leading to the next corridor. Inside, the light bulbs flickered and the paint peeled from the walls. Far to the end of the corridor I could see the shape of a woman standing near a window looking out into the night. I shuffled toward her with the scalpel leading the way, rolling my drip with my left hand. As I approached, the faint whispers became louder and I could finally make out the words, "DEFILER, COME TO THE RED

HOUSE," it whispered. My drip caught in a cracked tile on the floor, making an awful clanking sound. The woman turned and moved quickly toward me. My heart raced in terror as I prepared the scalpel.

"You shouldn't be out of bed." It was the nurse, a lit cigarette in her hand. She must have been smoking by the window. Her English was near perfect. She must have been the daughter of an American GI; many of them married Japanese women after the Second World War ended.

"Why were you whispering to me?" I asked, still pointing the scalpel.

"I wasn't whispering," she said, confused and frightened.

"You were whispering, you called me... 'defiler'. What does that mean?" I demanded, scalpel blade gleaming. Once again her face took on the same pale terrified look, the cigarette dropped from her hand.

"You're not safe here in Japan, or back in Vietnam. They'll be looking for you," her voice trembled as she spoke.

"Who... who'll be looking for me?" I implored her.

"I don't know what they call themselves. Every place has a different name for them. 'The Silent Plague' is the translation of what we call them here in Japan. All I know for certain is, they will be looking for you. Maybe you will be safe if you get back to America." Her words offered little comfort.

"You have to help me... you have to convince the doctors that I'm crazy," I said to her, almost begging.

"I will try... give me the scalpel" she said calmly.

I handed her the scalpel and, as quick as I had handed it to her, she slashed it across my arm. I roared out in pain. She dropped the scalpel and grabbed my hand, putting pressure on the wound.

"This is the only way," she said. I instantly realized her plan. Two orderlies came rushing into the old corridor from an adjoining corridor, alerted by my screams. "Get me some bandages, he's trying to kill himself!" she roared at the men. One of the orderlies ran for bandages, the other ran over to support me. I slunk down into the orderly's arms, more from pageantry than blood loss. The wound wasn't that deep; I had suffered much worse before. The nurse had done a good job.

I was put back in bed and stitched up. The next night I was visited by the psychiatrist, alone. He looked at me coldly, noted something on my chart, and asked, "Have you been hearing voices or … whispers?"

"No," I replied quickly.

"It's funny; we had a young soldier from Louisiana in here about three weeks before you arrived, he was also a tunnel commando. He claimed he was hearing … 'whispers', but he could never tell me what they said. We had to send the poor fellow home."

The psychiatrist maintained his usual cold, clinical composure, but his eyes seemed to burn with a fanatic rage. "If you did hear… whispers, and they told you something—a secret maybe—you would tell me, wouldn't you?".

"I'm not hearing any voices or whispers," I responded with as much resolve as I could muster.

The rage slowly faded from his eyes. "You are being transferred to a hospital in the US, You'll be assigned a psychiatrist there," he said before pausing, "I hope when you get home, you will find whatever it is in life you are searching for." And, with that, he smiled and walked away.

He knew I was lying to him.

That very night I was driven to the airport and pushed in a wheelchair into a C-130 by an MP. The flight was filled with men who were broken physically or mentally, and most likely a few guys like me; just desperate not to go back to Vietnam. Unlike them, I *was* actually hearing voices, but

I wasn't crazy.

The flight took off and I breathed a sigh of relief. I removed my dog tags, praying I would never need them again. I opened the zipper on my bag to put the tags inside and there, staring back at me, was a small, crudely made clay replica of the golden statue I had seen in the tunnels.

***

'So what happened when you got home?' I hear you ask. For a while, very little. I was kept in the hospital for about three weeks; the new psychiatrist seemed swamped with work and saw I wasn't really a danger to myself or others and so I was discharged. I tried finding Benoit as soon as I could but he had gone "off the grid" as they might say these days. In truth, disappearing back then was as simple as not listing your name in the damn phonebook. Despite living in the guy's pocket for eight months of my life I knew very little about him. I knew he was from a couple of hours west of New Orleans and he had a sister named Marie; not exactly solid facts to track a man down by.

Soon I gave up trying. I just decided to try and forget about everything: Vietnam, the tunnel, the woman's voice… but the damn statue was always there as a constant reminder. I kept it wrapped in cloth, afraid to touch the damn thing. Eventually, I did what every other person in New York did with something they wanted to get rid of; I threw it in the East River where it would find good company with all the discarded mob weapons and photos of ex-girlfriends.

I had a small amount of money coming in from my veteran disability payments. I topped this up by working odd jobs. When I could find the work, that is. New York in 1969 wasn't exactly a fun place to be; the city stank from uncollected garbage and there seemed to be a strike or a riot every other day—the teachers, the sanitation workers. Hell, it got so bad even the gays started rioting and they always seemed a peaceful bunch to me. I lived down near Greenwich Village so I was right in the middle of the mess. Crime was also a huge problem and I rarely left the apartment without my pistol. And that's how it went for about six months; I worked a little and tried to avoid getting shot or stabbed.

Then one night, out of the blue, the phone rang. I generally only got calls from "Cold Call" companies; it was a relatively new thing back then and every asshole outfit with a phone was trying to sell their crap.

I picked up the phone. "I don't wanna buy radiators, life assurance, or mortgage protection, so go fuck yourself," I calmly said. There was a tiny pause.

"It's Philippe… Philippe Benoit. I see you haven't lost your way with words," came the response.

"Benoit! Jesus, I tried tracking you down when I got back from Vietnam but I couldn't find a trace of you. Where the hell have you been?"

"New Orleans… look I don't wanna say too much over the phone but I received a very strange package in the mail. Turns out *someone* was able to track me down." My heart sank with the news. I didn't need to ask what was in the package; I could guess.

"Can you come down to New Orleans? I could offer you work and a place to crash if you need it. Do you have anything pressing keeping you in New York?"

I looked out the window as I listened to Benoit on the phone. Two NYPD officers were beating the everloving shit out of some guy with batons. A small group nearby were raining bottles at them.

"Yeah, I could do with getting out of New York for a while. I could be there in a few days," I replied.

Benoit filled me in on the details of where to meet; he didn't want to talk on the phone as if he thought someone might be listening. The next morning, I threw what little possessions I had into my old beat up Impala and hit the road. I didn't bother giving notice to the landlord of my fleabag apartment.

You might think me mad for taking the trip to New Orleans. I suppose I could have just hung up the phone and forgot about Benoit and the things we saw, but that's just not me. He needed my help and we had been through hell together in Vietnam. I don't mean that figuratively; I mean I felt we had literally descended into some kind of Hell in that tunnel. I wasn't about to leave the guy to deal with this shit alone.

It felt good to get out of New York; the journey was long and the summer was sweltering. I drove relentlessly, wanting to get to New Orleans as quickly as possible. I avoided the big cities and only stopped to sleep. On the last night of the journey, I stopped at a cheap motel near a one-horse town about an hour past Birmingham.

The reception building was small, the desk manned by a middle-aged man. I guessed he was the owner on account of there being a photo of him in uniform as a younger man on the wall. It looked like it was taken somewhere in Europe during the Second World War.

"You look a little worse for wear. Long journey? Where are you headed to?" the owner made small talk as he handed me my key.

"Houston," I lied as I fumbled with my things. I'm not fully sure why I lied; it's not like whoever these people with the statues were could manage to staff every shithole motel between New York and New Orleans on the off chance I passed through.

I was so exhausted that night, I fell asleep fully clothed as soon as my head hit the pillow. I awoke in a sweat to the whispers of a woman. It was still night out. I took my pistol from my bag and tucked it into the back of my jeans.

I left the room and followed the voice, the same phrase over and over: "Defiler, come to the red house." I walked down the steps to ground level. The voice became louder as I approached a soda machine at the corner of the motel, a light on top glowed red in the night.

"Defiler," the whisper came again, almost like it was inside my head.

"I'm not a fucking defiler," I mumbled back to no one.

"What was that, honey? You wanna 'defile' me? Well that's gonna cost ya. Usually my customers don't put it in that kind of eloquent language," she laughed.

It was a whore, a well dressed one at that; a little too well dressed and refined for this motel. She was leaning near the illuminated soda machine.

"Sorry, I was just talking to myself," I replied. The whispers had stopped.

"You looking for a date?" she casually enquired.

"No, I'm fine, thanks. Just came to get a soda," I quickly responded.

"You sure? It's a long way to New Orleans; I could help you relax," she said, licking her lips.

My mind froze with fear but I kept my composure, "I'm headed to Houston", I calmly responded.

"Funny, the owner said you were on your way to New Orleans," she dryly retorted.

"Well, the owner's mistaken," I replied, matching her tone.

"That's what I told him when he said you were headed to Houston. It took some of my *charm* to persuade him but he finally told me you had a map that showed a route to New Orleans when you checked in."

I said nothing in response.

"Sadly, what he couldn't tell me was where you were headed once you got to New Orleans."

"Yeah, well, maybe your *charm* isn't as persuasive as you think," I responded, all the while I was considering taking out my pistol and putting it to her head.

She tilted her head forward a little, her face glowing a fiery red under the light of the soda machine. She bared her teeth and her eyes took on the same look of fanatic rage I had seen in the psychiatrist's eyes at the hospital.

"Oh, you have no idea how persuasive I can be," she spat with unrestrained rage.

I reached for my pistol but she slipped around the corner and ran into the black of night.

"I hope you find whatever it is you're looking for," she said, laughing from somewhere deep in the darkness.

Running out after her into the night would have been a fool's errand. I ran in a panic to the motel reception building. Maybe she had divulged some tiny piece of information to the owner. I could be persuasive, too; broken ribs usually jogged people's memories. Maybe he wouldn't have any information but, either way, I was going to sternly educate him on the perils of spilling your guts to strange women who offered free blowjobs.

The small reception building was dimly lit and there was no one behind the desk. I rang the bell but got no response. Impatiently, I walked behind the counter and opened the back office door. As I opened the door, the metallic smell of fresh blood hit my nostrils, which I quickly covered with my hand. The owner lay dead on his back, mouth duct taped shut. Two glass shards had been rammed into his eye sockets.

Tough bastard; I didn't give him enough credit. He hadn't fallen for her hooker routine, so she had to torture him for what little information he had. Or maybe it was just to send me a message.

I wasn't hanging around for the cops. Maybe this was a setup. Either way, I wasn't sticking around. I wiped down the office door knob with my sleeve, my fingerprints being anywhere else in the building could be explained but not on the back office door. I walked to my room with as much outward calm as I could muster, packed my things, and got in my car. I drove out into the night. With luck, I'd make it to New Orleans by morning. I knew one thing for certain: these people, whoever they were, wanted that voice to keep whispering to me. They wanted to know where it was leading me. That was the only reason I was still alive; as soon as they figured that it might be less trouble to torture me rather than just follow me, I'd end up like the owner of the motel.

The pistol was digging into my back, so I took it from my jeans and opened the glove compartment to put it inside. As the glove compartment opened, a small clay statuette fell out. I didn't need to look at it; I already knew what it was. I put the pistol away and kept driving. Safety in numbers, I thought as I sped toward New Orleans. Benoit would have a plan. He always did.

***

I barreled my way through the night, praying the engine of my old Impala wouldn't give up the ghost from the hard ride. Day was breaking as I crossed Lake Pontchartrain. It glowed yellow with the rising sun but, in truth, it was a cesspool brown the closer I got to the city.

Benoit had just told me to get to the French Quarter and call a phone number when I got there. The French Quarter wasn't quite the tourist Mecca it is today but it was still popular, especially with service members on shore leave looking for cheap thrills. It was seedy as hell. But a city like that can be a blessing in disguise for men in my situation; seedy cities are easy to disappear in if needed and there's usually some unscrupulous ex-service member willing to sell you some extra firepower. And who was I to judge an unscrupulous man, I had just fled a fuckin' murder scene.

I parked the car near a payphone and got out. I fumbled with some change and dialed the number Benoit had given me. The phone rang for what felt like a lifetime, then someone picked up.

"It's me, I'm here," I said, not giving any other details.

"Good to hear your voice. I thought something might'a happened to you on the road," came Benoit's relieved response.

"Yeah, well, something did happen to me on the road. I'll fill you in when I see you," I replied while looking around the street through the dirty glass.

Benoit gave me an address a couple of blocks away but didn't say anything else over the phone.

I drove the car over to the address. It was on a quiet side-street. When I arrived, I thought I must have been mistaken. It was a small weird store, not an apartment building like I had expected.

Marie's General Goods and Supplies

Strangest general goods store I had ever seen; black drapes covered the windows, and there wasn't much sign of life. I pushed the door with apprehension. A small bell rang and I was hit by the smell of burning herbs. I walked into the store to find it filled with antiques and what I would refer to as "Voodoo shit", although I never quite grasped the difference between HooDoo, Voodoo, and all those other African religions.

"You made it." Benoit emerged from behind the counter with a look of relief on his face. He walked over and hugged me, beating his hand on my back so firmly it knocked the air outta my lungs a little.

"Take it easy, you'll break a rib," I said laughing a little.

"Sorry, just good to see you," he replied, releasing me.

"You hadn't called in a few days. I thought you might not make it."

"I almost didn't; something happened to me while I was on the road," I replied.

I wanted to fill Benoit in on all the details of my trip but I was more perplexed by the shop we were standing in.

"Marie's? Who owns this place, your sister?" I enquired, puzzled.

"It was my grandmother's. My sister is named after her; she died just after we were shipped out to Vietnam. My sister looked after the place while I was away. Almost as soon as I was home she moved to LA—she has a notion to become a singer. My grandmother left her some money and I got the creepy shop," Benoit said while sweeping his arm across the selection of weird merchandise in the shop.

"And people buy this… stuff?" I asked pointing at an odd selection of herbs.

"Business is good. The shop is kinda discreet so the tourists think they've found some genuine secret Voodoo shop. Don't worry; 95% of this stuff is completely harmless," Benoit said, smiling.

"And the other 5%?" I skeptically enquired.

"Yeah, that stuff's not for tourists. I keep those items in the back storeroom. Along with an item I got in the mail. Speaking of which, what happened to you on the road?" Benoit walked over to the front door and set the sign to closed, though he left it unlocked.

I filled Benoit in on the hospital in Japan, the statuette and the woman at the motel. The only details I left out were the murder of the motel owner and the whispers; I didn't want to freak him out or involve him in a murder I might get accused of. Benoit listened, looking concerned.

"I got the same statuette in the mail. It was sent to my old address so I don't know how long it had been there, probably since I got back from Vietnam. There's no way to know for sure since it had no postmark. Once I got it, I called you straight away. I got worried about the statuette, so I checked all the books here in the shop to see if any of them had any details on the statue or the woman in it, but I turned up nothing," Benoit continued. "I was stumped, so I called the University at Baton Rouge. They pointed me in the direction of a retired professor, some expert in ancient religions. So I paid him a visit, he lives about an hour from here in the middle of nowhere. Nice house but the land is practically a swamp."

"Did he recognize the statue?" I asked on tenterhooks.

"Kinda. He said that it wasn't really African or American. The statuette is a crude modern replica, but the woman depicted was probably 'The Silent Mother', some ancient god people worshiped in coastal communities the world over. The religion probably died away at least a millennia ago. Apparently, she can grant her followers eternal bliss if they worship at her temple. Trouble is, no one knows where her temple is. According to the professor, it probably doesn't exist. He told me to give him a couple of days to do more research."

"Those people in the tunnel sure didn't look like they found eternal bliss. Then again, it didn't look like a temple, either; just a small shrine," I mused. "And... did he get back to you?"

"And... that was a couple of days ago. I rang him all morning but he's not answering the phone," Benoit responded.

"Aw shit, we gotta drive over there… now… and bring a weapon," I said putting on my jacket.

"Should we just give him another day?" Benoit asked, perplexed.

"He may not have another day, Benoit," I said as we walked out the door. Benoit locked it behind him.

We drove out of the city to the west in Benoit's car. It was sweltering.

"In the tunnel in Vietnam, I thought you said you had seen something like that before?" I probed Benoit.

"Well, I was embellishing a little. Look… when I was fourteen, a local councilor was accused of some pretty serious stuff. Several local women made some serious allegations about the guy, but he was white and powerful and so was able to buy his way out of trouble. But the locals weren't satisfied with that outcome. One night, my Grandmother drove me out to the middle of nowhere, to a sort of… ceremony.

"My memory of the event is kinda hazy. There were lots of people chanting and there was this Voodoo priest. They forced the councilor to drink this weird liquid and the councilor's eyes took on a kind of dead look, like the lights were on but nobody was home. After that, the councilor responded to the shaman's every command; *'walk… Smile… jump.'* He was like a puppet and then they just released him and off he wandered into the night. The cops eventually found him and brought him home. According to newspaper reports, he seemed fine, if a little confused. He certainly didn't talk about any ceremony. A couple of days later, according to the same reports, he got a phone call at home. After the call his wife saw him he calmly walk into the kitchen, pick up a knife, and stab himself in the throat."

"Jesus, fun story, Benoit. Way to lighten the mood," I said with the mental image in my head.

"So, yeah; I didn't see exactly what we saw in the tunnels before but I have seen some weirdly similar shit," Benoit said as he pressed down harder on the accelerator, we both sat in silence as he drove.

After about an hour of driving, we turned off the small road onto an even smaller dirt track. Reeds grew high at the side of the road. The guy really did live in a swamp.

"Only a mile or so now," Benoit informed me as we bounced uncomfortably over the dirt road.

As soon as he spoke, we saw a small column of smoke rising in the distance.

"Tell me that's not his house?" I said, half hoping.

"His house is the only one on this road," Benoit replied with fear in his voice.

The dirt track turned to gravel as we approached. It was a small, old plantation house. Well, I say small; it was small as plantation houses go, but still imposing. It was also very much ablaze. Thick plumes of black smoke were billowing from the house but the fire had not fully engulfed it; it had clearly been started recently.

The car came to a halt on the grass lawn and we both hopped out. Benoit ran to the front porch where a barrel of rainwater sat near a gutter pipe. He dunked his head into it, drenching himself, then pulled his soaked T-shirt up over his mouth and nose.

"Are you fucking kidding? We're not going in there!" I roared.

"I'm not leaving the guy to burn to death. I got him into this mess," Benoit replied, his voice muffled by the T-shirt.

I hesitated for a second before following Benoit's lead, dunked my head into the barrel. We both stood at the doorway, our faces covered and ready to enter. 'This isn't going to end well,' I thought as Benoit kicked in the door.

The heat was incredible. Smoke was filling the house. Luckily, those old houses had pretty high ceilings; the smoke sat like an ominous black blanket above our heads. Soon, it would fill the house… and our lungs if we weren't careful.

Benoit lead the way. "His study is in the back; that's where he works," he shouted through his T-shirt.

We made our way quickly to the study. Benoit felt the door to check if it was hot. "It's warm, keep to the side," Benoit said as he quickly kicked the door and then ducked to the left of the door frame.

Luckily, there was no backdraft. The room was ablaze but it hadn't burned up all the oxygen. Flames engulfed the ceiling and licked the walls.

Then we spotted him. The professor lay dead in his chair, head slumped on his large wooden desk, a pool of blood pouring from his throat… and two shards of glass protruding from his eye sockets.

***

Flames licked the walls and the quilt of smoke rolled in thick black waves above our heads. Benoit and I stood over the body of the professor. We couldn't see each other's faces but terror clearly showed in Benoit's voice.

"Check the drawers, I'll check his pockets," Benoit ordered.

"What about prints?" I said in a panic.

"Are you fucking kidding? In five minutes there won't even be a body, let alone prints," Benoit screamed.

Realizing my stupidity, I began to rifle through the desk drawers as Benoit took the unenviable task of checking the dead guy's pockets. The entire building was a sea of sound as we worked, the fire roared and the building groaned under its own weight.

"Rubbings!", I said as I produced several thin sheets of paper from the desk drawer, I could barely make out the words with the smoke but I saw the phrase 'Silent Mother'. For those of you young enough not to remember, this was how people used to copy shit before everyone had copy machine in their house. Hell, maybe some of you are even young enough you barely know what a copy machine is.

Benoit's eyes lit up at the sight of the papers.

"We need to get out of here!" I shouted.

Benoit didn't answer. The house gave out an unmerciful groan like a death rattle. It was doing the talking now and neither of us needed to be told twice. We both sprinted for the front door as roof beams began to collapse.

We sprinted straight to the car. I took one glance back at the house; it was almost engulfed. The roof sagged and collapsed in on itself as I hopped into the car. Benoit was already behind the wheel.

The engine roared to life and we left a spray of mud and gravel as we tore off the lawn and down the driveway. The car bounced along the dirt track and we made it to the main road in doubletime, the house a raging inferno behind us.

"The rubbings?" Benoit enquired.

I pulled them from my pocket and examined them, scanning for anything that might be relevant. I could barely read the copied writing, my eyes stinging with smoke, but several blocks of text had been underlined with a red pen. I turned the papers over. On the back were some handwritten notes. I read one aloud.

"P.S. Mr.Benoit, it's worth pointing out that your statuette did appear to be hollow, did you consider breaking it open? Perhaps you hadn't noticed as you seemed afraid to touch it. I assure you it's perfectly safe from a historical point of view as it's a cheap modern replica. As to your question about 'The Red House,' please see my other notes."

"The Red House?" I questioned Benoit as he drove.

"Look, I didn't want to freak you out but I have been hearing voices telling me to go to 'The Red House,'" Benoit explained.

"I already knew you'd been hearing voices, Benoit. That creep of a psychiatrist told me at camp Zama. I just didn't know you were hearing the exact same voice as me... no more secrets from here on out," I said angrily.

"Alright, no more secrets from here on out," Benoit agreed.

"Oh... that nice motel owner I told you about, he was actually murdered in a similar fashion to our professor friend back there," I said waiting for the backlash.

"Are you fucking kidding? You're bitching to me about secrets and you had a murder hidden under your hat!" Benoit spat back at me with anger.

"Alright, alright; we're both agreed, no more secrets," I said while feigning reading the notes through my smoke burnt eyes.

We sat the rest of the journey in silence.

We arrived at the shop looking like shit. Benoit unlocked the door and we shuffled inside. Benoit made for the back room and I followed. The back room was large enough, it also had a restroom. I took the rubbings out of my pocket and put them aside on a desk for safety. We took turns splashing cold water into our burning red eyes, letting out sounds of relief as we did it.

After a few minutes, I slumped down at a pillar, exhausted. Benoit dried his hands and face then threw the towel to me as he sat down at the desk to examine the papers.

Benoit began to read aloud the underlined segments.

"The followers of the Silent Mother believed that she could offer them eternal bliss if they found her temple and released the 'Silent Plague.' The chosen few who followed her would then control this world in her name. The unbelievers would be empty husks ready to be commanded, their souls captured for torment by the 'Silent Mother.'"

"Shit, that sounds all too familiar," I said.

Benoit nodded thoughtfully as he skipped to another passage. "The Silent Mother's temple, it is claimed, could only be found by locating three golden shrines to the Silent Mother dotted around the globe. These shrines themselves were claimed to hold some weaker power over mortals and could enslave unbelievers foolish enough to touch them, which the Silent Mother would entice them to do. Those who resisted the urge to touch the shrine would be rewarded with part of the location of her temple. It must be noted at this point that that the shrines and the temple are believed by all reliable scholarly sources to be purely mythological. The only dissenting voice on this fact was a talented medical student named Arthur Blake, who traveled extensively in Northern Europe and East Africa studying the folklore in those regions during the mid-1930s. He claimed, in a paper for a historical journal, that he had found two of the shrines, and learned that the temple lay near a city by the sea fought over by all the great powers. He strongly believed that city was New Orleans. He refused to give any evidence why that city rather than many other cities that could match the given description. Suffice to say, his paper was roundly ridiculed for its vagueness, with many pointing out that no civilization spanned the diverse geographical areas he claimed to have found the shrines. Nor did it account for the fact that the stories of the Silent Mother's temple go back more than a thousand years and no great powers fought over New Orleans until the 18th century. The student quickly retracted his paper, stating that while traveling for scholastic reasons he had partaken in local rituals that involved psychedelics."

"Are you thinking what I'm thinking?" Benoit enquired, his hands shaking.

"Yeah, fate's a bitch. You've been living somewhere near a haunted temple your entire life," I replied.

"No, you idiot. That creepy fucking psychiatrist in camp Zama," Benoit said, pointing at the papers.

"Oh, shit. No wonder he's got such a hard-on for us; he's been searching for that third shrine most of his life and we blew the shit out of it."

Benoit began to read another one of the professor's hand written notes. "Although I was skeptical, I rang the Louisiana historical society and there is a building that was once referred to as 'The Red House,' it was an infamous brothel built in the bayou when New Orleans was first settled. The building has been abandoned since the 1920's but has not been demolished as it is a protected historical structure."

"He has an address written here," Benoit said, looking over at me.

"That detail wasn't copied from a book, so maybe our psychiatrist and his lady friend don't know the location yet… unless they managed to torture the information out of the professor," I suggested.

"Why kill the professor and burn the house unless they already had all the information they needed? Otherwise they still needed us to find the temple," Benoit replied.

"Maybe he lied to them or they just got sloppy. Hell, maybe we interrupted them when we arrived," I argued.

"We have to assume they either already know where the temple is, or are gonna follow us if we go looking for it," Benoit said, concerned.

As we both pondered the subject, I spotted the statuette on a shelf. I picked it up with the towel, wrapped it into a ball and smacked it against the top of the desk. I heard it shatter into pieces.

"Jesus, you could have warned me first," Benoit scolded me as I opened the towel and poured the broken contents onto the desk.

The shards emerged along with a small handwritten note:

If you find the temple, destroy it. Don't let the Followers of the Silent Mother release the plague. You've already destroyed one of her shines. Finish the work and release the souls she torments.

"I guess more than one group has been following us," I said, confused.

"Alright, fuck this shit. We go to the temple and fuck it up but I'm not going to that temple without some serious firepower," Benoit said with resolve in his voice.

"Do you know a guy?" I enquired.

"Oh yeah... I know a guy," Benoit replied, pushing aside a storage closet to reveal a small door.

***

Benoit opened the small hidden door and we both entered a dark room. He reached up and pulled a cord. A flickering incandescent bulb suddenly illuminated what could only be described as an Aladdin's Cave of armaments.

"Jesus, Benoit, when you said you knew a guy...," I said stopping as I marveled at the treasure trove.

"Yeah, well, remember when I said business was good? This is the real business," Benoit informed me.

I picked up and began inspecting an AK-47 style rifle from a collection leaning against the wall.

"Those are mostly AKMs, but there are a few Type 56s mixed in there as well," Benoit explained.

"I'm just disappointed you don't buy American," I said laughing.

"Yeah, well, what can I say? Communists make reliable rifles. Although, if you must insist, I do have something big, black, and all American, if you wanna see it," Benoit said smirking.

"Christ, I think I've already seen enough of that in the showers at boot camp, Benoit," I said with a look of disdain.

Benoit pulled the zipper open on a large kit bag on a table in the corner revealing a large, black M60 machine gun.

"Shit, don't you think maybe that's overkill? Hauling it around might be a problem for little guys like us. What about ammo?" I argued.

"Ammo isn't the issue; that's easy to source. The disintegrating belts that feed it are the problem. I only have one 50 round belt," Benoit informed me.

"No, we need to be able to move fast; it will only slow us down" I suggested.

"Good point. Alright, we'll leave it here," Benoit replied, stuffing 2 AKM rifles and 4 fully loaded magazines into a second empty kit bag.

I took a single claymore that was sitting on a shelf looking lonely and put it into the bag along with the rifles.

"A claymore?" Benoit said, surprised.

"Yeah. If we get there before them, I'd like to know when they arrive," I replied, smiling.

"Makes sense," Benoit agreed while placing some C4 and detonators into the bag.

"We all set?" he asked, zipping the bag shut.

"Looks like," I replied as we both put on our jackets and checked our flashlights.

I carried the bag, Benoit turned off the light and pushed the storage closet back into position, hiding the doorway to the small arsenal. We made our way to the front door, Benoit looked out onto the quiet street to see if the coast was clear.

"We're good to go," he said as we both emerged. I loaded the bag into the trunk.

Between all the time we spent reading the professor's notes and constructing our makeshift arsenal, it was sundown by the time we left the city. I was driving, at Benoit's insistence. He said we were much less likely to be stopped by the cops with a white guy behind the wheel. The steering felt sluggish with the heavy cargo in the trunk. I drove slowly so as not to attract any unwanted attention.

At a guess, looking at the map, the address seemed to be about an hour or so from the city, but it was deep into the swamp. We had to take a selection of back roads and byroads to get to our destination. Night was falling when we turned onto a small dirt road raised up from the water, swampland to either side. We drove on the road for a couple of miles; in the distance, a large building began to appear.

The Red House was, as the name suggested, red. It seemed to be made of sandstone. It sat on a small islet in the swamp connected to the raised road. It was a grand old building that looked more like a small fort that could have been lifted straight out of Paris or Saigon.

As we got closer, it became obvious that the building was in a serious state of disrepair but, frankly, it was a miracle it was still standing in a swamp after all these years. I wondered if some unnatural power kept a structure like this standing in such an area but I put the thought out of my mind and focused on the task at hand.

"Looks like we got here first," Benoit said, surveying the grounds as we approached. There were no other vehicles visible.

"Unless they arrived by boat," I suggested. The house sat on the water and might have had a jettie at the rear, it was hard to tell.

The grounds were overgrown, so we hid the car in a patch of overgrown reeds on the lawn.

Benoit opened the trunk. I unzipped the bag and removed the 2 AKM rifles, then loaded a magazine into each and slung one rifle onto my shoulder. I handed the other to Benoit and stuffed the claymore into my large jacket pocket along with a spare magazine. The bag was now empty save for the C4 and detonators. Benoit zipped up the bag and slung it over his shoulder.

We both walked up to the imposing building weighed down with our armaments and ascended the stone steps. The large wooden doors gave little resistance as I pushed them. We turned on the flashlights attached to our jackets as we entered a small lobby area with a coat room.

"I'm surprised junkies haven't taken this place over," I said to Benoit.

"People down south are afraid of buildings like this, man. Too many ghosts of the past; they stay well clear," he responded.

We walked through the lobby area to a corridor. The air was hot and smelled of mold, the old wallpaper was falling off, bits of broken glass and other detritus littered the old, baggy red carpet.

At the end of the long corridor, we reached more large double doors.

Opening them, we emerged into what looked like an auditorium. The room had a high ceiling and was laid out like a theater with a stage and lots of booths and tables. The galleries had lots of private boxes. The whole place was all adorned with badly worn red velvet drapes.

"I guess the place was converted into one of those classy burlesque whorehouses," I suggested.

"Yeah, must have been pretty swanky in it's heyday. I'm willing to bet rich folk and officers only; I can't imagine grunts like us would have been welcome in a place like this," Benoit responded.

"Yeah, well, back in those days, guys like you weren't welcome pretty much anywhere," I joked.

"Very funny. There's plenty of places we're still not welcome," he retorted.

"Where the hell do we go now? This doesn't look much like a temple," I wondered aloud. And then the familiar whispering voice began to speak.

"Welcome, defilers; I've been expecting you."

Benoit looked at me in fear. I could tell we were hearing the same voice and not just because she spoke in plural. The voice no longer seemed to be in our heads. It was emanating from behind the stage.

We ran up and mounted the stage. The voice continued to whisper but became louder. I put my rifle to my shoulder and pulled the charging handle. I parted the tattered stage curtain with the barrel.

The area was illuminated with our flashlights. We walked slowly through the backstage area as I darted the barrel of my rifle left and right at nothing but shadows. The voice whispered from below us.

The floor was covered with an old rug, which I pulled aside to reveal a cellar hatch with a metal pull ring handle. I pulled the handle with one hand, the other tightly pressing the rifle to my shoulder. We were hit with a foul smell, like rotting flesh.

"Look, whatever we see or hear down there, we just ignore it. We plant the charges and we get out as quickly as possible," Benoit said, fear painted on his face.

I just nodded as we started to descend the narrow stone staircase.

I suddenly remembered the claymore in my pocket. We paused as I took it from my pocket and placed it on the top step pointing toward the hatch. I pulled the hatch down and attached the tripwire to the handle on the inside of the hatch.

We continued down the narrow stone staircase. It looked all too familiar, like we were descending the same stone staircase from the tunnel in Vietnam. It seemed to go on forever. I led the way with my rifle. It was hot; sweat dripped from my face and the smell of decay became overpowering. The stairwell ahead stopped at a corner and turned to wood. We rounded the corner, where the wood was ornately carved like in a cathedral. We had clearly found our temple.

The wooden corridor ended in an archway, through which we emerged into what looked like a small wooden chapel. The chapel was lit by wall torches and had a high vaulted ceiling. The entire structure was made of ornately carved wood; only some unnatural power could keep a structure like this intact under a swamp; it should have rotted mere years after being built. Even the foul smell subsided when we entered the chapel.

The chapel was filled with wooden church pews and paintings adorned the walls in perfect condition. Benoit and I stared in silence. The paintings depicted the woman from the statuette. In one, she was smiling while handing bread to some children. In a second, she was comforting a sick, bed-ridden woman. In a third, she was protecting a group of peasants from soldiers in armor.

At the front of the chapel, there was a large statue of the woman but it wasn't gold; it was a simple wooden carving of the woman smiling. Aside from her legs being made of tentacles, she seemed warm and inviting. A small wooden box lay at her feet.

The voice spoke.

"Welcome to my temple… lost souls. You defiled one of my shrines, a beacon to protect the weak and oppressed. Vulnerable souls will suffer because of your sacrilege."

Her voice was warm and reassuring.

"But all is not lost; you have found my temple and can repent for your sacrilege. You must help me feed the hungry, tend the sick, and restore the lame."

"That's a lot of stuff, and neither of us are doctors," I replied like a scolded 5 year old.

"And I don't know anything about farming to grow food," Benoit told her in an equally ridiculous fashion.

"Fear not, children; simply open the box at my feet and read the prayer within and my love will spread throughout the world. It will fill the stomachs of the hungry, heal the wounds of the sick, and soothe the minds of those in despair," the voice said in a reassuring mother's tone.

I approached the box at her feet, Benoit following close behind. I reached out to open the lid with joy in my heart.

An explosion shook the chapel. The claymore at the foot of the staircase had clearly been detonated. I was disoriented for a second with the sound and shaking, just long enough to see the world as it really was. I retracted my hand, Benoit stepped back in fear looking around the chapel.

"This place… it's not right," Benoit's voice was filled with terror.

"I know… plant the charges," I responded.

Before my eyes, the wooden statue turned to solid gold and the expression of warm comfort on the woman's face turned to malice. The ornately carved wooden pillars of the chapel turned to bone and the paintings now depicted scenes of horror. In one, the woman hovered over an army of men with hollow eyes. In another, she stood before a temple made of human remains.

The chapel pews turned to stone and were no longer empty, they were filled with the skeletal remains of people all sitting upright, staring at the statue in adoration, the foul stench of something evil returned to my nostrils.

"Are you seeing what I'm seeing?" I asked with barely contained horror.

"Yes, cover the door!" Benoit screamed as he began planting the C4 behind the pillars.

I could hear screaming from above us, then two gunshots and the screaming stopped. They had obviously put whoever had been hit by the claymore out of their misery; they clearly meant business. I could hear the footsteps of a large group of people descending the stone stairs above.

"That sounds like a lot of people. I knew we should have brought the M60," Benoit said in a hushed but angry tone.

"Stop crying over spilled milk and plant those fucking charges," I said back, also wishing we had the M60.

I hunkered down behind one of the stone pews with the AKM trained on the archway entrance, which I could now see was made of stone and human bones. I reverted into the mode of a trained soldier, my hand steadied on the weapon and my breathing slowed as I could hear the footsteps draw closer.

A man entered the room pointing his rifle uneasily. He looked untrained; he certainly wasn't a mercenary, but maybe a fanatic. I didn't fire on him immediately, hoping his friends would join him. Two more men entered. The third man clearly had some training as he quickly spotted me hunkered behind the stone pew and raised his rifle. I fired three quick single shots, cutting each of them down.

No more men entered, but I could hear people in the corridor whispering.

"No grenades, you could damage the temple," I heard a woman whisper an order. I recognized her voice; it was the whore from the motel.

Benoit ducked over and hunkered down beside me at the stone pew.

"Charges are set, 10 minutes," he said pointing his rifle at the doorway. I prayed it would be long enough.

"I'm coming in. I'm unarmed, don't shoot. I just want to talk," came a man's voice.

"Ok, we can talk," I replied.

It was the psychiatrist from Camp Zama. He walked in with his palms open to show he wasn't carrying weapons.

"Thank you for leading us here. That old professor sent us on a wild goose chase. But we had some of our people tailing you as a precaution. I never imagined it would be this beautiful," he remarked in awe, looking up at the ceiling.

We let him talk but we knew we were on the clock.

"It's just as I had heard in the stories; a temple made of solid gold," he said while running his finger on a pillar near the entrance way, the pillar was made of stone and human femur bones.

Benoit gave me a sideways look.

I guess the Silent Mother promised different people different things. Two soldiers weary of war are shown a perfect, peaceful world, while the power hungry are shown a temple of gold and promises of infinite power.

"This is the true gift of the Silent Mother; she can grant infinite wealth and the power to rule over the world... she can even restore her followers to life if they sacrifice themselves in her name." As he spoke, his eyes took on the same fanatic rage that I had seen before in the hospital.

"Yes, mother... not much time... I understand," he mumbled seemingly to himself.

Then suddenly, he screamed like a banshee and ran toward us at what seemed like inhuman speed. The others waiting in the stairwell flooded into the room and began spraying assault rifle fire. I spotted three men and the woman from the motel in the chaos. We quickly cut the psychiatrist down but the others seemed to be imbued with the same fanaticism. The Silent Mother was whispering to them all. Who knows what she was promising them?

They were like animals advancing on us from behind the stone pews. Bullets snapped as they hit the pews we were hunkered behind. Two of the men tried to advance too quickly and Benoit put them down with a quick burst of automatic fire. I leaned out from the side of the pew and fired a quick shot at the crown of a head I could see poking up from behind another pew; a body slumped into the aisle. The woman had been flanking us and appeared at the side of our pew firing. A bullet snapped past my head, then she was hit by a volley of automatic fire that cut into her legs.

I turned to see Benoit's rifle, smoke emerging from the barrel. He ran over and kicked the pistol from her hand.

"We need to get out of here. We don't have much time," Benoit said, slinging the rifle over his shoulder.

We were ready to leave when we heard the woman crawling along the ground. She was still alive and dragging herself by her fingernails toward the statue. We looked down at her, moving at a miserable pace, dragging herself inch by inch to the statue. It was still a distance away from her and the attempt seemed worthless.

"Please… Silent Mother… please… I sought out one of your shrines… I did what you asked…," she pleaded, barely able to breathe, crawling slowly and leaving a snake of blood in her trail.

"Please… do as you promised… restore my child's life… please, Silent Mother… I beg you… I beg you…," she screamed with all her remaining strength through gritted teeth, crawling toward the statue.

I pointed my rifle and shot her dead.

We both ran toward the exit without speaking. The Silent Mother called to me while I ran, I assume she did the same to Benoit. We ignored her; perhaps her power was more effective on those who were desperate enough to believe her lies.

We bounded up the stone staircase. The clock was against us. We reached the top of the staircase; the top of the step and the hatch had been blown away by the claymore. I crawled out over the rubble, Benoit followed. We sprinted through the auditorium as the ground shook and a loud thud rattled the building. It began to groan angrily, it's foundations clearly shaken by the blast.

As we sprinted through the corridor, the building began to list dangerously. The damn thing was falling into the swamp. We burst out the front doors of the lobby, down the steps, and onto the lawn. From the safety of the lawn we looked back at the Red House. It was sinking on one corner backward into the swamp. Then, suddenly, as if a support pillar had collapsed, half the building broke off and fell into the swamp. The rest soon followed as we looked on in silence.

After that night, I never heard the whispers of the Silent Mother again, but I often thought of the desperation of that woman and what the Silent Mother had promised her.

February
—2017—

I've Been Seeing A Man In My Backyard For The Past Two Nights
By D.J. Creamer

To start, I need to give some background:

- I am a male who lives in relatively nice neighborhood.
- It's your average small town run of the mill suburbs area with not a lot of people.
- I am a college kid who's home on break while my parents have gone away, which doesn't help at all.
- I have a two-story house.
- I do not have gun, nor do I have any real weapons other than kitchen knives.
- I am not on any medication and I have no record of schizophrenia or any other mental illnesses.
- I barely have any relationships with my neighbors, most of whom are elderly and the rest I have minimal contact with.
- I do not have any people in my neighborhood (that I know of) who have reasons to attack or harm me.

***

Now, let's get into what has been happening. About two nights ago, I woke up very late in the night and I went to the bathroom to go take a shit. Now, my second story bathroom has a window that can see the entirety of my backyard. Directly behind it is a cul-de-sac which you can see directly into. There is a group of trees and pile of rocks and mulch that divides it. Usually I can see everything in my backroom without turning on my because lights from my neighbor's house dimly lights the room.

As I am using the toilet, I look outside and I notice there is a car parked directly facing my house in the cul-de-sac. Now, if you have ever seen a cul-de-sac before, you would know that when you park you always either park next to the curves of the sac or the sides of the street. This car was directly facing the curve behind my house. I thought this was extremely strange considering whoever parked must have been there to visit someone but, if that were the case, then why would they have not parked in one of the driveways? The people who lived behind me were both elderly so they probably didn't have some big block party I didn't know about and, even then, only an idiot would park like that.

As I stared into the car, I could distinguish a figure in the driver's seat, just sitting there. Since the lights were not on in my bathroom, whoever was in the car probably couldn't see me through that window. At this point I was determined to see just who the fuck was in there, so I went downstairs, got my binoculars from my dad's closet, and went back to my bathroom to see who was there.

Take in mind this is 3 in the fucking morning; what person would be in their car just sitting there in the middle of the winter? As I go into my bathroom, I look outside to find…nothing. The car had since left. I thought I was relieved seeing as I probably was just freaking out over nothing and the person was just leaving whoever they were visiting but, then again, what are the odds that the moment I notice the car that's the moment that the person leaves?

I finally calmed myself down and went back to sleep. The next day, a mix of boredom and paranoia got the better of me; I decided it was time for some investigation. I go to my backyard cul-de-sac to see if there was any trace of the person who was there last night. Nothing. I go to my neighbors to see if they had anybody over the other night; maybe it would clarify just why the fuck somebody would be parked there. I asked both the owners of the 2 houses on the curves the cul-de-sac, all of whom said they did not have visitors. I asked for their numbers and I left.

This is when my paranoia really started to kick in. This was fucked up, I had no clue whether the person was coming back later, and I can't call the police as they won't respond to a complaint that isn't even valid. I decide to wait until later to see if the person came back. I spent that night talking with my college friends about it over video chat, all of whom thought I was either making it up, or freaking out over nothing. I sign off and watch Netflix until it's pretty late. The entire time,, I just kept thinking about looking out my window to check but, since my friends had told me I was worrying about nothing and also since I am a bit of a coward, I just never checked it.

Finally, the clock ticked 3:24 am; the exact time I woke up the night before. I thought, 'Fuck it, might as well check to be sure.' This is where I absolutely shit myself; the same exact car was parked and there was a man in a black hoodie and a ski mask standing right next to it just staring at my house. I immediately ran to go get my phone dialed my neighbors, none of which answered. I ran back to the window, only to see that he was standing in my fucking backyard. This was no longer a burglary attempt because, if it was, he would be looking through my lower house windows trying to break in. This had to be some sort of a stalker.

I decided fuck this and opened up my window and screamed at the top of my lungs, "WHO THE FUCK ARE YOU?!" No response. "I'M GOING TO CALL THE FUCKING POLICE. GET THE FUCK OFF MY PROPERTY!" I yelled.

Finally the man spoke ,"HAVE A NICE DAY!" in like that cheery way a cashier at the store would say when you are leaving. The man waltzed (and I literally mean waltzed like a happy cartoon character) back to his car and left.

I called the police department immediately. They asked me if I had any friends who were trying to play a prank on me. I said no. Like I said, this town was relatively small and the police did jack shit. They told me that if it happens again to call them immediately. I am shitting myself right now. It's currently 11:00 pm, and god knows he'll be back tonight. I am going to be looking out my window all night waiting for him. I'll keep you all in touch if anything happens. Wish me luck.

Edit 12:24 am: I am currently staring outside looking out my window waiting for the man to come. I have informed my neighbors about his arrival and they have told me they are also on the lookout. I feel extremely nervous but at least I have my neighbors helping me out. I just want this to be over.

Edit 1:24 am: Nothing has shown up yet. Got a call from my mom about a half hour ago. I haven't told them about any of the shit happening. I just told her I loved her and hung up the phone. My friends have been snap chatting me asking me about this shit. I said that I'll try to get a picture of him if I can. If I do, I'll upload it so you guys can see.

Edit 1:34 am: Neighbors told me they see a car parked up the street from them. One of my neighbors who's in his mid-40s says he's going to check it out. My foot is tapping the floor like crazy right now.

Edit 1:37 am: False alarm. Turns out it was just the car of a family who just got home. Fuck me, this suspense is making me sick.

Edit 1:48 am: One of my neighbors says he is going to sleep. This isn't good. I just hope the rest of them hold out for me until the rest of the night. I don't know if I'm going to fall asleep at all. I've already chugged two cups of coffee and I'm as alert as possible.

Edit 2:11 am: I was looking out my window when I heard something in the bushes of my backyard. I couldn't tell whether it was the guy, the wind, or some animal so I shined turned on the light in my backyard and saw nothing. I think the paranoia is getting to me.

Edit 2:17 am: Alright, it's official; I am losing my shit. I heard something crash in my kitchen and I ran down to see what was happening. Some pan had fallen over from the shelf. Nothing notable but it scared the absolute shit out of me. I went back upstairs to start looking out the window again. At one of the streets right of my backyard which is about 200 yards away, through the trees, I saw a car at a corner flashing its brights repeatedly and then making a right driving away from the street leading to my house. What the fuck is going on?! Is this motherfucker taunting me?

Edit 2:40 am: I am currently at my neighbor's house staring into my backyard/the cul-de-sac. I walked out my back door and sprinted and rang the door bell as fast as possible. They saw me and opened the door immediately. Scariest shit I have ever done. I was worried he was gonna pull up any second. Now I just wait and hope for the best.

Edit 2:51 am: Nothing out of the ordinary has happened. I am dreading what will happen at 3:24, though. I saw 2 cars pass by my house. I couldn't tell if they were the same car as the one the stalker was using. At the same time, I can't tell if it was the same car passing by both ways. This guy is playing tricks on my mind. I am ready to dial 911 at any second now. I called my parents and told them what is happening; they said they will be on their way home tomorrow. God, please protect me.

Edit 3:01 am: This guy is definitely coming. A car came up the street on the cul-de-sac and started flashing its high beams again and left. He is trying to fuck with my mind. Thank god I left the house, because the direction he is going he is definitely coming back around to my house. Fuck, I'm scared and I'm not even in my house anymore. The moment I even see him outside his car, I am calling the police.

Edit 3:11 am: My neighbor and I both agreed we are going to leave the house and drive to the police station as soon as we see him park near my house. My heart is racing. I can't believe I had been just waiting in my house alone for the past couple hours. What the fuck was I thinking?

Edit 3:20 am: Still nothing yet. Even if he doesn't come, I sure as hell am not going back. I'm not even sure if I'll stay here. This is the scariest shit that has ever happened to me, holy fuck.

Edit 3:25 am: SOMEONE HAS PARKED IN MY FUCKING DRIVEWAY!!!!!!! I am getting the fuck out of here. I'll try to update you guys on mobile or later when/if they arrest this guy but I am leaving now. Thank you all for the support.

Edit 1:15 pm 2/19/17: For those who are concerned, I am alive. I went to the police station and I have been questioned and they are working on finding the guy. They haven't found him yet, unfortunately. I went to a hotel and got some sleep and I just woke up. I'll write more about this in a new post but for right now I am just taking some time to get this sorted out. Thanks to everyone for their support.

***

For anyone who has been reading this, I am alive and well but far from safe. As my neighbor and I were waiting for the coast to be clear, I saw my garage door open at approximately 3:27 am and, right then, my neighbor and I booked it to his car. As we were leaving, I saw the light turn on in my bathroom and I nearly threw up realizing how easily he got in and how I had been just a sitting duck an hour prior. I have been fantasizing over and over of how if I had stayed in there, my neighbors would have called me telling me he was in my driveway and I would had heard my garage opening with dread just knowing I was absolutely fucked. Once we were in the car, we sped off to the police station.

The police gave me the usual rundown of questions in this type of situation: Did I know this man? When and where was my first encounter with him? Could I identify his car or did I manage to write down his license plate? I told them he had only come two times prior and that both times it was too dark to tell even with the street light. When the man had parked in my driveway, one of my neighbors who had still been on the lookout said she that she saw the car was a gray Volkswagen with no license plate. She went on to say she saw the man type in the code to my garage, go inside, and turn on each of my lights, as though he was checking the whole house. The man had stayed there for 5 minutes according to her and proceeded to get back in his car without taking anything and sped off down my street. She notified the police immediately and they have been searching for him since then.

Nothing has come up. We returned to find that the house had been left relatively unscathed. The police did not find even a trace of DNA. Whoever this man was, he was meticulous as all hell and somehow had gained the knowledge of what my garage code was. It makes me shiver to think he may have been watching me even as I typed it in earlier in the week. God only knows what other knowledge he has to track me down. My parents have still yet to return home from their trip as their plane was delayed so, as of right now, I am alone and still at the hotel with only a bottle of Jack Daniels to console me. A couple police cars have been stationed around the area of my house looking for the guy and they are all waiting upon his arrival. I am not leaving this hotel until this fucker is caught. I don't think I will be able to sleep tonight. I am hoping this is the night he finally can't track me.

The police have advised me to stop using any form of social media that can be indicative of where I am. That means no Snapchat, no Instagram, no Facebook; nothing. They told me that I can use my laptop as long as I remain as low profile as possible. This means all I can do now is wait for the police to call me and tell me that the stalker has been caught. Now I am gonna try and figure out just who this guy is and why he might try to be stalking me.

Theory 1: My 9th grade Italian teacher. So, I went to a private school and this teacher had basically been one of the biggest lunatics I had ever met in a school system. He was very outspoken in the way he described politics and very mean-spirited during his time teaching. He would always make fun of students, had sometimes fallen asleep in class, and would always make perverted comments towards girls I knew. So one day, I decided to write an email to the Dean asking him to please fire the man from his teaching position and explaining the unacceptable behavior he had while working. It worked, and I have never seen the man since. Now, the reason I think he could be a possibility is because he never particularly liked me. In fact, I feel as though he singled me out in a lot of instances and picked on me. I don't know if he ever found out I sent the email but, if he did, I am extremely worried. I can't tell if it was him or not when he spoke in my backyard as I was in full adrenaline mode while I was screaming at him. I would say this is not a likely suspect but I'm just not sure.

Theory 2: My Christian deacon from back in second grade. I used to be part of this church program a while back when I was in elementary school. Out of all the head figures there one that always stood out to me: Deacon Anthony. He was a middle-aged man, very soft spoken, and he had always been very particularly nice to me and my friend Kevin. He would often bring us candy, talked to us about our home life, and treated us more fairly than the rest of the kids. One day my friend Kevin had told me that Deacon Anthony had asked Kevin if he wanted to go home with him to hang out. Kevin said no to him and told me. I told my parents about this and they had immediately contacted the church and told them about it. After that, I never saw Deacon Anthony again. My parents later told me that they had contacted the board and he was removed from the church. If this is the guy, he must have had a massive personality shift after that incident because the way the man happily told me to "HAVE A NICE DAY" did not match up with the one he had when I was younger.

Theory 3: My classmate Derek from 8th grade. Derek was one of those insecure types who would always get off by making other people feel small. He was your standard 8th grade middleschool shiteater who deserved nothing but a good ass whooping, which unfortunately never came. However, what did happen was I had started a rumor about him that I wish to not bring up, but it pretty much ruined his reputation and made him a laughing stock. He never found out it was me as far as I could tell but, from what I heard from my hometown while I went off to public school, the rumor hadn't stopped by high school and he turned into one of those quiet kids who never talked. Keep in mind, this kid literally had told my whole friend group to stop hanging out with me so, as far as I can tell, this revenge was extremely justified in my mind. This may in fact be the prime suspect as he would most likely know where I live. I tried finding any sort of social media about him but nothing came up. This guy is a ghost and I have no idea what he has been up to.

Theory 4: Some complete stranger who I have no association with. Maybe this is just a genuine old school stalker who takes pride in picking out their prey from a random crowd. No one I have seen in this town for the past week has seemed particularly odd. The only one that comes to mind was this weird cashier at 7/11 who seemed particularly in love with his job. He may have some form of Asperger's syndrome or just maybe he just takes pride in being a cashier but he was always very polite with his customers when he had been interacting with them. I had gone in to get a soda from the fountain and as the store was empty he had asked me:

"Hey, is that all you're getting?"

I said, "Yeah, this is all."

So he continues, "Oh, well, congratulations! It's free!"

I thought, 'Sweet, a free soda. This guy is the shit.' I thanked him a ton as he was smoking a cigarette outside and I said, "Have a good one," and left. Now, I know what all of you must be thinking. This is definitely the guy. He's a fucking cashier for crying out loud! Well, I am just not sure. This guy was probably in his thirties, seemed extremely grateful for his low end job, and just seemed content with what he had. He didn't strike me as a stalker, but then again I haven't been back to the store since so he may still be there or not there at all. Time will tell. I might have to stop by tomorrow and do a little more investigating.

As we speak, it is 11:00 pm again and I am staring out my hotel window scrolling through reddit. I am still dreading the moment I see a car with flashing high beams pull into the parking lot, so I will probably just be looking out my window all night again. I will post more updates if necessary. I appreciate you all. Bye for now.

Edit 12:43 am: I'm reading all your comments and, just so you guys know, I can't get ahold of a gun as easily as most of you think. I live in a state where that shit does not fly. The best thing I think I have right now is pepper spray and a baseball bat.

Edit 1:37 am: Call me a lunatic, but I left my room to get some fresh air. I couldn't stand being in this small ass hotel room one more second. I was bugging out like crazy, though. Every person I saw seemed like a threat to me. I started talking with this one guy in the hotel lobby. Says he's been traveling from state on some sort of self-indulged journey across the country. I asked him if he has any experiences with stalkers and he told me that he had been receiving anonymous calls a couple years back from some guy. I asked if he has ever encountered one in his backyard or anything and he just looked at me funny. I explained to him the situation and he wished me the best of luck. Nothing out of the ordinary but it was nice to have some real human interaction while I am losing my mind.

Edit 1:46 am: Alright, one of the janitors must be fucking with me. I spent the last 10 minutes searching for my phone and asked someone outside my room to call it for me. I listened for the ringing and it's in the fucking safe. The password is not the one they gave me. What the fuck?! This is fucking ridiculous! Whoever fucking did this is going to get torn a new one. I'm going to the manager right now to get this sorted out.

Edit 2:08 am: I'm demanding a different room. I am not staying in that same fucking room one more second. The whole staff is in there now trying to figure out the safe pass word. Meanwhile, the manager is looking for the janitors who have been in my room to ask what the fuck they were thinking. Fuck this. I'm tired, I'm worried, and now I just lost my fucking phone. FUCK!

Edit 2:24 am: It's not the garage code, guys; I checked. Even if it was, why would it be and how would the fucking stalker even get into my hotel room let alone rewire my safe?

Edit 2:26 am: Guys I'm not leaving the hotel, ok? I already paid the money to stay here. I don't have any other place to go that's not 100 miles away. I have no car, I got here in an Uber, and at least here there are over a hundred people. The stalker is not gonna come into a hotel full of people.

Edit 2:40 am: Ok, now you guys got me worried. I'm sitting in my hotel room, all alone with no phone. No way to call an Uber. No way to call the police. I'm starting to think one of the janitors got bribed to do this. I now not only have no way of driving away from here but I have no way of contacting any family or anyone for that matter who can get me away from the hotel. I'm going to wait another 45 minutes and, if they don't open the safe, I am demanding they call an Uber for me and I'm driving the hell out of here.

Edit 2:53 am: Someone just knocked on the door saying the safe is open. I told them alright and then they asked me to come get it. I asked him if he can slip it under the door but he said I need to go get it myself. I told him I would in a couple minutes and he said he'd be waiting. I don't know what to do, guys; you're all fucking with my mind.

Edit 3:10 am: The man said that my phone is in the main lobby if I want it. I am on my laptop next to my window and I could have sworn I saw a car flashing its high beams out of the corner of my eye. I don't know if I should hold out till morning or get my phone and leave...

Edit 3:14 am: Guys, I am not waiting until 3:24 for this guy to fucking come into my room and jump me. I am packing and getting the fuck out of here. I'll keep you guys posted on mobile when I get my phone back.

Edit 3:16 pm: Alright, guys. I'm staying a friend's place for right now. Just to clarify, when I said not a trace of DNA was found I meant that there was nothing that was found to trace this guy back. Like a glove or fingerprints on the garage key pad. The police did not do a full investigation, obviously. The guy still hasn't been found. My neighbors have told me no one has been back to the house and my parents are currently staying at my aunt's down south. I got my phone back and there was a missed call from some guy named Nick Sullivan. What's strange his name was never put in my contacts. I have never met anybody named Nick Sullivan in my life and I don't know how it was in there. I tried calling back and it just went to voicemail. Creepy shit none the less. Maybe I'm just paranoid, I don't know. I'll see if I can make another update tonight. Bye for now.

***

If you have not read my last update, I have since left my hotel and I took an Uber to my friend's house an hour away. As I got in the Uber, the driver had been waiting for me to come out and I got into his car. I nearly shat myself as he turned on his car to find that the car the one directly across from it in the parking lot was a gray Volkswagen. I couldn't tell if it was the same one from the night before because A) this one had a license plate and B) I have never gotten a good look at it up close before so it could just be any other person's car. As we were leaving, I looked up to the hotel and in one of the rooms there was clearly a figure looking out the window. I'm not jumping to any conclusions right now as to whether it was him. I'm not sure if it was the same room as mine. I honestly keep questioning myself at this point as to whether all this shit is real or just paranoia. Maybe the guy actually did find me and I was just about to be slaughtered, maimed, or worse; or maybe this is just a classic case of the Baader-Meinhof Phenomenon and I am just finding ways to freak myself out.

One thing that is for sure is that this guy is definitely still hunting me. I got a text from Mr. Sullivan, Nick, or whatever the fuck he wants to call himself and I am still petrified after seeing it. At exactly 8:34 pm today, he sent me a video and the only other thing he's said in the text was "I see you."

I am positively sure the house in the video is mine. Now I want to know when was the video taken. It probably was not taken last night as police were all watching my house, so that means he either took it the first two nights or as recent as today, and I'm really hoping that it's the ladder. If he took it today that means he probably still thinks that I am staying there. Unfortunately, though, this guy seems far from stupid and, if he has stalked me enough to know my garage code, he most certainly must have noticed I am no longer coming back there. Either way, he is trying to terrorize me and he is probably trying to get me to flee my house for his perfect moment to strike.

In some twisted way, I expected worse. I don't know what makes this psychopath tick; maybe dead animals, maybe dead people, or just seeing his victims crumble under all the stress he is inflicting on them. What I am dreading is if he actually manages to find me at my friend's place. This guy, we'll call him Tom (not his real name, obviously), took up the mantle of protecting me and, if this guy manages to find me, I will never forgive myself for putting this on him. I offered to pay him money but he refused so, for the past two hours, we have just been doing nothing but drinking beer and playing video games to calm my nerves.

Tom is a bit of a hick, I would say. He loves dipping, sitting on his front porch drinking beer, and he has a pretty large collection of guns (probably the best friend to have in a situation like this) just as you guys have been begging me to get ahold of. So, all in all right now, I am feeling the most secure I've felt out of all the days since this shit has started.

I have informed the police about my situation and the video and they told me they had not seen a car park near my house at all in the past day. I gave them the number and they told me they will do their best to try to triangulate its position.

Now that it's getting late, my friend and I have decided we need to start securing the place in case of intruders. His house has security alarms, he lives on a relatively busy street so no one can park near the house without parking in the driveway, and he has been staying off of social media as I have asked him to do for my safety.

The anxiety hasn't stopped, but this is the first time I have a friend by my side to help me with this situation so I feel a little better. He gave me one of his pistols and we started shooting in the range in his backyard despite me having never shot a gun before. We are currently on his porch talking as I write this down.

I am very grateful for all your support for the past couple days, guys. Updates will come as always, everybody. Have a good night, everyone. Hopefully nothing notable will happen for once.

Now we wait.

***

Last night when I posted the third update, many people in the comments had told me I needed to stop using reddit as it would only lead to my location, so I did. I turned off my laptop and put my phone on airplane mode for the past day. I decided my best course of action would to be to calm my nerves and finally get some shut-eye. I signed off of reddit, jumped onto my buddy's couch, and finally went to sleep.

At approximately 3 in the morning, my friend woke me up telling me I needed to check something out. I immediately grabbed the revolver I had left on the table next to the couch, and we went to the front porch. In the distance, we could see a car parked all the way down the road. I'd say it was about 300 yards away and still visible because of a street light. The following was the conversation best I could remember it:

Tom: See that car down there? I was dozing off and the moment I snapped out of it, the thing just showed up out of nowhere. It was just sitting there.

Me: How long do you think it's been there for?

Tom: I'm not sure. I saw it there and stared at it for a good 2 minutes. After that, I took my flashlight and started flashing it on and off. Then the car shut off, some guy got out, waved, and walked into the woods.

There is a wooded area near my buddy's house that, if you walk through it, you can go walk into a large open field in his backyard. There is a fence dividing the field from his backyard, but it can be easily hopped.

Me: Do you think we should go check it out?

Tom: No, this guy could be going into the woods and coming back round towards my back door. You have to stay here and I'll go check it out.

Me: Alright. If it's a gray Volkswagen, we need to leave immediately. I want you to record the license plate and look inside for anything notable. That means ropes, knives, duct tape; anything sketchy, we need to get out of here.

Tom: Alright. Wait inside and defend the house. Make sure no one gets inside.

I went back inside and stared out the window as Tom approached the vehicle with his 12 gauge. I went to the back of his house stared out his backyard window and saw some figure start walking across the field. This was particularly strange as there were no houses visible in this field and he just seemed like he was walking towards nowhere. He climbed over a hill and he was no longer in view from the window. I went back to the front window to look at the car and Tom was checking it out. I felt relieved for the slightest moment as I felt like maybe, just maybe, I was overreacting. Then Tom's home phone rang.

I looked at it and saw the caller ID. It was my area code, not Tom's. At this point, I had my phone still on airplane mode so I assumed it was someone from my neighborhood/family trying to contact me. I felt almost intrusive seeing that I was answering a call to a home that was not even mine, but now was not a time to take chances so I answered.

I picked up the phone:

Me: Hello?

Caller: (Silence for a few seconds)

Me: Excuse me, who this?

Caller: Oh, excuse me, sir. My apologies. Is this the owner of the household?

Me: No, I am just a friend of the owner. He is currently outside. Who is this?

Caller: (Silence for another few seconds)

At this point, I just felt that feeling you get in the pit of your stomach when you realized you fucked up. I just revealed that I am here alone and whoever is calling just realized that.

Me: Hello?

Caller: Who else are you with, sir? Is it just you?

At this point, I was shaking and I could barely speak without stumbling my words. I decided the best thing to do was lie like no tomorrow.

Me: Um, no; we are having a party and there are a couple other people here. I ask again, sir; who is calling?

Caller: Are you sure about that? I was just walking by and saw that there are only two cars in his driveway.

At this point, I completely lost my shit.

Me: Listen, just fucking tell me who you are. Why the fuck are you calling this house so late?

Caller: (More silence)

Me: Hello?! Can you please just fucking tell me?!

Caller: I apologize, sir. I may have the wrong number. Tell whoever owns this house to call back. Thank you.

Then he hung up.

Tom had come back and said the car was not a Volkswagen and had a license plate. He said the windows were tinted and the doors were locked so there was really nothing he could make out. I told him about the caller and he said he had no idea whose number that was. He called back, no answer. He called from a restricted number, no answer.

An hour passed by as we were sitting on the porch and we heard an audible slam from his back door. We both looked at each other and he motioned to follow him around back. We saw nothing out of the ordinary. We looked around everywhere for footprints, but still nothing. When we had gone back to the front porch after countless minutes of searching, it was approximately 4 in the morning. It wasn't until 10 minutes after we got back to the porch that we noticed the car 300 yards away was gone.

I haven't gotten any sleep since last night. I told Tom I wanted to leave his house because I need to keep moving, and he said he wants to come too. He locked up all his doors, brought some guns, and we drove off at 6 in the morning. Police still haven't done jack shit despite all the valuable intelligence I gave them, and I've been on the road all day with my friend. I drove a lot and he slept in the back. We are currently at a McDonald's as I type this. We were joking saying if we do end up getting kidnapped, murdered, attacked, these nosleep posts will make one hell of a "Based on a real story" script.

I'm just tired, guys. Tired of being stalked, tired of being hunted down, and tired of making these goddamn posts. I just want this to be over.

If anything happens tonight... I'll let you all know. Bye for now.

***

I'm sorry to inform you guys but I think it's about time we wrap up the show. My parents have returned home and both the police and my neighbors haven't seen the man ever since I left. I've been on the road for the past few days and I just want to stop running. My parents informed me that they got ahold of a revolver now and all I want to do is just go home, sleep in my own bed, and be done with this madness.

I'm starting to think that all of this has just been in my head. The guy hasn't made any notable appearances in my life since that night and maybe that video he sent was just from the first two nights I saw him. I don't know. I guess that's been the problem ever since the start of this is that I have just been over reacting to this whole phenomenon. Maybe this guy is just some deranged burglar. Maybe he came to my house thinking I was somebody else. I don't know for sure.

Tom and I have been on and off the road, only stopping to get food or to piss. A lot of comments have been telling me to either stop using reddit and to stake it out and confront the man myself. I've come to realize that I have been making a poor choice documenting everything that has happened on reddit; god only knows if this man has been using it to his advantage. But more importantly, I've been hiding and running away from him all this time. I thought it was finally time I confront him myself. Now, I am not going to make an effort to contact him or find him, but if he decides he wants to come and attack my house, my family, and myself, then he will finally meet his maker.

However, I thought a good start would be to pay the 7/11 guy a visit today and we decided to confront him. I just needed to be sure that it wasn't him. We parked in front of the 7/11 at about 8 at night, about 3 hours ago. This is the conversation we had to the best of my memory.

Tom: Is this the guy?

Me: Yeah, this is him. Let's just go in and ask him a few questions. We just need to scare him a little and see how he responds.

Tom took his pistol from the backseat and put it in his holster.

Me: Dude, is that necessary? Look, man, we aren't even sure if this is the guy. We can't just pull a gun on him and make him shit himself.

Tom: Just taking some precaution is all, and if this is the guy then we gotta be careful.

With that, Tom got out of his car and started walking in as I followed.

As soon as we walked in he asked:

Cashier: Hey, boys; how are we doing today?

We both gave him a stern look so he responded:

Cashier: Hey, guys, come on. What's the sour mood?

I looked at Tom and he looked back at the cashier and asked:

Tom: Lovely day, isn't it?

I could see that the guy was getting visibly nervous and began to sweat a little.

Cashier: Hey, man, I couldn't help but notice that gun in your holster. Pretty nice gun. That's an M1911 Colt, right? My dad had one of those.

We didn't break eye contact.

Me: Yeah, I would say it's a pretty nice day, isn't it? How's your day going, well?

I went directly in front of the counter and got face to face with him.

Me: Hey, can ask you something?

I could see the cashier swallowing and he coughed:

Cashier: Uh, yeah, sure. What is it?

Me: Do you drive here to work by any chance?

Cashier: Oh, uh, haha negatory. My friend drops me off.

I looked at Tom and he looked back at the guy.

Tom: You best not being lying to us.

The cashier broke:

Cashier: Look, guys. I don't want any trouble. If you are here to rob the place, that doesn't concern me. I'm just a guy who works here, alright? Just take the money and go if that's what you want.

Me: We aren't here to rob anything, just asking a couple questions if that's alright with you.

Cashier folded his arms and said,

Cashier: Sure, ask whatever you need. What's up?

Me: When does your shift end?

Cashier: Oh, usually around 3 in the morning. Hey, what's all this about? Boys, are you guys undercover cops or something?

Me: Have you seen a gray Volkswagen in the past couple nights you've been working here?

Cashier: Actually, I did. The night before you came in, there was a guy who came in after you.

Me: Did he buy anything?

Cashier: Yeah, he bought some cigarettes and dipping tobacco. He didn't say much, but he said he had a long night ahead of him.

Tom: I take it he gave you ID?

Cashier: Yeah, he did.

Me: What was his name, do you remember?

Cashier: I think it was Nathan Silverstein or something like that.

Me: Nick Sullivan?

Cashier: Shit, I'm pretty sure that was his name. What's it to you, by the way?

Tom: Can we see your ID for a second?

He showed us his I.D. and this guy seemed to be completely innocent.

Me: Alright, man, thank for your time. The police might come later to ask for your camera feed from that night, but I appreciate your help.

We left and that was the end of it. Finally, after all these days of running we finally got a decent lead on this guy. We called the police and they are currently going over the tapes. This was an amazing feeling now that we will finally have a good lead on this guy now. I can finally go home.

Tom has been such a good friend the past couple days. He has stuck with me through thick and thin, even through these rough times, and I am eternally grateful for what he has done for me in this time of need. After a long day of traveling, he told me that his girlfriend has been awfully worried about him, and this made me feel even worse about the situation. Finally told him that we needed to part ways, and that I wanted him to go home and rest and that I apologized for putting him in danger. He told me not to sweat it and that it was a pretty exciting experience for him despite it maybe putting our lives in jeopardy. I gave him some money to help him with his troubles. He is going to his girlfriend's house he said and he will be staying there for a while until this gets completely sorted out.

No more running, no more fear, no more stalking. I am finally done with this, guys. I can't wait to go home, see my family, and be safe and sound in my home again. I want to thank you all for your support through these past few days. It has really meant a lot.

At some point, I got texts from my parents saying it was safe to come home. When I called them, everything sounded normal. However, my Mom sounded somewhat worried and flustered about the whole situation when my dad put her on the phone. I asked her what was wrong and she had simply told me, "I'm just under a lot of stress," and followed it by, "Just come home, please. We miss you." I feel really sorry for them, I don't know why, but I somewhat blame myself for all this shit happening. If they haven't seen the stalker at all, then this must have to do with me and me alone. I must have done something to cause this man to torment my family.

As we speak, Tom has just left back home and I am finishing this last update at Starbucks. I'll call an Uber and I'll finally be home. If the guy gets caught, I'll link you guys to a news article or something but this is the final update.

Thank you all for the advice and enthusiasm. Peace.

Edit 12:12 am: Just came home and there aren't any cars in my driveway. I'm a little worried. Calling my parents.

Edit 12:14 am: Alright, no answer from my parents. Gonna try the garage code now.

Edit 12:16 am: Welp, my parents must have changed the garage code or something. I'm banging on the door and no one is fucking answering.

Edit 12:18 am: Jesus, it's fucking cold haha.

Edit 12:21 am: Alright, well, lights are turning on in my bedroom so they are obviously home.

Edit 12:24 am: Have a nice day everyone!

Edit 12:34 am: LOL guys I'm just kidding. Ya'll need to chill.

Edit 12:35 am: More updates to come, guys. Lots and lots of updates.

Edit 12:38 am: JUST WAIT FOR 3:24 AM EVERYONE!

EMERGENCY ALERT

By Preston Yates

EMERGENCY ALERT. THIS IS NOT A TEST. IMMEDIATE THREAT FOR RESIDENTS OF **[withheld]** COUNTIES. BE WARY OF: SEVERE WINDS, LIGHTNING, SEVERE RAIN, FLASH FLOODS. RESIDENTS ARE ADVISED TO STAY INDOORS. PLEASE LOCK OR BAR ALL ENTRYWAYS INTO YOUR HOUSE. RESTRAIN FROM USING ANY DEVICES THAT EMIT LIGHT OR LOUD NOISE. PLEASE ENTER A ROOM WITH NO WINDOWS. EFFECTIVE INDEFINITELY. ISSUED BY THE NATIONAL WEATHER SERVICE.

This was the message I was greeted by in the middle of an episode of Big Bang Theory in my living room. Frozen halfway through a forkful of Kraft Mac N' Cheese, I sat bolt upright and turned around to look out the window. The sky, as I thought, was crystal clear. A few clouds, but nothing crazy. No rain. No thunder. Nothing. Confused, I turned off the TV, erasing the alert from the screen. My two dogs came walking over to me and I patted them on their heads. One of my dogs, the other's brother, was shaking profusely from the buzzing noise that always shows up with Amber Alerts and the like. I left them in the living room and walked through my kitchen and onto my front porch. My neighbors, too, were standing outside their houses, all looking at the sky in bemusement.

An immediate threat? It didn't seem like it, I thought as my phone started buzzing with the same tone. One by one, everyone else's phones started ringing.

I should explain, I guess, that I have never experienced a severe weather warning for real. Not once in my life. I suppose it should come as no surprise, seeing as I live in Oregon of all places. I supposed maybe it was just a mistake but, just as the thought floated across my mind, I heard the siren.

The siren of the squad car coming down the street. An officer talked through the speaker, "This is not a drill. Please enter your homes immediately. Do not go outside under any circumstances."

Never the kind of guy to ignore higher authorities, I entered my house nervously, turned off all the lights on the above-ground floors, and took my dogs into my basement with a sleeping bag, some food, my phone, a charger, some spare batteries, flashlight, and other essentials. I called my brother, who lives a couple of blocks away, and asked him if he had gotten the message. He had. I considered saying we should stay together to wait out the storm, but then I figured we'd probably get in trouble for that. So I hung up, got comfortable on my sleeping bag, and started browsing Reddit. Eventually, I fell asleep, seeing as I was under stress and had woken up pretty early. When I woke up, I realized that I still didn't hear any rain. Seriously, nothing at all. More confused than ever, I decided to see if the alert had been called off. I turned on my phone and called my brother again. It went straight to voicemail, though, so I gave up. I decided to risk it and go upstairs. I had to squeeze between the door and the wall to keep my dogs from following me upstairs, but I won and they stayed in the basement. I walked through my kitchen to the front door and looked out the window part of it. As I squinted to see outside in the dark (strange, seeing as it was only 2:00 PM judging by my clock), the TV flickered briefly. I looked around at it and it flickered again, but this time every device on the ground floor flickered. Thinking little of it, I turned around and looked through the door again. Every house on the block had its lights turned off. Nobody was outside.

Except for one teenage girl.

A thin, short-haired girl wearing what looked like a pillowcase walked unsteadily down the street, very slowly, looking as though she was having some difficulty. I turned around, now extremely confused and worried, and got the dogs' food bowls, which I had forgotten earlier. When I looked up, one of the houses, the one diagonally across from mine (right next to the house across the street and to the left) had its lights on and one of its windows broken. I shuddered and rushed back into the basement as the lights flickered intensely.

I locked the door to the basement and sat on an old, tattered couch that I had brought down here—the basement is where I put everything I didn't have room for. So, yeah, it's packed. Oh yeah, I forgot to mention something that may be worth noting: I live in a small town. A very small town, probably with a population of under 500. Or less. As a matter of fact, it isn't even on most maps. We never make any news, we never have any scandals or anything. This is the first interesting thing that's happened, I think, since Mrs. [withheld] lost her dentures to a raccoon. So, it's possible this whole thing seems way worse than it is.

Call me crazy but, until a few minutes ago, I was thoroughly enjoying myself. I love these scenarios and my basement is totally secure, so I'm having the time of my life. Well, I was. I decided to turn on my radio—what harm could it do, as long as I didn't turn the volume up to high?

I was surprised to find that our local radio station was still up and running. They were talking about the weather, so I listened hard for any news that I hadn't heard. There wasn't any—they were just as confused as us. Not wanting to listen to crappy pop music indefinitely, I tuned into another station. This one was one I hadn't heard before.

"Could you give me the status of [withheld] county? Over."

"No new developments. Over."

"Okay. Any fatalities? Over."

"What part of 'no new developments' do you not understand, McClellan? A squad car will be passing through soon to scan the area for the target. Over."

"Any ETA on that? Over."

"No, not yet. Over."

"And any word from HQ, Jones? Over."

"No, McClellan. Not yet. Not since 013 first got out. Over."

"Well, let me know if and when they contact you. Over."

At that point, I lost the signal. Well, not really, but the connection got so weak that I could barely make out anything they were saying. I figured I must have found a police communication channel. And I had been left with no answers whatsoever.

That was about forty-five minutes ago, as of me writing this now. Guys, I don't know what's going on. Do any of you live near me? You'll know if you've received the warning. I'd say what county I live in, and which ones were affected, but I don't want to for privacy reasons. Anyway, I'll keep you guys updated, okay? Until then, wish me luck.

EDIT: Woah, guys, this has blown up. I'll be sure to keep you posted over the next few days!

UPDATE: Just a quick update before the first major update—about five minutes ago, a car alarm went off somewhere to the right of my house. I'm too freaked out to go check it out, but I'll go up and see how it looks tomorrow morning, and I'll update you then.

***

Hello, everybody and sorry for the wait. I know a lot of you have been waiting to hear more about my current situation. I have, however, been reading and responding to some of your comments, and I have some new insight into what may be going on. I still have access to the police radio channel, but I haven't had a good signal from it since my first attempt, and I haven't tried looking at it very much. About an hour ago, however, I did get into it. And I wrote down everything as I heard it.

"Officer Jones? You there? Over."

"I am, who is this? Over."

"Officer Sloan, sir. Do you have any intel from HQ? Over."

"'Fraid not. I just got done talking to McClellan and that SOB Kowalski. Any word over on your end? Over."

"Not since the last broadcast about forty-five minutes ago. Last thing I heard was about the footage of the wreck. Over."

"Yeah. Suspected as much. How are you holding up, Sloan? Over."

"Alright, all things considering. And you, Jones? Over."

"Well enough. I'll tell you though, if 013 doesn't turn up fast... I might just end up like poor ol' Officer Brown—with my brains scattered on the ceiling. Over."

"Rest his soul. Over."

At this point, Jones and Sloan went silent for a good ten seconds at least.

"Well, I guess I'd better get in touch with Kowalski—I put him in charge of examining the wreck footage. Wish me luck. Over."

"Yessir. Over."

Sloan disconnects and Jones waits a minute to call Kowalski.

"Kowalski? This is Jones. Over."

"Jones, hey. I'm just starting on that wreck footage. I haven't noticed anything out of the ordinary yet, but… time will tell. Over."

"Right. Look, Kowalski, I need you to focus. This is one of the weirdest parts of the whole ordeal. Think about it. A cop crashes into a telephone pole in a deserted road in broad daylight? Over."

"With all due respect, it might have been an honest mistake. I mean… come on, it's pretty dark out, what with the disturbances we were trying to prevent 013 from releasing. Over."

"Look, we all know 013 is an anomaly. That's nothing new. But I'm telling you, either he found her and she got the upper hand… Or… Let's just say I'm not ruling out suicide. Over."

"Whatever. Hey, let me get back to—"

The signal cut out.

Also worth noting: the emergency broadcast I received has now been updated to say that emergency services have been suspended indefinitely and leaving one's house is punishable by law. Also, I took a look of the format of the broadcast and the interface of it. It isn't one I've recognized before, but in my confused state I had been unable to tell. Weird, but what hasn't been lately?

I've been doing alright as of late, but I'm still paranoid at every sound I hear. As I started writing this, the wind picked up, and I can hear rain hitting the roof, getting harder by the minute. Looks like that weather warning wasn't entirely bullshit, huh?

So, I took my dogs up to the shower to do their business, as one of you suggested. I haven't gone upstairs yet but I have nothing else to report and I don't want to give you a half-assed update, so I'm going to go take a gander out the window and document what I see as I see it.

I just went upstairs. I think I'll take the box of Samoas down with me when I go back down. Hell, I'll take the Samoas AND the Thin Mints. Desperate times call for desperate measures. As you maybe can tell, humor is how I deal with stress. Unhealthy, I know, but whatever. It is what it is.

I just went to the window. I don't see anything, but the neighbor's window is still very broken. The street is very dark and all the lights are very off. Now it's raining, though—the streets are overflowing with water, almost, and—there, the first flash of lightning. Thunder came immediately. The storm's right over us. Right over our little town. The girl doesn't seem to be outside anymore, but I'll be keeping my eyes open. Weird, after that first lightning strike, the sky's lighting up every few seconds. Like I said, nobody around here, including me, is very informed on severe weather, seeing as it never comes our way, but I'm pretty sure that isn't common.

Okay, I just—what the fuck? Okay, the neighbor's door just opened. The one with the broken window. Nobody's there, though. Must've been the wind. I hope he noticed. Come to think of it, maybe I should give him a call and see how he's doing. We used to talk sometimes, after all. It would be nice to hear from someone going through the same shit.

Wait.

I can see him. He's lying on the floor. Oh shit, the girl just came through the door. I ducked (haha, I changed it but autocorrect said fucked) under the window. I don't think she saw me. I'm going to peek out the window just to check.

No, okay, she's walking down the street now. She just passed my house. I don't know why she'd willingly go outside in weather like this. In a scenario like this. But whatever. I'm going back into the basement.

I called my brother earlier. He hasn't gone upstairs in a while. Good thing, too. He said he heard a crash from one of his neighbors' houses a little while earlier, but nothing too loud. Nothing loud enough to cause serious concern.

Weird, as I'm writing, my dogs look worried. Haha, without them I'd have lost my mind by now. Without you guys, too—it's nice having people to talk to in a time like this. Hmm, maybe they have to go do their business again. It's risky though, seeing as my bathroom is upstairs. I'm going to take them upstairs, but I'll take my phone with me.

We just entered the bathroom. Nothing out of the ordinary. Okay, they're done. We're going back downstairs. I'm going to duck past the window, though. Come to think of it, I should really invest in some blinds for that window.

FUCK.

I just went into the basement, but as I passed the window, I saw her pass it too on the other side. I don't think she saw me, but holy fuck. Why is she out there wandering like this? By now it's crossed my mind multiple times that she is "013." And from this close… that pillowcase looks a bit more hospital gown-esque. Shit, guys. I'd phone the cops, but I don't even know their number. I need to go. I'll update you guys soon. Until then, assume I'm alive.

UPDATE: Okay, guys, so by now I've figured out that 911 takes you to the police, buuuuuut I also remembered that bit about emergency services being suspended. So there's that.

***

Hello, everybody; welcome back to my special hell.

It's been raining a lot lately. Rain and thunder. And the wind is really howling something terrible. But as of yet I'm alright. I haven't heard anything from the cops, who, according to some users who told me cops no longer use radio channels to communicate, may be something else, like an independent organization. Like storm chasers or something, but chasing escaped mental patients instead of storms.

Anyway, me and the dogs are doing fine at this point. Nothing has really transpired since my last update. I know, I know; I really should stop going upstairs. But today, I have to. I'll be real sneaky, okay? But I need to. I only have enough food for today—I GUESS I could stretch it to tomorrow if I really rationed it but, honestly, I'd prefer to get it over with now. ...Huh, the lights just flickered. I mean, sure, they've been doing it a lot lately, but that time it lasted a while. Anyway, I checked the alert on my phone again, but nothing about it was different. I recently ran upstairs to get some towels and plastic bags to deal with the dogs' defecation, but I didn't see the girl, whom I'm assuming is 013 and whom I'm just going to refer to as 013 for now. My neighbor's door was closed again, but that's the only thing that's changed.

As I'm writing, I can hear a siren. Not one I've heard before—closer to a police siren than anything else, but still a bit different. I considered going up to check it out, but you guys would kill me, right? I really hope this all ends soon. I only have, like, bread, ramen that I have no way of cooking safely, potato chips, saltines, water, and fucking salad dressings out the ass. So, if this goes on for more than two or three more days, I'll have to eat Pete or Maybelle.

I'm kidding. I'd sooner eat my own calf. By the way, I did Google my area. There was nothing in the news about it whatsoever, which was weird, seeing as our town wasn't ENTIRELY off the map. I called a few of my neighbors last night. None of them picked up. Two went straight to voicemail. I chatted with my brother. Things are no better by him.

I can't put this off any longer. I'm going upstairs to get some food. I'll take my phone with me.

I just put some food in a bag. I crawled past the window, of course. Went I went up there, the rain started coming down even harder. I could hear some of my neighbors, doors opening and closing. Some shutters shook in the distance. The shutters of the windows in my living room are open. I guess 013 could see in if she wanted to, but no way in hell am I fixing that shit right now.

Okay, I'm back downstairs. I'm going to try and contact the "cops" again.

Okay, so far I'm getting no signal.

Hmm. Okay, no luck. Hold on. I'm getting something, but it's really faint.

"Going…check [withheld] Street…" (That's my street.)

"Okay. …careful…ready…all times…"

"Okay…let me know how it goes…when… Over."

That's all the legible phrases I could get before I lost the signal, but now I know someone's coming down the street.

Also, you guys have told me that cops don't actually say "over" at the end of each sentence group. I have two theories, one being that they just don't know that, and the other being that they are trying to make themselves seem like cops so that if someone unauthorized finds the channel (oops) then they'll think they're just listening to police.

I don't know if these people are trustworthy, or if I should be concerned about someone coming down my street but, so far they haven't entered any houses, so even if they're paranormal Nazi spy demons, I should be good.

I don't honestly think 013 has any malicious motives—she doesn't seem to be the kind of test subject that lives in a five-star room, so she may very well be fleeing for her own safety, but I do know that she is undeniably, irrefutably dangerous.

Another thing: a lot of people seem to be picturing this girl as El from Stranger Things. However, when I said she was a "teenager," I didn't mean "13-ish years old," I meant anywhere from 16 to 20-something. And by "short hair," I didn't mean she had a buzz cut, just short hair and a choppy sort of fringe (not like an emo fringe, just unevenly cut).

So far, it doesn't seem like anything is going to happen today, but I still have some space to fill so I'll just tell you how I've been lately or something.

What the fuck? The radio just turned on. Oh shit, what the fuck. Guys, it just talked! It said:

"Open the door."

Guys, I don't know. This is getting weird as hell. It just turned on. I don't know if that was the cops or 013 or someone else but I'm fucking scared. We're they talking to me specifically? My dogs are staring at it now. It just said it again! It sounds so fucking calm. What the hell? Fuck.

My dogs just started barking.

***

Okay, guys, this is like five minutes later now. I just got my dogs to stop barking, but they're still growling. That was definitely loud enough for people to hear, maybe even through the rain and everything. I'm a bit more calm and collected now, but I'm holding a big ass kitchen knife just in case. This crazy ass psychic girl is gonna come in here and I'm going to fucking die, guys.

Okay, okay. It's two hours later now. She hasn't come in, so I think I may be OK. I almost broke the radio to stop her from using it, but I didn't. I might need it to stay posted on what the "cops" are doing. But now my power's out. I can only use my lantern and flashlights to light up the room now. I have to use my phone with data, and I'm not going back upstairs. Not a fucking chance. My phone probably won't last very long on just my power banks now. Guys, this might be it. I might be actually fucked this time. If I die tonight, well, my friends know my username. Some of them, at least. Guys, promise me that if you're one of the people who knows who I am, please tell my family that I love them and that I tried. I'll try to update you guys soon. Until then, assume I'm alive. Might be wishful thinking, but I don't know how this is going to end. Okay. Until I can make a full update, I'll make small ones on here. Wish me luck, guys. I'll need it.

Okay, guys. Hey again. I know I left off the last update at a bit of a cliffhanger, but I'm back now and I want to say that so far I am okay. I have a lantern lit and I have enough food to last until tomorrow afternoon, maybe tomorrow night. The dogs are doing good (better than me, in any event) and we're currently just laying low. I don't even want to risk going upstairs to get more food. Also, I don't really know what my thoughts are on the radio incident. If 013 wanted to get in, surely she could have by now. Unless she's like one of those old fashioned vampires who can't enter without permission, and I think my neighbor would disagree with that notion.

Oh, speaking of the radio, I did manage to tune in on the people I've been listening to. I got a better signal than last time, but I still don't have much more information to go by. Anyway, here's what I heard:

"Hello? Hello, Officer McClellan? It's—"

"Present. Over."

"McClellan. Hey. This is Sloan. Over."

"Sloan! Oh, are you ever a sound for sore ears! Over."

"Nice to hear from you too! Over."

"How's everything going over on your end? Over."

"Well, considerably better than things have been as of late. Do you think what Jones and the boss said is true? Over."

"What, about 013? I mean...I want to, so I guess. Over."

"Everyone WANTS to believe, but do you ACTUALLY believe it? Over?"

"Well, I mean...If Kowalski thinks he has a lead..."

"Man, fuck Kowalski. He's smart, okay? I'll give him that. Over."

"Look, I don't agree with everything Kowalski says or does. He's had good ideas and bad ones. Sure, I guess he's got some obscure views on what should be done about 013, but it's not like he's the first one. Personally, I'm right in the middle. I mean...I'm not here out of choice, and we're messing with human life here. Maybe Kowalski's right...Just a bit? Over."

"(Sigh) Sloan, it's not his opinion in 013. It's just... He always just sort of rubbed me wrong. Look, given the chance, I'd probably quit this shitty job and do something else. I don't really care what happens to 013. But Kowalski... Come on. Does he need to be here? Does he? He could get by totally unemployed, he's got money. So why's he sticking around? Over."

"Sean, stop. Sorry—McClellan. You're making some dangerous accusations here. I can't help but get the feeling this has something to do with—"

"002! Yes, Sloan! I'm telling you, Kowalski rigged the 002 experiment!"

"McClellan! Get it together, sir! Kowalski is a perfectly fine man. I don't know why you have it out for him. I can tell you that because we're friends—right? And besides, I didn't call to talk about Kowalski. I called to ask if you were going to investigate the radio disturbance on [withheld] Street. Over."

"Well, yeah, but... I don't see the point. 013 is causing disturbances all over, none of them particularly close to where she is. Over."

"Yeah, but maybe someone's been listening to us. I mean...usually, 013 sends out larger disturbances than that. You never know, and that's the Last thing we need. Over."

"Okay, I get it. Over and out."

"Bye. Over and out."

Now, I'm a bit concerned, because they mentioned a radio disturbance on my street, which could very well have been caused by either me or a neighbor listening to them. Also, if there's one thing I learned from that conversation, it's that 013 isn't the only one in existence, seeing as they mentioned a "002." Calling 013 an anomaly like in the previous update or the one before that, whichever it was, makes me think she has something the others are missing.

I've noticed that the weather has calmed down somewhat. I haven't heard anything but light rain coming from up above. Judging from that, as well as the conversation between Sloan and McClellan, I think this all might be called off soon. I think 013 is going to get found today. I really do. I'm really tired, even though it's early, because I barely slept last night, so I'm going to take a small nap. I'll wait to post this when I get up.

Okay, so I just woke up, about two hours, maybe three hours later, and the alert on my phone is now all weird. Like, it has letters randomly capitalized every now and then like some clichéd ransom letter. I'm just assuming it's a glitch or something, but still, it's a bit weird.

It's a little later now, and I'm officially out of food except for three granola bars and a single sleeve of saltines. Oh, and one water bottle. This basement smells like dog waste and BO, and I want out.

Guys, the alert changed again.

Now it's totally empty, except for the headline "*EMERGENCY ALERT*" and a URL. I really have a bad feeling about it, seeing as it's probably a virus, but practically squatting in a basement with just dogs to talk to, a phone that can only fully charge once more given the status of my power banks, and storing waste in Ziploc bags, so I decided to just say fuck it and click the link.

It took me to a weird site. It's just a black screen, totally black except for the Google bar thingy and some white text. To me, it looks like a transcript. Here's what it says:

The 013 Experiment
Notes:
- Subject is very uncooperative
- Subject refuses to eat

• Subject seems to display unique traits, possible anomaly.

DAY 1

Whitfield: Good evening, young lady. My name is Professor Whitfield.

013: Burn in hell.

Whitfield: Now, now, let's not get off to a bad start. Let us try again. My name is Professor Whitfield. And yours?

013: Fuck you.

Whitfield: [Clicks tongue] Dear, dear... They did tell me you weren't very cooperative. It's a shame. But I suppose I haven't brought you here to sip tea. I here tell that you are a very special young woman. And not in the way that every child is special...No, you can do things with your mind, can't you?

013: [Shakes head] My mind can do things with me. I can't control it. Keep me here any longer and my mind may just slip over your throat.

Whitfield: [Turns to observer] Shock her.

013: [Cries out in agony as electricity courses through her] Stop!

Whitfield: My name is Professor Whitfield. And you are?

013: Elizabeth Keller.

Whitfield: [Smiles] Perfect. Now, I would love to stay and chat, but I will allow you to get acquainted with your new quarters. [013 is locked in her cell]

013: Let me out. [Struggles to keep her voice calm] Let me out. Let. Me. Go. Open the door. Open the door.

DAY 2

Whitfield: Why hello, child. Elizabeth, was it?

013: Elizabeth, yes.

Whitfield: So it was. [Skims through papers] Were you by any chance related to a Mrs. Annie Keller?

013: No. Whitfield: No relation?

013: None.

Whitfield: Any notable relations?

013: No.

Whitfield: None?

013: I already told you, no, you bastard!

Whitfield: I advise you not to take that kind of tone with me. [013 is shocked again]

013: [Grimaces] Why are you keeping me here?

Whitfield: I have my reasons. Children like you aren't easy to come by. Now, you've been known to cause thunderstorms upon getting angry. Correct?

013: Yes.

Whitfield: And I have been told that you cannot control this. If you get angry... Noting can be done. Theoretically, of course, if kept in the right type of structure, it may be contained... But... I digress. Anyway... Tell me, Miss Keller, are you familiar with me? Do you know who I am?

013: Yes. You're the head of the local police.

Whitfield: That's what the people have been told. No, you see, we aren't police. This town has no true police. No, the people who run this town and enforce the law work for me but they are no police. We are the MEW Foundation. That stands for Mentally Engineered Weapon. Have you figured out why you're here?

013: Why can't you just let me go? Am I going to die in here?!

Whitfield: Relax. The twelve before you fated very well. I do not see why you should be any different.

Everything after that was all corrupted. I think maybe they found out it was leaked and tried to erase it. But... how and why did it leak in the first place? I can't help but think it was 013, in some bizarre attempt to expose the MEW Foundation. Anyway, I'm going to go now. I'll keep you guys posted until the next update. Okay, see you. Bye.

***

Hey, guys. I know I haven't updated in a while, but a number of things have happened. Now, seeing as this all happened before I was able to update, and the events were too big to fit into a small mini update, I decided to just compile them all in here. Okay? I doubt there will be many more updates after this, because I definitely feel like this is all going to be over soon, but until this all ends, I'll keep you guys posted. I should let you know now that this post won't be as outwardly scary as the other ones, seeing as some light has been brought to the situation in recent days, but it should be quite interesting for those of you who have made it this far. Let's just say I have a few more answers now.

There hadn't been a sound from outside in more than a couple of hours when I decided to go upstairs again. My power is still out, and my phone's battery isn't getting any fuller. But I don't think I'll be in my basement much longer. I even considered letting the dogs outside, but I'm not rushing into anything.

I went upstairs and looked out the window. The girl I had been seeing was crouched on my front steps, wet from the dying rain and extremely thin from malnourishment. I still felt a shudder travel up my spine upon seeing her, but I felt she had lost some of her ability to fill me with fear. I now knew who she was, assuming I could trust the transcript from the alert message.

I knocked three times on my front door. Through the glass part of the door, I could see her stand up and turn around. She looked at me, silently pleading, and I did what you've been warning me against doing this whole time. I let her in.

She walked in without saying a word, walked past me, and looked around. "Hungry?" I asked, and I noticed my voice was dry from barely speaking for several days. She turned to me and nodded.

Knowing full well I didn't have much to spare, I opened a cabinet and took out a bag of marshmallows. She tore it open and began eating it faster than I could imagine. Funny, I don't even like marshmallows. That's why I never took them downstairs. I filled a cup of water from the tap, an ability I had previously forgotten I possessed, and put it in front of her—she downed it in one gulp.

"Did you change my alert message?" I asked.

She nodded.

"Have you been hearing what I have on the radio?"

She nodded again. "They aren't cops." I noticed that her voice was raspy—she probably rarely spoke.

"I figured. Are you trying to run from them?"

"Yes."

"Okay," I said. "You can stay here for now. Do you have a house?" I'm a dumbass, by the way.

"No."

"Family?"

She shook her head. I walked over to the door and closed it. "Did you kill my neighbor?" I asked.

"He tried to hurt me. I didn't want to. I told him to stop but he had a shotgun."

"So you went to him for help. Okay. How long have they been keeping you locked up?"

She shrugged. "It was 2014 when they got me."

Two years. Shit. "OK. I can help you. I don't know if these people work for the government or not, but... If they don't, I can have them arrested and put away for good. If they do... I don't know."

"Thank you."

"I'm just about out of food," I said. "I'm going to go get some from my neighbor. He won't need it anymore where he's gone."

"Okay."

"Help yourself to whatever."

I left my house, despite every warning I had been given, and went across the street. I pushed open my neighbor's door, went inside, and stepped over his body. His neck was turned at an awkward angle, a shotgun lying next to him. I picked it up, cleared the chamber, put the shells in my pocket, and decided to keep it incase the MEW Foundation came a-knocking. I stuffed the big pouch on the front of my hoodie full of food and left, placing a washcloth over his eyes.

When I got back, 013—sorry, Liz? Betty? Beth? Lizzie? Just Elizabeth?—was passed out on my couch. I put a blanket over her and put some of my old clothes next to her. Then I locked the door and went back downstairs with my dogs.

I turned on the radio and waited to get a signal from MEW. It only took about five minutes.

"Kowalski?"

"Yes? Over."

"This is McClellan. Sloan and I are headed to [withheld] Street. Wanted to check the status on the radio disturbance examinations. Over."

"Well, they were coming from… I want to say house # [withheld]. Over."

"Interesting. We'll be sure to pay a visit. It looks like this may be finally over. …Over."

"I don't know. What if 013's escape gave the others ideas? The entire [withheld (name of my town)] Project could be compromised. Over."

"They know nothing about it. Those clones are idiots, Kowalski. Except 013… She's an exception, but that's probably because she's from a different person. At least, from what I gather. I never saw 14-26. Over."

"They're not idiots, McClellan. Just uneducated. Over."

"Yeah, you say that. What about 002? Strange things that went on, huh…? That one, though, man, was the dumbest of all. Over."

"Say what you want. I have my own opinion. I happen to think the clones should be treated fairly. And 002… That was unfortunate, to say the least. Over."

"I'll say. Didn't 002, like, die? Just… out if the blue, right?"

"McClellan…What are you getting at?"

"Nothing. Over."

"Hmm."

"Hey, what happened that day? If I remember correctly, you got knocked out for a little while. Over."

"I was working with 002. He came up behind me and hit me, and then everything went black. Over."

"OK. Kowalski? Why are you hear, man? You don't need this job. Over."

"I made a promise to Whitfield. I can't break it. Over."

"What kind of promise? If I remember correctly, you didn't want to be here at first. Over."

"Irrelevant, McClellan. Over and out."

After that, the channel went silent. I went back upstairs to find 013 awake. "Did you ever meet McClellan, Kowalski, Sloan, Jones, any of those?" I asked.

"All but Jones."

"Do you know why they hate Kowalski so much?" I asked.

"Because if the 002 experiment," she said.

"Did he mess it up?" I asked.

She furrowed her brow. "No," she said. "Well, they think so. But I know what really happened, because I stole the master file."

"Do the other people on the radio know about it?" I asked.

"Just Kowalski because, in a way, he's just like me."

"How so?"

"Well, take a look at the file. It has the names of all the people used for the cloning process." She took a black binder out of her shirt and handed it to me. "Here."

I opened it up. On the front page, there were four columns. In the first column: 001-006 Second: 007-012 Third: 013 (she was the only one not adapted from another person) Fourth: 014-026.

At the top of every column was a name.

1: Michael Kowalski

2: Sean [withheld]

3: Elizabeth Keller (too late to censor this one)

4: Henry [withheld out of respect—this is the boy who drowned and was declared dead later on]

"Kowalski was the person used to make 001-006," Elizabeth said.

"Was?"

"During the 002 experiment…He was attacked from behind. 002 killed him and assumed his job, his life, everything. He said the dead one was him—002—and not the original. I said so, but nobody believes me, and I didn't care. Why would I? "Kowalski's" almost as dangerous as me, but I think he's like-minded… Are you okay?"

I gulped. "My name is Sean [withheld]."

As of now, were waiting on edge for McClellan and Sloan to arrive, me holding a shotgun in hand, Elizabeth holding her powers in her mind. Until next time, wish us luck. Assume we're alive.

UPDATE: Upon further studying the book, I found that it names everyone in this town as pending cloning subjects. Apparently, in this town, they must take samples of your blood at birth or something. We're all ready to be cloned, but only a few already have.

***

Liz and I have been talking.

She knows it, I know it. This can't work forever. The people at MEW will never stop looking for her until she's found. Sure, I could take care of McClellan, Sloan, Jones, Kowalski if necessary. But I'm certain they have more man power—and who knows, the other experiments might not be as kind as Liz.

We just gave the radio a try. Nothing much, really, but we now have a time frame for the arrival of the "officers."

"Kowalski? Sloan here. Over."

"Sloan, hey. Have you and McClellan left for [withheld] yet? Over."

"Yes, we'll be there in… about two hours. Over."

"I just left as well. I'll be there in one and a half. Over."

"Well, tell us where you have and have not searched when we get there. We need to shut this down TODAY. Over."

"And Jones? Has he left? Over."

"Not yet. He probably won't be there for another three or so. Anyway, take care. Over and out."

The dogs are safely locked away in my basement for now, but I'm trying to convince my brother to take them to his house until things blow over. I've told him about Liz being a normal person. He didn't believe me at first, but I think he's coming around. Right now she's wearing a gray hoodie of mine over jeans, dark red converse, and a white Marvel T-shirt with a black Venom insignia. I don't think they'll be able to identify her without giving her a second glance.

A lot of you have been asking about the gun I found across the street. I did a little research, and the closest look-alike I found on google images was a Remington 870. I checked around my neighbor's house for more shells like some of you suggested, and I found about 4 more, plus two more full power banks. I didn't do a very thorough check, because we're on a bit of a deadline right now. Okay, my brother just got back to me. He'll take the dogs. He's still confused, but he'll totally back me up if I need him to when Officers Friendly, Smiley, and Joyful show up.

I'm not worried about running out of shells; if need be, Liz can probably make their heads explode or something. I'd rather she didn't have to because that would be difficult to explain to the authorities, especially when the authorities know about 013 and are the ones I'm getting ready to fight.

I really can't see more than one update after this. I think today it will all be over. I hope Liz makes it out of this okay, but it'll be a hell of a lot of work to keep them from her. If she's to be free, either everyone in MEW must die or she'll have to go on the run for real. In Mexico, maybe, or Canada—Canada's closer, so that before Mexico. Although, maybe if Whitfield dies, the others will leave her alone?

I don't know. It's been about 45 minutes since we listened in on the radio. Kowalski should be here in 45 more. Liz had a bright idea, too. What if we left a note for him? We found some sidewalk chalk in the basement, and we took it out to the street and wrote "002" in large letters. When the others show up, either we can wash it off with a hose or with some rain courtesy of Liz. But I think it's a good idea. What if Kowalski wants to fight just as little as we do?"

Okay, 15 more minutes have passed, and I'm really getting anxious. I think we should do one more sweep for supplies.

Okay, so we went back across the street and picked up a machete and a small revolver. I put the revolver in my pocket for now—I might give it to Liz even though I doubt she'll need it—and put the machete on my back. I don't know why all the other neighbors are being quiet. Should I give them a warning? I asked Liz if she killed them, too. She said no.

My brother showed up and got the dogs. Here, I'll give you the gist of our conversation:

"Holy fuck, Sean!"

"What?" I asked him.

"You aren't enlisting in the military; you don't need a fucking arsenal!"

"You want one?" I asked.

"Fuck no!"

"I'm serious," I said. "You might need it. These people are going to check all the houses on the block, probably!"

"I'm good," he said, turning to Liz. "So, you're the one who kept walking around outside?"

"Yes," Liz replied.

"What's going on?" he asked me. "Are we involved in some messed up government experiment or some shit?"

"Well, frankly, yes," I told him. "You got my—our—back?"

"'Course," he said. "But I better not go to jail for this, buddy."

"Jim, calm your ass," I said, motioning for him to calm down. "Just take the dogs to your place, maybe come back here. And be ready for a fight."

"Okay," he said, calming down slightly. "Okay."

"Okay, hurry up," I sad, and he ran into the basement to get the dogs. A few minutes later, he was pulling out of the driveway.

"Your brother seems nice," Liz said.

"He's an ass, but you'll get used to it."

Fifteen minutes before go, he came back. I handed him the machete when he refused the revolver. I offered the revolver to Liz, but she said she wouldn't need it. I agreed.

I have my kitchen knife, too, in my other pocket. We all had one of those, actually. Also, I forgot to mention that the revolver had a full cylinder.

Okay, in five minutes, Kowalski should be passing by. I'm really nervous now, but I should be okay. I don't think he'll be a problem.

Okay, Kowalski showed up. I'm looking through the window at him. He's looking at the chalk message, and he looks like he's getting worried —nervous, confused, whatever.

He just saw me.

Okay, I'm back. I went outside with the shotgun in my hand and he took several steps back, his hands up. I questioned him a little, and he admitted to killing the real Kowalski. Then Liz came out. We checked him, took a handgun off of him (I'll try to find out what kind) and took him into the basement to tie him up. He's currently sitting across from us, bound and gagged, my brother pale as a sheet.

"We just kidnapped a guy," he muttered.

"We're probably about to kill a few more," I said, "so buckle up."

I noticed the insignia on his lapel. "MEW" written in white against the dark gray fabric of his shirt.

I decided to go wait behind my dead neighbor's house for McClellan and Sloan. Liz and Jim waited at the house.

Okay, they're here. They just got out of the car, but there's four of them. McCLellan is a guy of average height and brown hair, moderately built, and Sloan is a slightly short woman with black hair in a ponytail. The other two are both tall and of average build, one with blond hair and one with black, both male.

One of the big guys just came my way. Sloan and McClellan are walking in my house's general area. The other big guy is walking down the street away from me. I'm going to put my phone down.

Okay, guys, I just shot the guy.

He came around and saw me, and before he could take out his gun, I shot him with the shotgun. McClellan and the other big guy were both in houses, but Sloan was outside, so she saw him fall down, although they probably all heard the shotgun. My ears ringing, I stood up and got ready to run, shaky from the fact that I now had this man's blood metaphorically on my hands. I shot at Sloan but missed, and she caught up with me as I was running. I shot her in the thigh, and she fell over, but sat up and started shooting at me.

McClellan must have decided to stay put, and the big guy was nowhere to be seen, so I crouched down behind the nearest house, Sloan crying out in pain. "Why...?" she asked me, looking at me angrily. "You ass hole..."

"You can't have 013," I said. "I know what you're doing in that place."

"I'm a police officer!" she said.

"But then why does your shirt say 'MEW?' And why did you keep saying 'over' on the radio?"

"All cops say "over,"" she said.

"I used to think so, too."

"Look, I don't care if 013 gets captured. But I need to do my job."

"I'm giving you an out," I said. "Stay quiet, lay low, and let me take care of it."

She was looking behind me. I turned around as big guy numero dos came around the corner of the house with his gun held out. I took out my knife and stuck it in his shoulder—he fell over and I got on him, sticking it between his ribs.

"I don't want to do this!" I said.

He fell limp, and I looked at Sloan. "If you can't call them off, nothing can be done. If it's something that can be stopped, then stop it."

Through her radio, I heard a voice. "This is Professor Whitfield to Officer Sloan. I will be there shortly with Jones. In due time... Over."

I took the shotgun, hit her with the barrel, and knocked her unconscious, my head swimming.

***

Guys, this is the last one. For some of you, this is good news. For me it is, too.

A lot has happened since the last update, which I admittedly ended quite abruptly. To make things easier, I'll pick up from where I left off.

Sloan's walky-talky continued to crackle after she slumped over on the ground, but no more words came through. I took out my phone and called Jim.

"Sean! Hey, what happened?"

"I just killed two of them, man, and one of them's out cold," I said shakily.

"Fuck, what did you do that for?"

"I didn't have a choice!" I said. "They jumped me, man—but that's not why I called. Tell Liz that Whitfield's on the way."

"The fuck?"

"Just tell her! And how's Kowalski doing?"

"Alright, considering he's tied up."

"Okay," I said. "Stay put. I'm going to see if I can find McClellan."

I hung up the phone and put it in my pocket, strafing around the house, my eyes scanning for any sign of McClellan.

"Sloan?!" someone called from somewhere to my left. Must be McClellan.

I remained silent and looked around for the source of his voice.

"I estimate that we will be there within fifteen minutes," Whitfield said curtly through Sloan's radio. "Over."

"Fuck..." I muttered.

"Sloan!" McClellan repeated. "You alright?"

I sprinted across the backyard and crouched behind a bird fountain.

"Sloan! Hello?"

I could hear his voice getting closer. Finally, I could see him nervously inching closer to me. I stood up to move, and his eyes locked onto mine. He drew his pistol and fired.

The bullet whirred by my shoulder and I ran, cocking the shotgun and firing it in McClellan's direction. I missed, and he came running at me. I cocked the gun again and fired, but only a few balls of birdshot landed in his left arm.

"Fuck!" he cried, clutching his arm. "Stop running, you fucker!"

"Get out of here!" I said. "I know what you're trying to do here!"

"Oh yeah? And what will you do about it? Kill me? Kill fuckin' Whitfield? Good luck with that one, pal! What did you do to Sloan?!"

"She's unconscious," I said, "but alive. At least until you put down the fucking gun!"

"You're one to talk," he said. "Drop it!"

I lower my gun, and he lowered his. "You're treading on thin ice, prick," he said. "If you don't stop, you're going to have to face Whitfield in the flesh. And you'll find he isn't as understanding as me. Now where are Maloney and Schmidt? Kowalski."

"Big guys?" I asked. "Dead. Kowalski, too. I'm sorry, they drew on me."

"Fuck," McClellan said, raising his gun again. "How do I know you're telling the truth?"

"I know where 013 is… but I won't tell you because I know what's going on in that place. I read the transcript of the first couple of days 013 was in there."

"The fuck did you get that?" he asked.

"It got put on that bullshit emergency alert message. If I had to guess, she put it there to discredit you guys."

"Whatever you read, you have to believe me—013 is dangerous. Okay?"

"Well, it's not like you aren't."

"Look, kid, put your gun down. I won't hurt you, but you need to let me know where 013 is."

"I'm not dropping my gun," I said. "But she's in there." I pointed to my dead neighbor's house.

"For real?" he asked. "You're not playing me?"

"No," I said. "I'm being honest."

"Okay," he said.

He turned around to enter the house. "Okay. I'm trusting you here."

I nodded. "Be careful, man."

"I know what I'm doing."

While his back was turned, I quietly started backing away.

"You know what?" McClellan asked. "I'm not gonna turn my back on a guy with a gun in his hands, so why don't you put that shit down, huh?"

"Okay, okay," I said, dropping the shotgun.

"Thank you," McClellan said in exasperation, turning around again as I continued to back up. "Now you stay put so I don't have to do something rash."

"Yeah," I said, continuing to back up.

"You hear that?" he asked, turning around.

"Hmm?" I asked.

"A car," he said.

I listened for the noise in question, and I found it—tires on gravel.

I turned around and saw a car pulling into a driveway three houses down from my house.

"That's probably Whitfield," McClellan said. "I advise you to act on your best behavior, kid, 'else you're gonna have a bad time."

"McClellan!" said a man in the passenger's seat of the car as he opened his door. "Who's the kid?"

"Civilian," McClellan said. "Killed the others, except Sloan."

"Oh, fuck—Christ, McClellan, you're not cuffing him?"

"What's going on here?" Whitfield asked, exiting the vehicle. I studied Jones and Whitfield. Whitfield was tall with long, gray hair and a slightly wrinkled face. Jones was tall, as well, but with short-cropped hair and a strong jaw.

"He's saying this kid killed the others, boss!"

"Listen," McClellan said, "he says 013's hiding over there." He pointed to the house I had tipped him off on.

Whitfield closed his eyes, focusing, it seemed, on something. "No," he said.

"What?" Jones asked.

"You lying?" McClellan asked me.

"No," I said, "I swear."

"Yes, you are," Whitfield said, opening his eyes and pointing to my house. "I can sense her from this distance, and she is in there."

"Well," I said, "I thought she was in the other one."

"McClellan!" came a voice from in the distance. "Jones! Whitfield!"

Sloan, I thought. Fuck.

Jones ran off toward Sloan's cries, and Whitfield and McClellan turned to face me. "So," McClellan said, "this kid says he knows about MEW."

"Does he?" Whitfield asked. "Well, something will have to be done, won't it...? Give me his gun."

"Uh...sir, are you certain?" McClellan asked.

"Yes, McClellan, now give me his gun. We don't have all day. The sweepers will be here soon to wipe out the town. The copies will be placed shortly thereafter. Now give me that gun."

"Sir, he may be of some assistance. You know, with the cloning."

"He knows too much to live," Whitfield said as my heart pounded in my chest. "Pick it up and give it to me."

McClellan swallowed hard and bent over to pick up the gun. He grasped it in his hands and stood up straight again. "Fine then."

With a *crash*, my living room window exploded across the street, bursting into a million tiny fragments and sending long, jagged blades of glass soaring through the air.

One sliced through McClellan's neck, bringing him to his knees and then to his stomach as blood spurted from the cut. Another lodged itself firmly in Whitfield's back.

"Well," Whitfield said as McClellan writhed on the ground. "That's unfortunate." I bent down, pried my gun from McClellan's hands, trying to ignore his gurgling, and aimed it at Whitfield. I pulled the trigger. And birdshot erupted into his body.

"You insufferable child!" he cried, turning to face my house as he pulled the glass out of his back. "Escaping the lab will be the last thing you ever did. And you..." he turned to me. "Why don't you give me that gun?"

The bullet holes in his body were beginning to cover themselves. I fired again, and this time his face met lead. Skin gone, giving way to bone and muscles. "Give me that gun, you fuck!"

With a flick of his wrist, he beckoned the gun towards him, and it left my hands for his. "Now, boy, you will meet your literal maker."

He cocked the gun and prepare to fire.

013 ran out of my open doorway before the door hit the wall and reached out for a telephone pole—it uprooted itself and went flying at Whitfield. It cracked over his head and fell onto the ground in two pieces. He moved the barrel of the gun away from me and fired at 013.

Liz fell to the pavement in tatters.

"Fuck!" I shouted. "You asshole!"

"What?" he asked. "Did you really think you were going to win? You, along with… let me guess… your brother and a runaway freak? Please. We have more power than you could ever dream of, and you owe everything you have, ironically, to us. We are responsible for your creation. Every single one of you. All using the same original entity as a base. Even I owe everything to the immeasurable 000."

I reached for my kitchen knife and found it in my pocket. I grasped it in a reverse grip and ran blindly forward.

"Don't you understand?" he asked, pushing my onto the ground with his mind. "This story has no happy ending." He took my knife and threw it over his shoulder, blood still pouring from the holes in his head. "I could kill you know…but I want you to see what I mean. You'll see the sweepers come through. You'll see how they erase this town completely. It will be as though it never existed. And then, a week or so later, the clones will take over, and nobody will know the difference."

I tried to sit up, but he kicked me in the chest and sent me onto my back. "Goodbye, Sean [withheld]. You will not be missed. Jones! Get Sloan, and let's get out of here! The deed is done."

I stood up only when their car was leaving the block. I limped towards my house, stepping over Liz's lifeless body and knocking on the basement door. "Jim! Get the dogs. We need to leave."

People were starting to leave their homes when we left. I advised them to evacuate. Many of them did. The others, as of me writing this, are probably mostly dead or imprisoned.

We've been on the road since we left. We managed to get into the next state, so far. We took the dogs and our necessary items, as well as a few small luxuries and stuff. We're both totally messed up from what happened, and we haven't mentioned Liz once since leaving. There won't be any more updates after this.

This is the last one.

Thank all of you for staying with me through this. I know it fell apart towards the end, but it is what it is.

I don't know what comes next for us, but it won't be easy.

The alert was finally taken off my phone. for a while, that is.

While sitting in a Wendy's parking lot and waiting for Jim to get back, I received another alert. This one was different, to say the least.

EMERGENCY ALERT I am informally issuing an emergency alert for the following counties: [withheld]. Citizens should be wary of all "government officials." The town will be "swept" for survivors with clear memories of recent events. Nobody is safe here. I advise you all the leave as soon as you can. Do not talk to any police officers if their uniforms are marked "MEW." They are NOT police officers! Effective indefinitely. Do not go to [withheld] County. It is not safe there.

I wish you all good lives, and bid you adieu. For as long as you remember this, assume I'm alive.

UPDATE: Guys, I just got out to use the bathroom. When I got back, there was a full box of Thin Mints in the back seat.

Patient 314

By Aaron Hilgen

Have you ever wondered what it feels like to die? Is it painful when your body lets go of its last stores of energy? Are you aware that you are dying or do you think it will pass? Maybe you are one of the many that have thought it great to never be *able* to die. Like a superhero. Saving beautiful women from horrible men and little children from burning houses. Oh yes, that would be nice.

Now let's imagine you are walking up some stairs. The damned elevator is broken again and you have to trudge up five flights to get to your office building. Step up, step up, step up. After two flights, you are a little winded perhaps, maybe you take your phone out and check emails to save time. That is when your foot catches the stop of a riser and for a split second you panic. Your heart races, your blood flowing fiercely through your body which causes your body temperature rises significantly and you break out into a sweat. In the next moment your foot finds the step and your panic recedes although you feel a little sheepish and hope no one witnessed the miscue. A few stairs later and your face is no longer flushed with the excess blood, your heart has returned to a normal rhythm, and all is right with the world. You may tread a little more carefully for the next minute or so, maybe even putting your phone back into your pocket or purse, and you forget about that moment in time.

These are all normal responses for a normal human being. Your body senses danger, your balance is thrown off and your mind knows the great distance you could fall should you go backwards. All normal. But what if I told you that **everything** caused your body to react that way. Every properly executed step. Every change in the wind's direction. Every noise your ears perceive and every flash of color taken in by your retinas. What if your body could not differentiate between normal interactions with the world around you and emergency situations? I suppose, then, you would be me.

My mother told me once that all I ever did was cry for the first few years of life. She couldn't understand it, the doctors couldn't understand it. Pain, the doctors told her. He is always in pain. There was nothing they could do because they couldn't find the cause. The only indication they had was my heart—it constantly revved up like I was in pain and then stopped very briefly before resuming a normal beat. She had raised four children already and knew exactly what each needed based on their cry, except for mine. It didn't take long for her to stop taking me places and pretty soon I was left alone in a dark room with the door closed and a primitive baby monitor keeping me company.

I was small and weak, physically and mentally. Going outside for even a moment was enough to send me into shock. But I survived. I kept on going. As I grew up and my capacity for communication increased, I was able to relate more of what I was going through with my mother and doctors. Unfortunately it was far too late for any real help or hope. The debt of constant hospital visits and specialists crippled my mother. My father only lasted a few weeks before giving up and leaving us. I told my mom to stop looking for a cure and focus on my brothers and sister; thankfully, she did.

I spent the next fifteen years by myself for the most part, except for those my laptop connected me to. School was out of the question, so I enrolled in online learning that was an at-your-own-pace style. It was hard considering just touching the mouse or clacking on the keyboard sent my heart racing and stopping suddenly, mind crashing into mental walls of anguish and blinding light overtaking all of my senses. It is hard to describe but it was as if I tasted more than I could handle, heard more than I could process, smelled so much I became clogged, felt every molecule colliding with my body, saw so clearly the spectrum of visible light separated for me for a split second. It was overwhelming every time. But I kept going. I survived. The episodes slowly grew worse, longer, harder to handle. I had to do something but I no longer had doctor visits or specialists calling the house or coming by to see if they could figure things out. I was on my own armed with the internet and a determination to prevail.

Fast forward to today as I speak this aloud for my computer to transcribe. I have my answer, my cure. Death. As you are probably aware, there is some very taboo stuff on the internet and, as a person who literally spends his every waking moment online, I have stumbled across a lot of it. I began studying death more deeply some time ago and it intrigued me. Something about it seemed so familiar but I wasn't sure why. I studied what death was, how people died, what religions thought about it, what people with near-death experiences describe. It slowly became clear to me that I was dying. With every touch, sound, blink of an eye I died. And came back. Again and again and again. Eventually my heart won't be able to take the constant trauma and I will die for good unless I can find enough *helpers*.

As I said, I found a cure, but it isn't an easy one to obtain and I happened upon it by accident. Yesterday, I was determined to make another attempt outside for research and to see the world. This would make my fourth visit that I can remember to the world outside of my home. Wearing special sunglasses that block out almost all light and noise-cancelling headphones, I took it very slow, my powerchair cruising at the slowest speed. I had "died" twelve times by the time I made it to the end of my driveway. Glancing up ever so slightly to one side and the next I made sure the road was clear and began the slow crossing. As I crossed the yellow line in the middle of the road, I heard the loudest sound I'd ever witnessed, dying for twentieth time. When I came back to myself I could feel the heat of the car crash a ways down the road, hear the screams of those inside the car and those running to help. I died nine more times trying to get away as fast as I could before the car exploded.

Seven people died that day because of me. Four in the car and three who attempted to rescue them before it blew. I could feel the blast on my neck as I powered away at a brisk 3 miles per hour. But I didn't die. Not that time. In fact, I made it all the way back inside my home before I succumbed to another instance of my malady, caused by the high-pitched sirens of emergency vehicles arriving on the scene.

I was filled with fear, filled with hope. It was time to experiment.

***

I knew I should feel horrible. I should be full of remorse and regret and guilt for being the cause of such a terrible accident. But I didn't. I felt alive! I felt genuine happiness. For the first time, I was able to enjoy the sensations of life without pain or anxiety. I heard things without repercussion, felt the air ruffle my hair, and watched a bird land outside my bedroom window (which was open for the first time ever). Although it didn't last very long, it was the greatest few hours I'd ever had and I needed it back. Over the course of the next twenty four hours, I tested the effects the car accident had on me.

- For three hours, only extreme sensations caused me to "die"

- The remaining twenty one hours slowly tapered back to a more normal response from my body, however I noticed slightly less sensitivity by the end of the day What caused it? Was it an overload of information? The massive amount of heat, burning flesh, screeching tires and crunching metal, BOOM of the engine and screams of those inside and those running to douse the flames, the sirens of eight emergency vehicles coming on the scene? I couldn't say for sure but I was about to find out.

I had never seen my father in person, just a few old pictures my mom kept for some reason. He had been in contact a few times to try and visit, make himself feel better about leaving us. Last time he called was about a year ago and he really wanted me to meet his new wife and kids. Yeah, sure I'd love to meet the family that was good enough for you. But that was then, and this is now. Now I had a reason to see him—*Look at me, dad; I'm better! You can finally teach me how to play catch.*

"Hey, uh, Dad?"

"…wow… I can't believe you are calling here. Is everything ok?" I could practically see the tears welling up at the corners of his eyes.

"Yeah, yeah. Everything is fine, dad. More than fine. I am better! I can do things like go outside now."

"How, how is that possible? What did the doctors say?"

"It is easier if I just showed you. Want to bring Vikki and the kids over tomorrow for lunch? I'll make something for us."

"Yea, of course; lunch. I'll take the day off work and bring everyone by. We just got a puppy, Pickle. Want me to bring him, too?" The tremble is his voice was almost too much for me to take. He was just so happy.

"Sure. Can't wait to see you, Dad."

With that, I hung up the phone and slowly made my way through the house, getting it ready for them tomorrow. Mom would be home soon from work and I had a lot of work to do. I wanted everything to be perfect for my first visit with my dad.

I had to get up at 5AM to ensure that the house was ready and lunch made in time for their visit. I made it just in time. Just as I laid out the last fork, I heard a knock at the door. My heart was racing and I wasn't even being effected by any outside stimulus. I was nervous, excited, ready. Pausing at the door for a minute to regain my composure and let my heart settle down, I slowly opened the door and let them in. All the excitement of five kids and a puppy hit me hard and I had to catch my breath after several "deaths" all in a row. Dad looked at me with sad eyes, knowing what pain and agony I just went through and realizing that I wasn't actually cured of anything.

Don't worry, Dad. It isn't as bad as it used to be and I am in the middle of an experiment that relieves my condition. I'll show you.

Once they were all in, I ushered them over to the table and they took their seats. I asked dad to say grace and then we dug in to some delicious pancakes and eggs (it is all I really know how to make). Halfway through my second pancake, I reached out and grabbed the knife for some more butter but instead plunged it deep into my fathers' neck. The cold metal and warm blood would normally send my body into spasms and my heart would race, stop, race, stop. But not this time. I felt strength and a calming of my nerves just like the after the accident. His new wife screamed at the top of her lungs and tried to get up but only succeeded in crashing into one of her brats. I pulled the knife out of his neck with blood pumping out all over my arm and moved slowly around the table to his wife as she scrambled to get away. Kicking her in the face once, twice, then bending down and ramming the knife into her pleading eyes with all my force. She stopped moving immediately. Pickle was barking and whining, going from snapping its teeth at me and licking the blood off of the ground.

I turned, aglow with renewed vigor and life, towards the closest child. We had a huge bottle of extra strength superglue that I had coated the chairs with just before they arrived and it was doing its job. I reached out and snapped the neck of the closest and sprang away down the hall after the oldest. Her legs were long enough to reach the ground from a sitting position and she ran, hunched over, towards the front door. I caught her by the hair and flung her backwards. She landed on her back, face covered in tears, mouth split wide in a scream. I stuffed the knife straight down her throat until I felt it connect with the vertebrae. Running back (amazing how trivial this seems to most, but it was my first time doing so) to the last of them, I made their cries stop quickly. Pickle was last. I honestly didn't know if an animal life would benefit me or not and I am still not quite sure. I was so high, so full of their life essence that I couldn't tell one way or the other.

My body was strong, agile, not a single sensation caused my heart to race or stop. My experiment was a success!

I spent the rest of the afternoon cleaning up the mess and enjoying my new found freedoms. It wasn't until the next morning when I had my first relapse, which was minor in comparison to what it used to be. Even now, as I type this with my actual hands, I have yet to fall back into the state I once was. It is possible that either the violence of the death or the close connection I had to the dying caused it to be that much more medicinal. Of course, I have much more experimenting to do before I know whether it is permanently cured or not. Fortunately, I have many doctors who can help me.

My mother was astonished when she came home. The entire house was clean, sparkling. Every curtain was drawn back to let in the bright sunlight. It had been so long since this house was brightened by anything other than incandescent bulbs. Dinner was laid out on the table for her and I to enjoy.

She walked over to me, weeping joyful tears. "Hunnie, what is all of this? Are you… are you… better?"

"I just woke up and felt different. Momma, I'm cured." Of course I couldn't tell her the truth.

"Oh sweetie, oh my baby!" She stood behind my chair, hugging me tight and covering my head in tears.

We ate together, her staring at me between bites, still unable to comprehend the sudden and drastic change in me. It was so nice to see her smile again. She has a pretty smile. I offered to clear the table and wash the dishes but she had a better idea. We hopped in the car and went for ice cream! This was the first time I had ridden in a car that wasn't heading toward a hospital. I ordered a PB Blizzard Blast, extra-large, and she bought a waffle cone with two scoops of butter pecan. Do you remember the first time you ate ice cream? Do you remember the cold filling your mouth and stinging your teeth a little but immediately washing away with wonderful flavors dancing along your tongue? I do.

I made my momma promise not to say anything to anyone yet, not even my doctors. The next morning was my scheduled in-home visit and I wanted them to see it for themselves when they came. We stayed up late playing card games and watching classic movies that I had missed out on. I was starting to wear down a little bit after the third movie. Maybe it was because it was so late, but I didn't want to chance it.

"Momma, I'm going to go the bed. I can't keep my eyes open anymore."

She kissed my forehead. "Ok, Sweetie; good night."

***

I woke up the next morning refreshed but still a little worn down. I was unsure whether the effects were not permanent or if I just pushed myself too far with my newfound lifestyle. I would find out soon enough. I laid in bed for a while contemplating this when a wonderful smell made its way into my nostrils. I got dressed and was greeted with omelets and coffee. How could I have never enjoyed coffee before? Seriously, it is amazing. My first sip hit me the way Mario must feel whenever he gets a mushroom or power-up. Dark, rich, and hot. My mouth burned but I didn't care—I let it sit on my tongue for a while just savoring it. I drank three cups along with my eggs and a slice of toast while waiting for Dr. Ramsus to show up.

He was shocked, to say the least, when I answered the door on my own two feet with no signs of heart agitation. I led him into the kitchen and pulled out his chair, offering him some coffee.

"No, thanks. Coffee and I don't mix. I suppose I don't know what to say. When did this change occur?"

"I woke up yesterday morning feeling different. I suppose 'strength' would be the right word; I felt strength in my body."

"Can you describe what you feel? What differences you perceive?"

He asked me a lot of questions that I did my best to answer and then took a few blood samples to take back to the lab for testing. He also did a quick physical—listened to my chest, blood pressure, looked in my mouth and ears. When I led him to the front door we shook hands and he promised to get in contact with me as soon as he had a look at my test results. I thanked him and he left.

I figured I had two days before he would want me to come in for more extensive testing so I began to plan. I still felt a little weak, although eating a big meal helped some, and an excessively loud action scene in a movie I was watching set my heart off to the races so I knew I wasn't cured completely. I would need more deserving helpers.

It was a nice day and I wanted to enjoy the sun on my skin so I went for a walk through the neighborhood. Kids were out playing, the mailman tending his route, and a woman dog-walker trying to keep control of the ten or so mutts she had out in front of her. She was on the same side of the street as I was and I caught up to her pretty quickly, seeing how her dogs kept taking off in different directions. As I passed, I recognized her; a friend of my older sister—and a constant source of teasing when I was younger. My, my, my... she had matured nicely. She did a double-take when she saw me. We chatted for a bit while we walked and I explained the miraculous change. She was majoring in human anatomy at the local university so she was *very* interested in the whole thing. I invited her over later that night to talk more about it and she agreed. I watched her butt sway back and forth as she walked away down another street.

***

Vanessa rang the bell (something I used to despise hearing) and I let her in. She was gorgeous, radiant. Her hair flowed easily around her shoulders and neck and her eyes twinkled whenever she smiled. She was wearing yoga pants and a loose, flowy shirt that looked like it was 80s fashion.

I led her to my room and we sat across from each other on my bed. She asked me all kinds of questions and it was a lot of fun making up the answers. Instead of answering one of her questions I leaned in and quickly kissed her on the lips.

It was my first kiss! I knew I didn't have anything to lose so why not, you know?

She was kind of startled by it but she kissed me back. Oh, it was heavenly. What a day! My first taste of coffee, my first kiss, and, later, my first orgasm.

I'll spare you the details but I am sure you can remember the first time you experienced it. What a rush! I am not sure if I enjoyed having sex with her or killing her more, but both were incredibly satisfying.

***

The next day, I got a job walking dogs (because, clearly, Vanessa no longer could) and I used the opportunity to learn my neighborhood better.

Who lived where, who had pets, kids, that kind of stuff. One of the dogs was especially unruly and disobedient, so I decided he would be my test subject of the evening. Late that night, I snuck into the backyard where the dog lived and found my new helper snoozing.

We did some experiments and then I went home, a huge smile on my face. It was great to know that animals could give me strength, too; although not quite as much. Armed with new knowledge about my disease, I laid out my plan for Dr. Ramsus and the others that had failed me thus far in life.

I can't wait to show them everything I have discovered!

***

Mt. Whitney Psychiatric Ward
Dr. Feldman

2/6/2017—4:12AM

Transfer of [REMOVED] from Mayo Research Clinic, completed.

Admittance of [REMOVED] into Ward 11, completed.

[REMOVED] assigned to PID# 314

48 hour initial observation of 314 has begun.

2/6/2017—9:01AM

First contact interview between Dr. Feldman and 314—logging...

Patient 314 is laying on the cot with eyes closed.

Dr.: I trust the flight was not too rough. How are you feeling this morning?

314: Screw you.

Dr.: Are the lights too bright? I can have them dimmed more if you prefer.

314: Screw you.

Dr.: I see. Command, please increase lumens by eighty, thank you. I'll be back in an hour.

Patient 314 spits on the observation window and resumes laying on the cot with eyes closed.

2/6/2017—10:04AM

Follow-up interview between Dr. Feldman and 314—logging…

No change in Patient 314.

Dr.: I would like to discuss what you did to Dr. Ramsus and his colleagues. Will you please explain what caused you to act so destructively towards your doctor?

314: He promised to cure me fourteen years ago. I was just making sure he kept his promise.

Dr.: How can he keep his promise if he is dead? Are you suggesting that you are cured?

314: For now.

Dr.: Please elaborate.

314: Screw you.

Dr.: We can't help you if you don't explain why you did what you did and what you mean by him curing you. Please, elaborate.

314: Do you even know what is wrong with me?

Dr.: You suffer from a unique condition in which your senses overload your brain causing massive heart trauma, which has now been called [REMOVED] Disease. Additionally, you suffer from mental instability and delusion (in this case, Cotard Delusion) possibly caused by a lifetime of extreme stress, and mental and physical anguish. Furthermore, you are now labeled as schizophrenic and/or bipolar.

314: So, no?

Dr.: Let's move on for a moment and talk about what happened at the clinic. What drove you to do that to Dr. Ramsus and his staff?

314: Each person cured me a little longer. It isn't rocket science, Doc. And you are wasting time brightening my room. I've got a few weeks before they wear off.

Dr.: I suppose we will have to wait and see, won't we? Command, please increase lumens by one hundred and initiate noise program. Thank you. I'll return in an hour.

Patient 314 shows no noticeable signs of distress.

2/6/2017—11:09 AM

Second follow-up interview between Dr. Feldman and 314— logging…

Dr.: Command, please discontinue noise program. I am going to read to you the transcript issued to us by security at the clinic. Please interrupt at any time if a detail is incorrect or if you'd like to explain. I'll pause periodically to ask questions, as well. [Dr. Feldman begins reading.] 'Patient was lead to Observation Room 1 where Dr. Ramsus and twelve staff members waited to perform testing and observations based upon the recent change in physical ability. The patient sat down in the chair, which was centered in the room and surrounded by equipment, monitors, and staff. Dr. Ramsus began asking several questions when the patient grabbed a scalpel and surgical drill. The patient proceeded to stab nearby staff with the scalpel while placing the drill to the head of Dr. Ramsus and

—

314: I had already drilled through his eye before I ever stabbed a staff member.

Dr.: Noted. 'Patient then threw scalpels and other surgical items at staff while chasing down each one with the drill. The room was put on lockdown while security rushed to the scene. At one point, two nurses tackled the patient from behind; however, the patient bit and ripped out the throat of one nurse while jamming the drill into the stomach of the other. By the time security could get a Taser on the patient, Dr. Ramsus and ten of his staff were dead. The remaining two were critically injured and died in transit to surgery.' [Dr. Feldman looks up from his clipboard.] Before this incident, you could not even leave your room without extreme cardiac distress. How were you able to murder thirteen people within 90 seconds?

314: When they lose their life, I gain mine.

Dr.: So you are saying that you steal their life force?

314: I have no idea how it works. I just know that when I cause their death my issues fade.

Dr.: Hmm… Is this fading permanent or temporary?

314: Well, I'm not sure. My experiments were interrupted.

Dr.: Don't worry, we will get to the bottom of your disease together. How did you discover this phenomenon?

314: By accident, really. I caused a massive car accident a while ago. Immediately, I felt different. From there I began my experiments and here I am.

Dr.: Was your father and his family part of your experiments?

314: Yes.

Dr.: Thank you. Your lunch will be brought to you shortly. I'll be back this evening to discuss your daily schedule of testing. Get some rest. Command, please reduce lumens by one hundred and eighty. Thank you.

Mt. Whitney Psychiatric Ward

Dr. Feldman

2/7/2017—6:15AM

Experiment preparation—logging…

Patient 314 receives breakfast, eating rapidly.

Dr.: Good morning, 314. How did you sleep?

314: Mind if I finish eating first? It is rude to interrupt a meal.

Dr.: Of course. I'll skip the pleasantries and explain what we are aiming to do here. All you need to do is listen.

314 continues eating, however his eyes never break from Dr. Feldman

Dr.: We want to perfect your 'cure', 314. Right now, we know only rudimentary ideas about how your disease works but that is going to change. Dr. Ramsus, quite frankly, didn't appreciate the opportunity he had. He squandered his chance at placing his name in the forefront of the medical community. I, however, will not let that chance get by me. Now, I am going to ask you a few questions about the circumstances of your disease. All you need to do is nod "yes" or "no".

314 has finished his meal.

Dr.: Any amount of sensory stimuli would cause heart palpitations and mental anguish, correct?

314 affirms.

Dr.: Until the car accident, you had never witnessed a reversal of the condition, correct?

314 affirms.

Dr.: Your first experiment involved your estranged father and his new family in which you attempted to recreate the effects of the car accident, correct?

314 smiles, then affirms.

Dr.: Tell me about the outcome of that experiment. please.

314: It worked, at least for a while. My experiments were interrupted, so I can't be sure about any quantitative or qualitative statistics. I *believe* that a personal connection, positive or negative, enhances the experience. When I killed my father, I felt much more strength flow through me than when I killed his skank or kids. Of course, I also thought it could be tied directly to the size of the individual, or their vigor. Again, I was interrupted before conclusions could be made.

Dr.: Do not fret. Together we will pinpoint the exact range with many testing variables. Did intercourse with Vanessa give you "strength" or was it simply the euphoria of orgasm?

314: It was my first time. I have nothing to compare it to so I can't answer that. Are we almost done? I'm bored.

Dr.: One more question: If you are never cured completely, will you kill forever in order to have a 'normal' life?

314 affirms.

Dr.: Wonderful, thank you for your cooperation. Your room records everything you say and do and we would like to know your thoughts throughout the process of these upcoming tests. If you say, 'Journal Entry, start,' and, 'Journal Entry, end,' your words will be logged separately. Lunch will be served [looks at watch] in approximately four hours. After lunch, your first experiment begins.

2/7/2017—11:00AM

Lunch delivered. 314 eats in silence. Still no change in demeanor and monitors not detecting a heart episode yet.

2/7/2017—12:07PM

314 has begun to explore his room. 314 appears to be exceptionally patient and thorough in exploration. Discovery of observation glass doubling as a television has ended the exploration. 314 is now sitting on the cot watching world news—it is the only available program.

2/7/2017—2:15PM

Automatic light intensity program initiated. Television volume increased by four. 314 appears to be slightly agitated.

2/7/2017—3:15PM

Light intensity increased. Television volume increased by four. 314 begins pacing, continues for two minutes, then resumes exploration of the room.

2/7/2017—4:15PM

Light intensity increased. Television volume increased by four. 314 is now face down on the cot, blanket draped over his head. Monitors show one small instance of heart palpitation.

2/7/2017—5:15PM

Light intensity increased. Television volume increased by four. Dinner is presented to 314. The sound of the metal tray sliding on the concrete floor creates a heart episode. 314 slowly makes his way to the food and eats even slower. Three more episodes occur during the meal. The last episode is stronger.

2/7/2017—6:13PM

314 appears to be anticipating the increases. Dr. Feldman watches his reaction and the monitors when the increases occur. A massive heart episode causes 314's body to twitch and shiver.

Experiment 1 complete. Light intensity reduced to normal. Television off, observation window now opaque.

Dr.: I am sorry for the discomfort. Before any real testing could begin, we had to first bring you back to a baseline. I didn't know if more sensory information would speed up the process—now we know it does.

314: Screw you!

Dr.: Now, now, now, any good scientist knows the need and importance of a baseline. How else can we draw any real conclusions? Please, [a small child enters the room of 314] believe me when I say that we want to cure you *and* understand your disease properly. Now, you know what to do.

314 launches at the small child, grabbing the hair with both hands and twisting forcefully. The child drops lifelessly to the floor. 314 stares down for a moment, then returns to his cot.

Dr.: Better?

314: Who was she?

Experiment 2 complete.

Mt. Whitney Psychiatric Ward
Dr. Feldman

2/8/2017—5:30AM

Observations from experiment one and two—logging…

Patient 314 can be manipulated into submission with extreme sensory input and enhanced by the taking of life. Still unsure of the cause, whether it is life force, chemical reaction in the brain, or simply a deranged perception. If it is life force or a chemical reaction, we can control it and perfect it. If 314 has created this illusion it won't be so easy to control. Maybe even impossible to control. Today we attempt to measure how much a life is worth.

2/8/2017—6:15AM

Experiment preparation—logging…

Breakfast delivered. 314 eats in silence. Immediately following the meal, another child is presented. 314 watches the child warily for several minutes, glancing at the observation window occasionally.

314: Who are you?

Child does not respond. 314 circles the child, then casually snaps its neck.

Readings are taken, compared, logged.

Light intensity increased by 180, white noise volume 8.

Readings are taken, compared, logged. Light and noise discontinued.

2/8/2017—8:15AM

A child is introduced to the room. 314 looks up from the floor.

314: Didn't I just kill you?!

314 grabs child by the neck and strangles it to death.

Readings are taken, compared, logged.

Light increased by 180, white noise volume 6.

Readings are taken, compared, logged. Light and noise discontinued.

2/8/2017—10:15AM

The final child is introduced to the room. 314 screams in what seems to be rage. 314 grabs the child by the face, pressing one thumb into each eyeball. 314 repeats *"Just die!"* over and over until being overcome by sobs.

Readings are taken, compared, logged.

Light increased by 180, white noise volume 5.

Readings are taken, compared, logged. Light and noise discontinued.

2/8/2017—11:15AM

Lunch is brought to 314 but Patient shows no desire to eat. The food is removed at 11:45AM.

2/8/2017—12:15PM

A woman is introduced to the room. 314 does not seem to notice.

Dr.: Please, 314, only a few more before this stage of testing is over.

314: Why did the little girl look the same? Why are they all the same? WHAT DO YOU WANT?!

314 pounds on the glass.

Dr.: Kill her.

314 spins and lunges in one fluid motion and snaps her neck cleanly.

Readings are taken, compared, logged.

Light intensity increased by 180, white noise volume 8.

Readings are taken, compared, logged. Light and noise discontinued.

2/8/2017—2:15PM

A woman is introduced to the room.

314: Who are you?

Woman: I am Test 3.2. Please kill me.

314: Why do you want me to kill you?

Test 3.2: So that you can be cured.

314: But don't you want to live? To experience life outside of these walls?

Test 3.2: I live only to be killed. Please kill me.

314: Why do you look just like the last woman?

Test 3.2: Please kill me.

314 begins striking Test 3.2 in the face and chest. 314 screams in pain due to a broken bone in the hand. While clutching the hand to his chest, 314 kicks Test 3.2 until she drops. He stomps repeatedly. An orderly and

a nurse enter the room, pulling 314 away from the crushed skull to treat his hand. The body is removed and floor cleaned.

Readings are taken, compared, logged.

Light intensity increased by 180, white noise volume 6.

Readings are taken, compared, logged. Light and noise discontinued.

2/8/2017—4:15PM

The final woman is introduced to the room.

314: Mom?

Woman: Oh, [Removed]; I thought I'd never see you again. Are you ok? What is this place?

314: Some kind of lab or something. They are experimenting on me. I... I've done bad things, Mom.

Woman: Hush, now; everything is alright. Mommy's here. [She holds 314 close, stroking his hair.]

314: I think I broke m—

Dr.: Kill her, 314.

314: Wait, what? Kill my mom? No, no way! Are you kiddi—

Dr.: Kill her.

Woman: Who are you? What are you doing to my son?

Dr.: Kill her, now.

314 is shocked with 50,000 volts. He is shaking his head, tears in his eyes. The woman is striding toward the glass. She pounds on it, then moves to the wall where she entered the room, pounding on it.

314: I love you, Mom.

She crumples to the ground, neck broken.

Readings are taken, compared, logged.

Light intensity increased by 180, white noise volume 10.

Readings are taken, compared, logged. Light and noise discontinued.

2/8/2017—5:15PM

Dinner is brought to 314.

Dr.: Please, eat. You need your strength.

314: Screw you.

Dr.: Oh come now. I thought we were past all of that nonsense. There is only one more test today and then you'll be moving on to the next phase in testing. I promise you'll enjoy it much, much better. Now eat your dinner and I'll bring you your dessert soon.

314 slowly eats the food. As soon as the last bite is eaten, Dr. Feldman enters the room holding a plate with a large slice of carrot cake. Dr. Feldman sits next to 314, offering him the cake. 314 begins eating.

After two bites 314 takes the fork and jams it into the throat of Dr. Feldman. Blood spurts out all over the carrot cake and 314's face.

[Clap, clap, clap.] Dr. Feldman can be seen just beyond the observation glass.

Readings are taken, compared, logged.

The observation glass switches to television mode, displaying CCTV footage with timestamp matching the present time. The footage is of 314's home. His mother passes by one camera, emerges on another in 314's room. She sits and cries.

314 takes a bite of carrot cake.

Readings are taken, compared, logged.

Experiment 3 complete.

Mt. Whitney Psychiatric Ward
Patient 314 Personal Log

2/8/2017—8:17PM

I feel like I am being conditioned, like I am a bad dog in obedience school. To a degree, I understand what Dr. Feldman is doing and why but I hate not being in control of the experiments. I felt like I was getting closer to a cure on my own! I didn't need this beady-eyed prick force-feeding me little kids and raping my eyes with blinding lights. Eff it. At least he said today was the last day for all of the back and forth shit. Tomorrow would be fun, he said. I'd like to say I don't trust him but what choice to I have? It is going to happen one way or another. What I don't get is how they have clone tech. Like, I know it wasn't my mom but at the same time it was impossible not to think it was her. Her voice, expressions, everything was perfect. Then that smug bastard throws a clone of himself in here. Probably testing me to see how much I hate him. A lot, man. A whole effing lot.

Dr. Feldman

2/8/2017—10:00PM

Observations from experiment three—logging...

Patient 314 has stabilized. There was concern at first due to the nature of our testing, of course, but his resolve is incredibly high. This is most likely caused by the extreme isolation he has already endured. Testing has determined that size or age of the individual is not a factor in the amount of strength 314 gains from each kill but, rather, emotional bonds. It is still undetermined whether positive emotions or negative emotions such as love and calm versus hate and fear change the amount but we will revisit that at a later date. A most interesting note—the highest amount of strength gain did not come from killing me but actually his mother. Very much looking forward to testing my theory on why that was.

By the end of the day, we determined the amount of sensory stimulation needed to bring 314 down to his zero point: the point where he does not hurt from sensations but is not above normal human ability. We also determined that 314 actually goes slightly beyond the normal levels of human strength, speed, and agility after killing, thus enabling the next kill to be easier.

Tomorrow will be an exciting day.

2/9/2017—6:15AM

Experiment four—logging...

Breakfast delivered. 314 eats hungrily. Readings are taken, compared, logged.

Six individuals enter the room. Each one is faceless and naked.

Dr.: Good morning, 314. Before you is the first round of tests for the day. If you would please kill one, then wait until my signal, kill two and wait for my signal, then the last three. I also need you to be consistent in your actions.

314: Why don't they have faces?

Dr.: We are trying to eliminate any emotion behind the acts today.

314: How do they see?

Dr.: One day I will explain everything but, for now, please kill the first individual.

314 studies Dr. Feldman's face for a moment before walking over to the first. He stops an inch away, almost nose to nose (if it had a nose).

314: It isn't breathing. Strange.

314 snaps the neck and steps back. Readings are taken, compared, logged.

Dr.: Proceed.

314 moves in front of the next, quickly snapping the neck of one and then two. Readings are taken, compared, logged.

Dr.: Proceed.

314 snaps all three necks almost too quickly to see. Readings are taken, compared, logged.

Dr.: Thank you, 314. I'll return once the results for this test have been analyzed. Relax and enjoy some news.

The observation window switched to television mode and news is displayed. A blurb about the President, unseasonable weather patterns, an ISIS terrorist attack at Mayo Clinic, a Yellow Fever outbreak.

2/9/2017—9:27AM

Experiment four, continued—logging…

Dr.: Have you ever fired a gun before, 314?

314: My doorbell used to send me into shock. You think a gun firing six inches from my ear would be pleasant for me?

Dr.: Of course, a silly question indeed. Six more individuals will be entering your room. One has a gun. Please take the gun and kill them all.

Readings are taken, compared, logged. Six of the faceless come in, the last holding a gun outstretched toward 314, handle out. 314 takes the gun, slides his hands over it, studies it. The first shot misses however each subsequent shot hits the target. 314 is smiling. Readings are taken, compared, logged.

Dr.: Excellent, thank you. How did it feel to use a gun?

314: Different. Powerful. Surprisingly cold, like the gun is trying to steal all of my warmth.

Six more of the faceless come in, each one grabbing a deceased test subject and carry them out. They return, the last holding a large hunting knife.

Dr.: Please, again; this time with the knife.

314 takes the knife and sprints from the first to the last, knife flashing out. Each drops lifeless with a slit across the throat. Readings are taken, compared, logged.

Dr.: Did that feel different to you? The knife?

314: It did. I could almost feel the heartbeat when I ran the edge across their throat, the warmth of blood on my hand.

314 glances down at his hands to find them devoid of any blood.

Dr.: Interesting, yes, yes. Quite marvelous. [Slowly walks off talking to himself]

2/9/2017—11:15AM

Lunch delivered. There is also the most recent issue of Time magazine. 314 eats and reads.

2/9/2017—4:00PM

Experiment four, continued—logging…

One of the faceless enters 314's room.

Dr.: Good afternoon, 314. This test will be a little different. I'd like for you to kill the subject with your mind.

314: My what? Mind? How the hell am I supposed to do that?

Dr.: I don't know; maybe you can't. But please humor me and try.

314 stares at Dr. Feldman, eyes narrowed, and then focuses attention on the Faceless. Nothing happens. Two minutes pass. Still nothing. Readings are taken, compared, logged.

Dr.: May I ask what you are thinking?

314: I am thinking this is the most retarded test I've ever heard of.

Dr.: Have you truly tried to kill the subject? Focused intently just as if you had a gun or a knife in your hand.

314: Sure, yeah. Ok.

314 focuses on the Faceless. Eyes close. 314's vitals slow. The Faceless twitches momentarily. Then nothing. 314's brow is glistening lightly with sweat. The Faceless leaves the room. Readings are taken, compared, logged.

Dr.: Thank you, 314. You may rest now. Dinner will be by shortly.

2/9/2017—5:15PM

Dinner delivered. 314 takes the dinner and sits down to eat. A man enters.

Confusion crosses 314's face momentarily, then recognition, then a smile.

The man drops dead. He looked just like his father.

Experiment 4 <u>complete.</u>

Mt. Whitney Psychiatric Ward
Patient 314 Personal Log
2/9/2017—10:23PM

I guess I need to eat my words a bit. He said today would be fun and it WAS! Sure, yeah, it started out kind of slow but shooting a gun was invigorating, mesmerizing even. The power inside of that tiny little weapon is astounding. I wouldn't mind taking it up as a hobby someday, but who needs a gun when you can visualize severing the spinal cord and it actually happens? Well, I guess I don't know if the spinal cord severed but the dad-clone died so whatever I did to it killed it. How did he know I could do that? I guess since I am patient 314 that means there were 313 before me but the real question is where they *like* me or were they all different? Like, different abilities and stuff? I am going to ask some questions tomorrow.

Dr. Feldman

2/9/2017—10:59PM

Observations from experiment four—logging…

Patient 314 has shown more promise in four days than any other patient in a month's time. I do not think that we have seen anywhere close to his maximum potential. 314 is also becoming a bit more interactive—this can only be taken in a positive way. Only two other patients have reacted positively once testing began. He appears to be settling into his routine nicely.

As I theorized, an isolated kill is very static, and only fluctuates with emotional connection. This is important for a great many applications where emotion must be removed from a situation. When multiple beings are killed there is a multiplier factor of 1.3. This is possibly linked to adrenaline or a similar effect to "runner's high"—more testing will be done to determine the exact cause.

It should also be noted that the method of killing plays a factor. Patient 314 gained more from killing with the knife than he did with the pistol. He does seem to favor using his hands when killing. This might tie in with the emotion aspect.

Most exciting of all is having another patient with the mental ability. Patient 313 was a complete failure in the testing environment however the discovery of her mental abilities led us to Patient 314, so I shouldn't be too hard on her. Where she failed he has succeeded! Autopsy on the Faceless that 314 failed to kill showed some damage to the neck similar to whiplash and minor internal bleeding on the brain. Autopsy on the clone showed a cleanly severed spinal cord. If we can somehow find a way to translate that result without the personal/emotional connection... I am getting ahead of myself.

Tomorrow will be interesting.

2/10/2017—6:15AM

Experiment five—logging...

Breakfast delivered. 314 appears contemplative and relaxed while he eats.

Sixteen subjects enter the room just as Dr. Feldman begins to speak.

Dr.: Good morning, 314. Today we will attempt to verify a few theories I have. In front of you is a mixture of Faceless and clones of your Father, Mother, and myself. Each one is holding a different weapon. Those without a weapon you will kill with your bare hands, except the very last which must be killed with your mind. On my mark move to the first subject. Please wait thirty seconds between each kill. Proceed.

Readings are taken, compared, logged.

314 moves to the first subject. When he finds himself in front of the last, he locks eyes with the subject. Blood seeps slowly out of the mouth, nostrils, eyes, and ears of the subject as it crumples to the clean, white floor.

Readings are taken, compared, logged.

A powerful strobe lashes out, blindingly bright, accompanied by a thunderclap of sound.

Readings are taken, compared, logged.

Dr.: Wonderful, simply marvelous! Sixteen more are coming in now. This time I would like for you to try and mentally kill the first subject

AND the last subject. Proceed.

314 approaches the first subject. Sweat begins beading on his forehead. His breathing grows harsher.

Dr.: 314, enough. Use your hands and move on to the next.

314 moves down the line with more violent intent. When he steps in front of the final subject, the neck twists swiftly in a full 360 degrees. 314's hands never left his sides.

Dr.: Perfect. Thank you, 314. I am sure you need some rest so I'll have a snack brought and we can resume at 8.

314: How did you know I could do that? You know, with my mind?

Dr.: I suppose you deserve a few answers. Patient 313 had similar mental capabilities. Once an ability is discovered in one Patient, we check every Patient for those abilities as well.

314: Are there other Patients here? Can I meet them? Can I meet 313?

Dr.: You've already met Patient 313.

Dr. Feldman walks away and a tray with sliced meats and cheeses is brought it. 314 eats in silence.

2/10/2017—8:00AM

Experiment five, continued—logging...

Dr.: How are you feeling, 314? Have you had any headaches or eye strain?

314: Not yet, no. Was that an issue with 313?

Dr.: It was, among others. We are going to continue the testing now if that is ok.

Three clones of Dr. Feldman enter the observation room.

Dr.: If you would, please try to kill each one mentally.

314: [mumbles] Like this world needs more crazy doctors running around...

Patient 314 stays on his cot but focuses on the first clone. His knuckles turn white as his grip tightens on the edge of the cot, then the clone crumples to the floor. Readings are taken, compared, logged. 314's neck bulges and strains as the second clone drops to the floor, twitching slightly twice. A large vein is standing out on 314's forehead and gleams with sweat. Readings are taken, compared, logged. A guttural yell escapes the lips of Patient 314. His concentration has forced him to stop breathing, his head vibrating back and forth.

Dr.: Breathe. Recollect yourself. Then try again.

Patient 314 leans back, drawing in a large breath. Again. Again. The color in his hands and face start to return to normal. He locks eyes with the last clone—twenty seconds later, it drops lifelessly to the floor. Readings are taken, compared, logged.

Dr.: I believe we have found your threshold. There will be one more test today but it can wait until just before dinner. A second channel has been added to your television. Please try to rest.

2/10/2017—11:15AM

Lunch delivered. Patient 314 awakened by the sound of the tray. Television mode is activated while 314 eats.

2/10/2017—4:00PM

Experiment five, continued—logging...

Six Faceless enter the room.

Dr.: This is the last test of the day. I would like you to kill four with your hands. Then try to kill the remaining two at the same time with your mind.

314: Are you kidding? At the same time? How am I going to do that?!

Dr.: How do you kill one? You visualize the action and carry out the action with your mind. Try to visualize them both.

314 sighs and closes his eyes. He rubs his temples for a minute before looking up at the Faceless. Breathing is slow and even. Eventually two thuds resonate through the room. Readings are taken, compared, logged.

Dr.: [whispers] Yes… [to 314] How do you feel?

314: Tired. Could I meet 313 again?

Dr.: I am afraid that isn't possible anymore. You killed her yesterday.

[ADDENDUM TO LOG]—Patient 314 killed her two days before. See Day 3.

2/10/2017—5:15PM

Dinner is delivered. A comedy movie is playing on the television.

Experiment 5 complete.

Mt. Whitney Psychiatric Ward
Dr. Feldman
9/13/2016—5:15AM

Observations from experiment six—logging…

Patient 313 continues to decline. She has not slept the past three nights and still refuses to eat. Today we will be forced to run an IV and tube feed her to regain her strength based on our interactions in the coming hour. She must remain alive. It is hard to judge whether she is refusing to use her mental capabilities or if she is too weak to use them effectively.

Experiment three showed such promise. It seems like a lifetime ago when I was excited about her test results. Today we will repeat experiment five again in hopes of determining whether or not multiple subjects can be terminated.

9/13/2016—6:15AM

Experiment seven—logging...

Breakfast delivered. Patient 313 makes no indications of getting up.

Dr.: 313, please eat. You need your strength.

313: Don't act like you care about me.

Dr.: You know that I—

[313 interrupts]

313: You abducted me from my home, my son left all alone, locked up in a room defenseless. You keep me isolated in a small room with nothing but news and hospital food to eat. You are a monster, *Doctor.*

Dr.: You don't like the food? I'll look into that. And, like I have said before, your son is safe and being watched after. He doesn't even know that—

[313 interrupts again]

313: That you replaced me with one of your fucking clones? No, of course; that makes it all better. MY SON NEEDS HIS MOTHER. NOT A DAMNED CLONE!

The lights begin to flicker. A small crack forms in the center of the observation window as Patient 313 moves deliberately towards it. Fifteen Faceless rush into the room to apprehend Patient 313. Twelve are killed before a needle finds a home in her neck. The crack has become a massive spider web in the glass. She is taken to a maximum security cell where a feeding tube and IV are administered.

She is kept in an induced coma for seven days while her body is replenished with nutrients and back in balance. Drug Z is implanted.

9/20/2016—8:07 AM

Medical evaluation of Patient 313—logging…

313's eyes fluttered open as the last of the IV fluid left her system. She slowly turned her neck one way, then the other.

Dr.: Good morning. Don't try to sit up yet. It will take most of the day for the grogginess to fade completely. There is some food next to you when you are ready.

313: What did you do?

Dr.: You were malnourished and in a very agitated state when we last spoke. It was necessary to remove you from the observation room while we made the necessary improvements to it. I don't think you'll be cracking the observation window any time soon. Nor do I think you should try.

313: I'll do whatever the hell I want. Kill me if you don't like it.

Dr.: I have better options than killing you, but I certainly hope it doesn't come to that. You are special, 313. We can learn a lot from you.

313: You'll get nothing else from me, you bastard. I promise you that!

Patient 313 begins sitting up, slapping the meal tray away and pulling tubing out of her arms.

Dr.: I see. It was a pleasure working with you.

Dr. Feldman activates Drug Z. The change in Patient 313 is immediate.

11/1/2016—10:30 AM

Observations from experiment twenty-eight—logging…

This will be the last observation log for Patient 313Z. She has done as much as she can in her current state of mind. There is only so far a controlled mind can go when testing mental capabilities. Below is a summary of her accomplishments:

- Able to kill up to six individuals at once
- Able to push thoughts into an individual's mind
- Able to block out pain up to a pain threshold of a gunshot wound
- Able to learn at a heightened rate

Tomorrow we will do a full medical screen for genetic markers and scan for matches. Once the scan is complete, the full autopsy can be scheduled.

11/2/2016—6:45AM

Patient 313Z medical summary—logging...

We found some very interesting things; very interesting, indeed. Patient 313Z has a marker we have never seen before which may contribute to her ability. Much more testing needs to be done to determine if this is the case but preliminary research indicates the marker determines higher brain functions. Her autopsy is postponed until all research is complete.

2/5/2017—8:57PM

Patient 313Z medical summary—logging...

We found a match to Patient 313Z. Mobilizing a task force for immediate transport.

2/8/2017—4:14PM

Patient 313Z sent to observation room 1.

2/8/2017—4:17PM

Patient 313Z sent to autopsy room 1.

Mt. Whitney Psychiatric Ward

Containment Protocol—Facility Lockdown

2/11/2017—11:12PM

ALL CHANNELS OPEN—logging...

Security channel: Sub-Ob 3 breach. All units to central loft. All units to central loft. Patient 3 is active. Patient 3 is active! All units to central loft.

Chief Security Advisor: P3 Unit to the fore. Stand ready. Units one thru four flanking position. Weapons ready.

[Central loft comes to rest and doors open]

Dr. Feldman Personal Log

2/11/2017—11:13PM

Patient 3 is not in the loft. It is coming for me. It's not alone.

[Dr. is rifling through papers, searching.]

[Massive data dump onto unknown server.]

Office should hold but just in case... initiate Phase 3 on my command...

[Groan of metal can be heard.]

2/11/2017—11:13PM

Chief Security Advisor: Where is it? FUCK! This wouldn't happen if we had video in Sub-Op. Security to operations, this is CSA. Do you have a visual on Patient 3?

Operations: Negative, CSA. Thermal scan in progress... Heat signature outside Dr. Feldman's office.

CSA: En route. Units with me, protect Feldman at all costs.

2/11/2017—11:14

[Metal screams in anguish, audibly twisting and conforming against its will.]

CSA: P3 Unit forward. Engage. All units backup formation.

[Weapons crackle and sizzle, men screaming.]

CSA: ALL UNITS ON ME! TIGHT CIRCLE; PATIENT ZERO IS PRESENT!! PATIENT ZERO IS PRE—

[Weapons open fire in all directions.]

[A single tentacle breaks through, bits of metal still attached to its suckers.]

Dr.: Access code: Kite Bravo Six Zero Field Six One Hippo Tango

Security Channel: Phase 3 confirmed.

[The tentacle pulls back. Inhuman shrieks mixing with human screams fill the compound.]

P3 UNIT: Patient 3 neutralized. Patient Zero at large. All remaining units to Feldman's office. Office hull is breached.

[A deep groan issues thought-out the compound. Generators begin whirring]

[Dr. Feldman's body lies facedown behind his desk. Blood spills from his head at both temples.]

P3 UNIT: Feldman is dead. All personnel, be advised; Patient Zero has assumed his form. I repeat, Feldman is dead. Open fire immediately upon contact with Dr. Feldman.

2/11/2017—11:16PM

Patient 314's observation room opens. Dr. Feldman walks in.

Dr.: Sorry to disturb you at this late hour, 314. If you would please follow me.

314: Follow you where?

Dr.: I'll explain on the way. Come along now.

2/11/2017—11:21PM

[All data received at Site 2. Phase 3 in progress.]

Water floods the facility, filling every square inch of every room. All power is diverted to the coils, 1,000,000 volts cooking anything left alive. Explosive charges begin to go off. Floor by floor, the facility collapses onto itself.

2/12/2017—12:04AM

Patient 314 watches from the back of a high-speed railcar. The mountain seems to shudder slightly.

Zero: As I was saying, I am not Dr. Feldman. In there, I was referred to as Patient Zero just as you are Patient 314. I was the first, the reason all of this is even happening.

314: So who are you, really? How did you know how to get out of there?

Zero: Who I am is not important, young man. What I can do is the important thing. Dr. Feldman and I were colleagues once, doing research for our joint thesis on the human potential. I was trying to find out more about myself, my ability. He was trying to make himself better.

314: And what is your ability?

Zero: To put it in basic terms, I absorb information and I never forget anything. The downside is that whatever information source I absorb is destroyed in the process. If I read a book, the pages are wiped clean. If I take someone's memory, they die. I was careless with it early on in my life before I understood the need for such caution and it caught up with me. Dr. Feldman was a brilliant man. He figured out there was something special about me during our short time together as researchers. What I didn't know was that he was already working for Mt. Whitney Research.

314: But you look like him, too. So you shape shift?

Zero: The reason a living thing dies when I absorb their information is because I take ALL of it, down to the DNA that dictates how they look. We went for a weekend camping trip to take a break from our thesis but it was a setup. I was locked away in that mountain ever since. He figured out how to extract the information I had absorbed and built almost everything off of that information. He designed an implant that mimicked my ability. It absorbed information without destroying it. With each new Patient, he was able to put together one piece of the full human potential puzzle at a time. You might have been the last piece.

314: Me? Why?

Zero: Because with you, he could unlock the secret to escaping death. While I absorbed *information*, you absorbed *life*! If he could harness that and manipulate it in the right way, it would enable everlasting life. Not to mention the nifty tricks you can do with your mind. He hit the jackpot when he found you and your mother.

314: Mom… [314 looks out the window at the rapidly fading mountain.] Why did you save me?

Zero: Because Feldman activated Phase 3. All his research was transferred to Site 2. His clone is probably already at work trying to locate the next Patient. We're going to stop it.

Zero's Personal Log

2/12/2017—3:17AM

Patient 314 is sleeping. I have reviewed all of the mental memory from Feldman—we are just under eight hours away from Site 2. According to the Phase 3 time table, we should make it there before they are in full swing. These fuckers are quick. Task forces are already being reassigned to the new site and the data dump that Feldman did is being uploaded. Until that is complete, they won't have any real security features online that can contain us once we are in. My hope is that we can get there before the upload is complete.

2/12/2017—6:42AM

Patient 314 awakens. I hand him an energy bar. "Eat this, you will need your strength."

"Thanks. So what is the plan? Why do you even need me if you have all of Feldman's memory?" 314 begins eating.

"Having all the knowledge, schematics, access codes; those are all important. But you are the weapon. I know *about* the abilities of the other Patients but I can't *do* them. Feldman didn't get very far with your mom or you on *how* you do what you do, which means I can't do what you do either. What I did know is that I couldn't trust any of the remaining Patients to help me do this except for you."

314 shakes his head. "Wait, what do you mean 'get far with my mom?' He took my mom?"

"Your mother was Patient 313. She had the same mental ability you have. That is how he even knew about you in the first place."

"So… that wasn't a clone, was it?" I shake my head, watching realization come to his face. "I killed my mom…"

"I'm very sorry," I say. "But that is how I knew you'd help me stop this bastard."

314 buries his head in his hands, entire body heaving with silent sobs. I put a hand on his shoulder before walking away towards the other end of the train car.

2/12/2017—7:09AM

314 looks up, eyes bright red and puffy. "What's the plan?"

I smile.

2/12/2017—11:10AM

The train glides to a stop inside of what looks to be an abandoned warehouse. 314 and I exit the train and are greeted with nothing but a metal staircase leading down.

"Alright, follow me," I say. "If we cross paths with anyone, let me do the talking."

314 nods and we begin the descent downward, feet echoing loudly in the narrow stairwell. After ten flights we arrive at the concrete landing. I approach the large steel door and place my hand onto the palm reader while staring into the retinal scanner. The computerized voice of the systems speaks, "Dr. Feldman recognized, access granted."

The airlock releases in a quiet hiss, massive bolts sliding into the walls, ceiling, and floor—light filters out into the dim landing as the door opens.

2/12/2017—11:32AM

Site 2 Security Channel—logging…

Motion detection active.

Video surveillance active.

Video-transcription software complete.

Facial recognition software incomplete. 51%

Voice recognition software incomplete. 34%

Thermal recognition software incomplete. 18%

Cognitive recognition software incomplete. 2%

Defense systems offline.

Two humans enter through Train Entrance 3. One (Human 1) walks with purpose, the other (Human 2) follows. Couple moves to Floor C. Another human (Human 3) approaches from the east.

Human 3: Ah, Dr. Feldman, it is good to see you. I'm glad you've finally made it over here to Site 2.

Human 1: Kill him.

Human 3 drops to the floor. Dr. Feldman and Human 2 drag the body into the closest room, then continue south towards the offices. They stop in front of the office of Dr. Feldman. He palms his way into the office and Human 2 follows inside. The door closes.

Zero's Personal Log

2/12/2017—11:44AM

"Shit, he isn't in here," I whisper, trying to control my frustration. "He must be wandering around, overseeing the progress of everything gearing up. I am going to access his computer and try to absorb anything else he may have on there that wasn't in his mind. Stand guard while I am linked up. I'll be vulnerable while it is going."

"What do I do if Feldman's clone tries to come in?" 314 asks.

"Knock him out. We may need him still."

2/12/2017—1:39PM

Site 2 Security Channel—logging…

Motion detection active.

Video surveillance active.

Video-transcription software complete.

Facial recognition software incomplete. 98%

Voice recognition software incomplete. 71%

Thermal recognition software incomplete. 37%

Cognitive recognition software incomplete. 12%

Defense systems offline.

Human 4 is entering the loft. Loft has stopped on floor C. Human 4 proceeds towards the offices. Facial recognition software complete. Searching...

Human 1 is Patient Zero.

Human 2 is Patient 314.

Human 3 is General Talbot.

Human 4 is Dr. Feldman.

Dr. Feldman approaches his office.

2/12/2017—1:41PM

The clone of Dr. Feldman walks in to see 314 directly in front of him and falters mid step. 314 focuses on breaking his knees, knowing Zero told him to keep him alive. Confusion creeps across 314's face when nothing seems to happen. In an instant the clone is lunging forward, fist outstretched. 314 tries to move out of the way but takes a glancing blow to the cheek and the lunging body follows, crashing into 314 as both bodies fall to the floor. An object, blurred by the speed, crosses 314's vision. Blackness envelopes him.

2/12/2017—5:06PM

Dr.: I see you are finally waking up. Let me be the first to welcome you to Site 2.

314: Site 2? Wha… what? Uhmmm.

Patient 314 rolls over gingerly, holding the side of his head. 314 slowly brings his head up to look around. Four walls, one observation screen, one cot.

Dr.: I must thank you. In coming here, you've allowed us to pick up where we left off at Site 1. I wasn't quite finished with your testing, you know.

314: Zero. What happened to Zero?

Dr.: Ah, Zero. You can thank him for making all of this a reality. Without his ability, this facility would probably not exist. It was unfortunate to have to kill him, especially in such a vulnerable state. He didn't even look up when I wrapped my hands around his throat.

314 trembles with rage. Tears stain his face.

314: I won't help you. I won't!

Dr. Feldman takes out his phone and presses a few buttons. A blinding light and horrible screech fills Observation Room 1. It seems to go on forever.

Dr.: Oh, I think you will. Without a kill, you'll be in the same sad, pathetic state you were just a few weeks ago. Any passing fart will send your weak heart into convulsions. Do you want to be like that again, 314?

314: I lived my whole life like that. I'll suffer it if it means you don't get what you want.

Dr.: Hmm. Be that as it may, if you don't mind, please feel the nape of your neck for me. [314's hand slowly moves to the back of his head.] Do you feel that slight bump? That is the Z implant. If I press a button, it is activated. If you try to take it out it is activated. Do you know what it does, 314? It gives me complete access to your mind. You are my little zombie pet, hence the 'Z'. I can make you do anything. *Anything*, 314. So I dare say that you will help me whether you want to or not. I was able to test on your mother for quite a while before her lack of will became a roadblock. But, you see, now I know your ability is hereditary. You will be my factory, impregnating thousands of women so I can test on all of your special offspring. Oh yes, I will get what I want.

A Faceless walks into the room.

Site 2 Test Facility
Dr. Feldman

2/12/2017—8:44PM

Dr. Feldman personal entry—logging…

The look on Patient 314's face when his ability didn't work on me. There is no greater rush than power. I was unsure if the neural disruptor would work, considering our tests were cut so short at Site 1 but I was very pleased with the outcome. I felt a tug somewhere in my neck but only briefly. It is possible that 314 didn't have enough "strength" to overcome the device. More testing will determine the true extent of the device. Tomorrow begins a new chapter in his testing.

2/13/2017—6:15AM

Experiment one—logging…

Breakfast delivered.

Dr.: Good morning, Patient 314. I very much look forward to working with you. For the next few days we are going to focus on that beautiful brain of yours. You'll be given Faceless to kill as you please in order to keep your strength up; however, your tests will not involve killing. Are you familiar with Star Wars, 314?

314: The movies or the government projects? [Eats slowly, deliberately, warily.]

Dr.: The movies. [314 nods.] Good. The Jedi have certain abilities they like to use to get their way. In a similar fashion, you should be able to, as well. With practice and careful tutelage, of course. When you are done eating, I will ask you to take a seat in the chair. Once in the chair, a cerebral cap will lower down and fit over your head. Don't be alarmed by it—it is only there to help map your brain activity.

Three Faceless enter the room, one holding a chair.

Dr.: You may kill two of them in whatever manner you choose. The third will subject itself to your directions. These directions must be spoken internally only. Understood?

314 finishes his last forkful of hashbrowns and nods slowly. Setting the plate down he moves slowly to the first Faceless, snapping its neck. The second is dispatched similarly. Once in the chair and the cerebral cap strapped on, he looks to the observation window. Readings are taken, compared, logged.

Dr.: Good. Now give it a command to do something out of the ordinary.

Patient 314 turns back to the remaining Faceless. The cerebral cap begins reading his internal monologue.

I don't want to do this. I can't help this man. How can I get out of this? I should play along for a while, come up with a plan. How? He killed Zero. I'm alone. Alone. I've always been alone. I figured this disease out on my own. I can do this. Focus.

314 looks up into the blank stare of the Faceless.

If I can control this, I can get to Feldman. I can kill him. Hurt him. Make him suffer. Why couldn't I kill him earlier? Was I too weak? Focus. Focus.

The Faceless seems to contort slightly, pinching and pulling at the skin where its mouth should be. A thin crease forms in what looks to be a smile.

Dr.: Oh, most excellent. A smile on a Faceless! You are more twisted than I am, 314. You may kill it now.

The Faceless crumples as if no bones were present in its body. Readings taken, compared, logged.

Experiment one complete.

2/13/2017—9:20PM

Dr. Feldman personal entry—logging...

The speed with which Patient 314 learns and performs is astonishing. I wouldn't believe it unless I saw it with my own two eyes. It helped to be able to hear his thought process—such focus! A lifetime of isolation and suffering honed his resolve to far beyond anything I have seen in previous patients. 314 has shown considerable command over mental coercion in the first three experiments. In addition, several gaps in my understanding of his ability have been filled. After review of the data collected by the cerebral cap, I now have pinpointed several neural paths that only his brain seems to take. Tomorrow we will attempt to perfect mental coercion and begin reading minds. If I am correct that will give me enough data to complete mapping his neural paths and design an algorithm to match it.

2/14/2017—6:15AM

Experiment four—logging...

Breakfast delivered.

Dr.: Good morning, 314. Please have a seat in the chair once again and we may begin.

314 sits and eats, the cap descending down onto his head as the last bite is swallowed.

Dr.: You progressed very well yesterday. So well, in fact, that I think you are ready to begin pulling from their minds instead of pushing into their minds. Try to ascertain what the Faceless are thinking. I have programmed them to think of several things, each one for twenty seconds before thinking of the next.

A Faceless walks in with a chair and sits three feet from Patient 314. The blank "stare" gives nothing away.

What are you thinking? What stupid, pointless thought does he have flashing across your brain right now? Focus. Where did I push thoughts yesterday? Yes, ok. What are they saying? Focus! How can you read the mind of a doctor if you can't read the mind of a blank-faced zombie? FOCUS! Animal. Four-legs. White? Wooden. Paint. I must have run out of time, new thought.

314: The first was an animal; maybe a white, shaggy dog.

Brass. It's large. Focus! Hinges.

314: A door.

Fast. Powerful. Click-click-clack. What is that? A sound? A game? Typing!

314: A computer.

Dr.: Good, keep going.

Red. Short. Heat. Inferno. Water. Dog. This makes no sense… what is this? Focus! Metal dome. A siren.

314: A fire hydrant.

Dr.: An excellent first attempt, 314. Of course, people don't think at such a slow rate under normal conditions so the next test will be 10 seconds per thought and each thought will be more involved. Now I'd like you to push a thought into the Faceless's head so that it kills itself.

314 looks from the Dr. to the Faceless.

Stop breathing.

The gentle rise and fall of its chest ceases. A tremor slowly builds in its body, muscles give out from a lack of oxygen. The Faceless drops in a heap to the floor, the last thought still lingering in its mind long after.

2/14/2017—11:12PM

Dr. Feldman personal entry—logging…

The mapping is complete. By the end of the day, Patient 314 was able to successfully determine 90% of thoughts at one second intervals. Even with this accelerated testing, he never seemed to wear down. Of course, more testing would be preferable but my timetable has changed. With a complete neural map I should be able to stop both incoming and outgoing information from my brain with the disruptor. Tomorrow I'll put it to the test, as well as testing whether or not I can duplicate his ability.

2/15/2017—6:15AM

Dr. Feldman opens the door to Observation Room 1 and closes it behind him. Patient 314 watches warily from his cot as the doctor sits down in the chair he has grown to hate as much as the cell.

Dr.: Good morning, Patient 314. I apologize for a lack of breakfast this morning but I did not see much point in it. Today is a big day for us. I'd like for you to try and read my thoughts.

A moment passes before 314 grimaces in pain.

314: I can't.

Dr.: I see. If you would please, push a thought into my mind. Tell me to hurt myself in some way.

Another moment goes by. Sweat forms on 314's brow and pain

flashes across his visage.

Dr.: Good, the device is working. You see, by watching and mapping how your brain works when you push and pull thoughts I was able to create a means of breaking that connection. I was fairly certain the device would work but the real test is right now.

314: Oh? And that is what exac—

314 can no longer move. Fear fills his eyes like a spooked doe in the open field. Dr. Feldman stands up slowly and walks up to 314, placing his hands on each side of the teenager's head. Memories, thoughts and ideas, the very structure of Patient 314 flows into the man that looked like Dr. Feldman.

Patient Zero lets go of his head and steps back, the body tipping back lifelessly. He stares at the body he now mimics and smiles as a Faceless walks into the room.

Zero: Ah, just in time. Dispose of the boy. I have a plane to catch.

I've made a horrible mistake. Whatever this... thing that's after me is, it's going to win. He's gathered everything he could possibly need to destroy me, but it's not dying that I'm so afraid of. This monster wearing Dr. Feldman's skin won't kill me, and that thought scares me more than anything. It's going to try and take everything from me. Mind, body, and my very soul. I don't know how long it'll be before they find me here, so I have to keep this somewhat brief before moving on.

About three months ago, I discovered something strange. I found dead birds, mutilated and positioned around my property. Not only had a number of them had their heads and wings removed, there was a terrible smell like natural gas and decay. The experience was quite unsettling but, since it only happened over two days, I didn't think much of it. Just over another month went by completely normal before anything else unusual happened.

I got a call from my boss early in the morning to tell me there was a small electrical fire at our job site, and that I didn't need to come in for the day while the fire department and electricians were dealing with the mess. I normally sleep in until almost noon on my days off but I was already awake from the call, so I went for a jog instead. About twenty minutes into my run, I saw a hawk land on a telephone line just ahead of me. Stopping to get my phone out for a picture, I was suddenly overcome with that horrible smell once again. I gagged, eyes tearing up, and vomited onto the road. But what came out of me wasn't vomit.

I expelled a small cloud of black matter the likes of which I've never seen. It was like tar trying to become gaseous. As it left my mouth, it expanded out briefly like a cloud of smoke, before dripping slowly to the ground. I kept spitting, trying to clear my mouth of whatever the fuck was coming out of me. There was strangely almost no taste to the material, just a slight copper tang, not unlike blood. I stood straight and took in a deep breath, trying to not panic. I looked around in a bit of a daze, wondering about what just happened to me. Then I noticed it. The hawk was gone, but the black mass that left my body has somehow gathered itself into a small shape. The shape of a hawk, but completely black and featureless. I stood there, just staring at it dumbfounded. As I stared at the hawk-thing in front of me, it began to melt back into a puddle of thick back fluid. I turned and ran home as fast as I could.

When I got home, I locked my door, ran to the bathroom, and plunged my fingers down my throat, inducing vomiting. Once again, a thick black mass billowed out of me before slowly becoming a pool of black fluid in my sink. I stared down at it, morbidly curious about what was happening to me. As I considered whether to go to the hospital, a small bubble appeared in the fluid's surface. Painstakingly slow, inch by inch, a small form began to gather out of the pooled substance. After several minutes, there was a fully formed, inky black hawk standing in my sink.

I still don't understand how I got to be like this, but what I've figured out in the two months since is that I can expel this ink without much effort and that it will take the form of whatever sentient creature I last saw. With a lot of practice, I figured out how to make the beings I create follow my basic commands. I'm still not sure if it's telepathy, or that they're somehow part of me. I even made a copy of myself one day and shot it in the foot with my rifle to see if I'd be affected. The bullet hit and stopped dead, caught on the surface of my copy's ink-black skin. Once I realized the potential of this, I started training as much as I could every day after work. Now, I can create a copy of myself materialize in eight seconds just by looking in a mirror, focusing, and spitting. I kept my newfound talent a secret and continued my life as normally as I could.

This morning there was a knock on my door just after sunrise. I got out of bed and tossed on some track pants and a hoodie before walking down the hall to the front door. I stopped dead in the hallway when I saw the silhouettes of at least six people on my porch. Each one of them had handguns at the ready, trained on my door. The pointman knocked again, this time with the butt of his gun.

"Mr. Clarke, we know you're in there. Please come out immediately with your hands on your head; there doesn't need to be violence."

I didn't respond, instead choosing to take the initiative. I made a copy in seconds. The moment it was formed, it entered full sprint, charging straight through the door. The door exploded into splinters like a wrecking ball had just gone through my home. My copy stopped all momentum instantly, spinning in place and striking each man once in the head. Six men were left in crumpled, bloody messes in mere moments. I took a deep breath and turned to begin packing an escape bag. I rushed through my house, grabbing some clothes, dry food, water, and a compass. I ran to the front door to grab a pistol and the ammo from the dead men, when I heard a man's voice boom over a loudspeaker.

"315, we have you surrounded."

I felt sick to my stomach. Feldman kept his promise. I ran for my back door, making a copy as I threw my shoes on. The copy opened the door and was met with a hail of gunfire. I stepped directly behind my copy, and began to walk forward, bullets bouncing off or being caught in its inky skin. Ahead of me I heard a man scream "HOLD FIRE!" and the storm of bullets ended. With a single thought, a small hole opened in my copy's chest and I began firing with the handgun on the four men in tactical gear that I could now see before me. At near point blank range, the men had no chance to even flinch before I shot them down. I reloaded and ran for the edge of my property as fast as I could. I could hear other mercenaries shouting commands on the other side of my house as I hit the treeline that borders my home. I ran for almost an hour through the forest before I reached the highway.

I hitched a ride with a trucker and went two towns over before parting ways. I'm sitting in a bar right now writing this, and I saw the update on 314. Feldman—no, Zero—isn't going to let up this hunt. So now my copy and I are on the run. I'll keep you all updated as I can. Wish me luck.

My name is Matt, and I refuse to become Patient 315.

Mt. Whitney Psychiatric Ward
Dr. Feldman Personal Log

5/18/1985—7:30AM

Today a new chapter is opened—our research will make massive strides forward. My colleague and friend, Irithmus Thar, has kindly volunteered to be our first human test subject. As much as we have gained in the five years experimenting with the local flora and fauna, we will gain in weeks or even days with Patient Zero. That is, if my hypothesis is correct. Irithmus has this amazing talent for absorbing knowledge. It seems as though he needs to read a book once to commit it to memory in its entirety. I began questioning how this could be when we started to work together more closely on the human potential. He had no books, no library of any kind, never took notes or recorded conversations or lectures. Somehow, though, he retains all he took in without the slightest error.

Of course, there are physiological explanations for this, disorders that could cause it as well, but usually result in a loss of function in some other fashion. Without any apparent losses, I can only speculate that this is a singularity unto Irithmus himself and must be examined in a more secluded and contained environment. Today our journey into his mind begins.

5/18/1985—8:00AM

Experiment One—logging…

Dr.: Good morning, my friend. I pray you are feeling well.

Zero: What have you done, Jacob? Where did you take me?

Dr.: This is where real science takes place. You wanted to study the human potential; let's study it!

Zero: You don't know what you are doing. You can't just take people, Jacob. This isn't you.

Dr.: Oh, I do and I can. On the table next to you is a book. Please pick it up and being reading.

Zero: I am not in the mood for reading, Jacob. Let me out!

Patient Zero approaches the observation window and begins pounding on the glass. The shock collar affixed to his neck is activated, sending him crashing to the floor.

Dr.: The observation glass is rated to withstand an angry bear. The collar around your neck can be turned up high enough to kill such a bear instantaneously. Please do not disobey my orders again. Now pick up the book, Zero.

Zero: Zero? [He gingerly makes his way to book and picks it up. A small after-tremor from the shock shakes his body.]

Dr.: Now, begin reading.

As Patient Zero turns the pages they become a blank.

Dr.: Just as I thought. What did page twenty eight explain?

Zero: The chemical reactions in the brain that dictate short-term, long-term, and ultralong-term memories.

Dr.: In your professional opinion, would you say that you only create ultralong-term memory?

Zero: Yes.

Experiment One complete.

Dr. Feldman Personal Log

6/24/1985—7:21PM

I love being right. After weeks of work, I finally replicated Zero's ability to extract and retain information and have begun collecting his memories. I love this digital age. Once digitized, we can then implant the memories back into Patient Zero. On second thought, maybe I should only give him some memories back. I suppose, depending on what we need him for, he could be given information and have things taken away at any time. Yes, that would make the most sense.

I have begun to experiment on myself to see if I can start forcing memories into becoming ultralong-term. That must make me Patient One. [Feldman chuckles to himself.] Of course, I'll never be on the other side of the observation window. Hmm… what was I talking about? My memory does seems to be a bit off since the experiments. Would ultralong-term memories even be desired without a fast enough recall? Patient Zero never seems to hesitate when bringing forth information. There must be more to his ability—instant recall, perhaps. Oh good, something new to test.

6/25/1985—6:15 AM

Experiment Two—logging…

Breakfast delivered.

Dr.: Good morning, Zero. I am excited for the results of today's testing. Are you?

Zero eats his food silently. Four orderlies walk in with an exam table loaded with equipment.

Dr.: Once you are done eating, these fine gentlemen are going to hook you up so that we can track your recall ability. Does that sound good?

Patient Zero continues eating in silence. Once completed, Zero is ushered to the table and strapped in. Electrodes are placed in various locations on his body, predominately on the head. Patient Zero is given an encyclopedia.

Dr.: Please read the book. When you are finished, I will ask you questions regarding the information contained therein.

Patient Zero reads through the book in twenty-seven minutes. Each page takes approximately half a second to be understood.

Dr.: Page one hundred seventy-one, paragraph three.

Zero: These specialized plants employ a variety of mechanisms to capture prey, ranging from the passive pitfall traps of pitcher plants to the adhesive leaves of sundews and butterworts to the "snap traps" of Venus flytraps and aquatic bladderworts. Most carnivorous plants attract and digest insects and other invertebrates, but some large pitcher plants have been known to digest frogs, rodents, and other vertebrates.

Dr.: Page nineteen, paragraph one.

Zero: Just prior to the beginning of the Neoproterozoic, Earth experienced a period of continental suturing that organized all the major landmasses into the huge supercontinent of Rodinia. Rodinia was fully assembled by one billion years ago and rivaled Pangea (a supercontinent that formed later during the Permian Period) in size. Before the beginning of the Cambrian, Rodinia split in half, resulting in the creation of the Pacific Ocean west of what would become North America. By the middle and later parts of the Cambrian, rifting had sent the paleocontinents of Laurentia (made up of present-day North America and Greenland), Baltica (made up of present-day Western Europe and Scandinavia), and Siberia on their separate ways. In addition, a supercontinent called Gondwana formed, which was made up of what would become Australia, Antarctica, India, Africa, and South America.

Dr.: Page nine hundred and two, paragraph four.

Zero: Black Panther Party, original name Black Panther Party for Self-Defense, African American revolutionary party, founded in 1966 in Oakland, California, by Huey Newton and Bobby Seale. The party's original purpose was to patrol African American neighbourhoods to protect residents from acts of police brutality. The Panthers eventually developed into a Marxist revolutionary group that called for the arming of all African Americans, the exemption of African Americans from the draft and from all sanctions of so-called white America, the release of all African Americans from jail, and the payment of compensation to African Americans for centuries of exploitation by white Americans. At its peak in the late 1960s, Panther membership exceeded 2,000, and the organization operated chapters in several major American cities.

This continued for two more hours

Dr.: Excellent. Thank you, Zero. Lunch will be served soon.

Experiment Two complete.

09/01/1985—08:31:15

FROM: Richard.F.Talbot@51.gov

TO: J.Feldman@MWPW.gov

SUBJECT: Entity Transfers

Good morning, Dr. Feldman,

I'd like to thank you, on behalf of the United States Military, for your exemplary service and dedication to your work and this great country. Based on the most recent logs received, we believe that your research far and away exceeds the expectations initially placed on your facility. As a result of this, we will be transporting two entities to your facility to help further your cause. The attached documents will outline the precautions needed with housing and testing of your two new Patients. Henry Finebar is already on a flight out to assess your facility and send a report back to me on what you will need. In addition, a barracks will be built in order to house a regiment. These men will be available for whatever needs you may have in addition to security.

Please continue providing weekly reports directly to me. Once Henry builds the report for your facility, we will have construction crews out immediately to get you up and running quickly. I would expect your new Patients within the month. Once again, thank you and congratulations on your recent successes. God Bless America.

General Talbot

ATTACHMENT 1: SUBJECT A

Description: Humanoid in shape. One hundred and eleven centimeters in height, one hundred and eleven pounds. Skin color is a matte gray that absorbs light. Subject A has no reflection nor casts a shadow. Each hand ends with three fingers and a thumb, however, each finger has far more dexterity. Subject A is capable of bending each finger in any direction and can carry out two tasks per hand in comparison to a human. Feet are similar in nature.

Abilities: Subject A has incredible strength, quickness, and agility. Adept at blending in to its surroundings, although it does not change in color or appearance. When motionless, it simply fades away from vision.

Conclusions: Based on its adaptability and apparent need to vanish into its surroundings, it is determined that Subject A is most likely in the middle of the food chain in its place of origin. The terrain is either extremely mountainous or densely forested and bleak in color.

Precautions: Subject A does not blend well with the color red—therefore it's holding cell should be colored as such, as well as any transportation devices used to move it back and forth. It should be noted that a color change is advised, at least on a semi-annual basis. Subject A could become accustomed to a new environment and begin blending properly with red. Alternate between reds, yellows, and oranges. Subject A has strength equivalent to a fully grown gorilla and quickness rivaling a mongoose. Ensure all forms of containment can withstand 100,000 psi and has a set of two doors, an inner and an outer.

ATTACHMENT 2: SUBJECT B

Description: Slightly smaller in size than a giant squid, but similar in all regards externally. Approximately six meters long and three hundred and twenty pounds. Blue in color. The beak is larger and extremely powerful. Two were found, one dead from impact.

Abilities: Subject B is highly intelligent. It has its own language and learned English within three months of captivity. Although it is difficult to understand due to the difference in anatomy, it is intelligible. It does not need to be in water to survive.

Dissection: The brain is roughly the same size as a human brain and each section proportionate to ours, as well. There are no lungs or other unknown internal organs, so its skin must be similar to that of an amphibian. It should be noted that each individual sucker has tiny barbs that emit poison from a sac at the base of each "attack tentacle". Testing has confirmed that there are two different poisons. One is an aphrodisiac and the other a sedative.

Conclusions: In the water, Subject B is an extremely dangerous and formidable foe, most likely at the very top of its food chain. The intelligence and power that it possesses alone make it deadly but the addition of the poisons make it a truly remarkable predator. It is possible that it uses the poisons solely for mating but that seems unlikely. Its place of origin is clearly similar to ours based on its amphibious nature.

Precautions: DO NOT PLACE IN WATER. On land, it is much

more slow and cumbersome, although still fierce and formidable. Subject B does not like electricity. Excessive use will result in permanent cognitive damage, just as with humans. Keep temperature at a constant sixty degrees Fahrenheit to ensure longevity.

09/09/1985—14:21:55
FROM: Henry.U.Finebar@51.gov
TO: Richard.F.Talbot@51.gov
SUBJECT: Mt. Whitney facility assessment
Staffing—Understaffed; however, with only one patient, that is to be expected. Suggesting two companies of troops stationed initially, scaling up to the full regiment by year five.

Security—Adequate, but outdated. A full revamp will need to take place if the site will be ready for Phase 2. Suggesting a second emergency exit be installed and blast doors on each entrance. Handprint, voice, and retinal scans at each entrance, as well as internally for restricted areas. A flood system and shock system will need to be installed in case of site failure, as well as charges on each floor. Expand the no-fly zone.

Accessibility—There is only a gravel path currently. We will need to install roads, a helipad, and high-speed rail for patient transport. In addition to the barracks, the area will need outposts and fences installed to keep hikers and campers far enough away.

Data/IT Infrastructure—Very basic server room connecting a few desktop computers. With the extent of research that will soon be happening, we will need a similar setup to Site 51. This is not my expertise so an expert should be sent to assess.

As a side note, I believe a second site should be built in case of emergency evacuation of Site 1.

Cost—Total cost will range from $300 million to $900 million

Mt. Whitney Psychiatric Ward
Dr. Feldman Personal Log
11/28/1985—2:53PM

Forgive me for not making a log sooner. The system has been down or intermittent for some time due to all the construction and changes being made here. Patient 2 and Patient 3 have just arrived and are in their new homes! I always knew but now it is confirmed! Life outside of this planet—wow! And I, Jacob Feldman, get to test and experiment these marvelous creatures for the betterment of humanity.

I can't wait to see if Patient Zero can absorb their information the same way he can Earthly beings. Of course, I have to figure out how to scale back his power first. Don't want to absorb everything and lose one of the most precious test subjects in the history of the world! What a day, what a day. Today truly is a day of Thanksgiving. So much to do before dinner with the troops.

Mt. Whitney Psychiatric Ward
Dr. Feldman Personal Log
1/1/1986—1:58AM

I can't do anything with these stupid things! "Be gentle, don't push it, we only have one." Stupid obtuse close-minded ninnies! How do you push the bounds of science without taking risks? Just give me one day with them unhindered and I'll know all I need about their race, culture, hierarchy, whatever! Hmm... what if it wasn't the only one? What if I made more? Where did that wine bottle go? [low mumblings]

Dr. Feldman

1/20/1986—9:11PM

Experiment C observations—logging...

What an excellent way to start the year off! Patient Zero and I have been working tirelessly since my revelatory thought to perfect his ability to absorb cognitive information only and not the physical information. Of course, that was quite easy for us and we moved on to searching for specific bits of information to absorb instead of all of it which leaves the victim essentially useless. While still not perfect in administration, we have come to a fairly efficient method of pulling small parts of information out of entities without turning them into empty shells.

Our breakthrough came when I could translate that ability onto the system and do it myself. No need to put Zero in harm's way unnecessarily, right? Longevity of Patient Zero aside, the real beauty of the process is that I can copy the information and then stick it back into the entity so that they lose nothing. What truly makes this a breakthrough is now our system can replicate physical life forms! By taking the physical information that make up Patients 2 and 3, we can then imprint that information into a living host.

So far, the hosts have not taken kindly to the new information and die out before more than one or two changes can take place. I have high hope that we will find someone or something that has a higher resiliency to the changes but if necessary we will need to create a host of our own.

Dr. Feldman

4/9/1986—5:02PM

Experiment C observations—logging...

There are only so many lost hikers to choose from before you need to give up and move on to something else. Patients 2-10 all failed miserably at retaining the physical information—Patient 4 was quite glorious in his explosion. The research team has been working with Macrocystis pyrifera to see if we can either steal the growth rate from it and apply it to a basic bacteria or imprint the information onto Macrocystis pyrifera in such a way that it maintains its growth rate while taking on all the other aspects we want it to have.

Dr. Feldman

4/27/1986—10:12AM

Experiment C observations—logging...

We were going about this all wrong from the beginning! The whole point of this is to replicate any being many times over. If I take a human, a mosquito, and a sheep and I give them the same information, I should get the exact same end result from each so how can I do that? Symbiotic parasite! If you design the parasite as simply the mode of transportation and carrier of information to the host, you can then implant whatever information you want into that parasite and it does the changing for you. Again, timeframe is a factor here so we will need to improve that, but initial testing has been successful when the host has been less complex than the information it has been given.

Dr. Feldman

6/19/1986—6:16PM

Experiment C final observations—logging...

With our first successful clone walking around the building, I believe we can put the wraps on Experiment C. Continued improvements will certainly be made and we shall observe my clone very closely for the next year for any signs of degradation or failure. It is quite enjoyable to watch a faceless human walking around sneaking up behind new staff. From this point on, all mentions of Experiment C will be referred to as Patient 11.

- Patient 11 must be administered to a living host.

- Patient 11 needs similar biomass to be effective. Too little biomass results in double or triple the incubation time.

- Patient 11 incubation time ranges from three (3) days to nine (9) days depending on biomass.

- Patient 11 can only be accessed by S-class personnel.

Dr. Feldman
8/3/1986—12:59PM

Patient 11 experiment observations—logging...

Improvements made since the last update:

- Patient 11 incubation time ranges from thirty six (36) hours to ninety six (96) hours.

- Patient 11 has successfully cloned Patient Zero, 1, 2, and 3, as well as dozens more of itself.

- Patient 11 has not yet shown any failures or regressions.

- Patient 11 is exceptional at performing mundane, dangerous, or obscure tasks.

- Patient 11 now has a new "form"—that of Staff Sargent John Dansk.

John was the fortunate, or unfortunate depending on your reference point, winner of the strength and fitness competition we held. Instead of keeping all of these fine young soldiers here at the facility, we decided to make a staff of clones that we could easily manipulate and control. In winning the competition, it was clear he had the best physique and form and, therefore, was chosen to be the face of Patient 11. My dark humor is getting the best of me. Staff have begun calling Patient 11 as "Faceless" and it does seem to be catching on quickly.

The troops stationed here have been reassigned to new bases and a clone of SS John Dansk promoted to Captain. He will be some of my eyes and ears outside of the facility for new Patients.

Dr. Feldman Personal Log
9/2/1986—6:12AM

Our clone in Russia has paid off nicely thus far. It seems as though they are trying to determine the human potential, as well, but in a vastly different way. Steroids, pft. They must think getting into space was more important than getting into the human brain. Obviously space travel is important but knowing everything about our race, planet, et cetera should be higher on the-to do list than traipsing out into the great void. We know of two alien races already and, if we ever ran into them on a larger scale, they would wipe us out, easy peasy. Just two hundred of Patient 2 would probably be enough if they landed without our knowledge. Who knows, we may have more of Patient 3 in our oceans right now and they are watching and waiting. The ocean is enough mystery for me. Let's focus on that, huh Russia?

Task Force 1 Communication Log
5/11/1992—1:52AM

Team Lead: Circle the home, secure all exit points. Do not use lethal force.

All members: Understood.

Team Lead: Two of you, on me. We enter through the front, left to the kitchen and down to the basement. Let's go.

Splintering wood can be heard on the comm. Grunts and then heavy footsteps for 78 seconds.

Team Lead: PUT DOWN THE SAW, NOW! ON YOUR KNEES!

Man's voice: No need for yelling, officer. I am putting down the saw and placing my hands behind my head while moving to my knees.

Team Lead: Check to see if she is still alive. Sweep the home, check for anyone else. All units hold exits.

All members: Yes, sir!

Team Lead: Do not move. I am putting cuffs on your hands. If you so much as twitch, I will use force to subdue you. Do you understand?

Man's Voice: No need for force. I'll come willing. I wish you would have waited another week so I could have finished my work.

The soft clink of the handcuffs can be heard on the comm.

TF 2: Home is clear, sir.

Team Lead: Let's go, on your feet.

Sirens can be heard in the background.

Team Lead: All units move out.

Mt. Whitney Psychiatric Ward
Dr. Feldman
5/12/1992—6:15AM

Breakfast delivered.

Dr.: Good morning. I hope breakfast is adequate for your tastes.

98: Oh yes, fine. The egg was a little undercooked.

Dr.: My apologies. You may be asking what you are doing here instead of in a prison cell. Let me assure you, your work will be completed. It might not be in the exactly the same way, but it will be completed.

98—I must admit I was a little perplexed when I was thrown into the back of a van instead of a police cruiser and then put on a train of some sort. Would it be a fair assessment to make that those were not police officers last night?

Dr.—Your genius has not failed you, 98. You are indeed correct. The men who brought you here are my own creation and you are here instead of rotting in a cell for the next eighty years because of your gifts.

98—A fan of my work, yes? Splendid. May I ask why you call me "98"?

Dr.—You will be unhindered in your research here. Anything you need, we will provide you with so long as you cooperate with my questions and tests. You are very unique, 98. Your ability to sense others' pain, know exactly what is causing it, if it is life threatening. Truly remarkable. I would like to understand how you do these things and the full extent of your abilities. To answer your question, you are the ninety-eighth patient to be tested here in my facility. A great amount of research and scientific breakthroughs have happened in the very room you now occupy. I do hope we can learn more together.

98—I see. I will be a lab rat performing on lesser lab rats.

Dr.—You have a personal log that you can access simply by saying "Patient 98 log". Make a list of everything you need to perform your experiments and we shall bring them to you.

Dr. Feldman
Patient 98 Observation Log
5/30/1992—9:21PM

Patient 98 is the first to seem somewhat happy here. It is a nice change of pace from the yelling and screaming and sobbing. His abilities are incredible to say the least. He certainly chose the right profession as a surgeon. Each day we have brought in a new terminal subject with varying issues from cancer to aneurisms and internal bleeding from car crashes. We have also brought in several with a simple head cold or other minor ailment.

So far Patient 98 has correctly identified each situation as life threatening or non-life threatening by simply looking at the subject. He then describes in detail the cause or lack thereof and what needs to be done in order to save the subject's life. At first, I believed it to be Patient 98 reading the mind of the subject in order to ascertain the information but soon ruled that out by secretly administering terminal diseases into subjects and bringing them to Patient 98 for analysis.

What I now believe to be happening is Patient 98 *sensing* the "pain" to such a degree that he can pinpoint the location and cause of that pain, even if there is no pain felt by the subject. If true, it will revolutionize the way we look at pain in the future. For example, subject 21 was given an active strain of HIV. When subject 21 was introduced to Observation Room 1 with Patient 98, he grimaced and told her he was sorry and he would do everything he could for her. He then proceeded to hook her up to a clone for a full blood transfusion. We are still waiting on the prognosis of that test.

He also "senses" and even removes fear like some animals do. Even with horrible news like contracting HIV or stage four pancreatic cancer, the subjects never show much sign of worry or fear. His bedside manner overwhelms them with confidence and hope in an almost mystical way.

Patient 98 has stated that he "sees" how things are connected like pain and fear and likely other emotions from brain to body. I believe this is separate from his other "senses" in that it is an overarching feeling of how all of his abilities work together. This is not altogether unlike reading peoples mind but, instead, reading the neurological pathways as they travel in the body and connect emotions to physical.

Lastly, he can not only sense these things but, in some ways, manipulate or control them. In most cases the subject will not need anesthesia, stating they feel no pain or discomfort. Much more testing needs to be done but at this moment Patient 98 appears to have nine senses.

- Sight
- Hearing
- Touch
- Taste
- Smell
- Fear
- Pain
- Death
- Neuroception

I am very much looking forward to fleshing out these senses to their fullest. There are many applications for them if we can find a way to harness and utilize them. Imagine being able to just shut down pain, shut down fear. The Faceless will be much more useless with such talents added...

I awoke in a haze, wracked with pain from head to toe. I haven't felt like this in... how long had it been? Days? Weeks? I honestly have no idea how long I was kept in that room.

There was an extreme pressure on my wrist. I was being pulled, dragged actually. Unbearable light penetrated my eyeballs and the squeak of my bare heels dragging along the clean linoleum floors sent horrible pains through my eardrums. It was almost too much to bear; however, I had come too far and endured too much to give in now.

Mashing my eyelids together to block out the light, I gathered my strength and pushed off the floor while twisting. The grip on my wrist loosened, then broke. I had taken my captor by surprise and didn't hesitate to capitalize on it. My hands leapt forward and groped for purchase, finding a familiar medium to mold. With a twist, the neck snapped and strength flowed through me. I opened my eyes and let go of the Faceless tasked with my disposal.

I took in my surroundings, trying to determine where in Site 2 I was. Eventually, I just wandered around until I found the central loft that I was familiar with and headed up to the top. Fortunately, I ran in to a few more Faceless along the way which helped build my strength back up. At last, I came upon a large door that opened up and beautiful, natural sunlight filtered down from ten flights above me. I climbed up the metal stairs and was greeted by the train that brought me from Site 1.

A sound caused me to duck and dive behind the nearest cover, which wasn't much, just a metal railing. Someone was poking around in the train. I couldn't quite make out the face but I didn't recognize his features as anyone I had encountered during my experiments. He was young and moved with an uncertainty as if he wasn't quite sure what he was looking for. I sat, crouched down, and watched as he made his way to my end of the train. If he was going to exit out of the train, he would spot me instantly so I moved, low to the ground, over to the doors and waited for an opening.

It was at this point that I realized how stupid I was being. Why not just read the guys mind and see what he wants? I focused on him, searching for the information I needed. He was from Reddit! It seemed like so long ago when I was posting my experiments to that site. Feldman must have taken over my account and continued posting. Why the hell would he do that? Ego, I guess. Anonymous notoriety? Karma? That stuff is a bit addictive once you get a taste. This guy knew just about everything that had gone on with me in that place.

I broke the connection and stood up. At that exact moment he lifted his head up from the control panel of the train and we made eye contact. I didn't have to read his mind to know he peed his pants a little. The look on his face was enough.

"It's ok, I know you are on my side," I said. "You know me as Patient 314."

"I, uh, umm hey. How can I be sure you are you and not Dr. Zero?"

I shrugged. "If I were Dr. Zero why would I be hiding in my own train station? And if I were Dr. Zero, I would have just sent up a few Faceless to kill you or bring you down for testing."

He nodded. "I suppose that is true. I guess we will just have to trust each other, right?"

"Right. Why did you come here? More importantly, how did you find it?"

"It is kind of a long story, but there are a lot of people rooting for you. Feldman and Zero are monsters and we all want to help. I figured I would try to put some pieces together. Hey, umm," he squinted at me, "I don't really want to call you Patient 314, so what's your name?"

"My name. Yea that is probably the one thing you don't know." I extended my hand. "I am Harrison. Nice to meet you."

"I'm /u/Sandman9913. Let's get out of here. You have a lot to catch up on."

Sandman handed me his phone with the Reddit app open and I began to read all of the posts that Dr. Feldman and, later, Dr. Zero made on my account.

***

I can't begin to describe what I felt as I read about what had happened to me. Surreal just doesn't cut it. I never knew the doctor's thought process during the testing and that was quite enlightening. The guy was smart, I'll give him that. The origins threw me for a loop, though. Area 51? Aliens? I am sure there is a lot more we don't know about and maybe one day I'll come back and try to learn some of them.

I admit it. I cried when I read about my mother. That sick bastard screwed with my head more than I thought was possible. The one thing that helped as I read each entry was the comments. So many people hating on Feldman and Zero. So many hoping the best for me. Sandman went so far as to search for me and another guy even challenged Zero. Not smart, I'll admit, but admirable. After reading everything, I just had one question for Sandman.

"You read that last entry, right?" I asked.

"Yeah, I read all of them, why?"

"At the end of it, Zero killed me, or at least he thought he did. What made you think I'd still be alive?"

Sandman shrugged. "I don't know, man. I guess I just couldn't believe that, after everything, it would end that way. But, like, why didn't you die?"

"A very good question. I am not sure if I truly know the answer but my guess is that Zero wasn't very thorough when he absorbed my information and my condition made it seem like I was dead. For all intents and purposes, I do die each time I get stimulation overload but, for whatever reason, the end result of death doesn't come. Maybe I can't die, not fully. Maybe I am already dead." I look out the window of the train, watching the scenery fly by. "So, where are we headed now?"

"We are going to find Zero and save Patient 315," Sandman said.

Spring is a beautiful time of year. I had never witnessed it firsthand before so, to you, this revelation might seem a bit odd but we all have little times like these in our lives, right? When we "stop and smell the roses," so to speak. The cruel, cold death of winter faded before my eyes as new blooms opened and greeted the warm sun rays. Skinny trees began to fill out with new foliage that provide cover to the nests high up near the tops.

Our train sped along in the general direction we needed to go and I sat back enjoying a process I hoped to witness more than just once. This was my spring—a new life ready to bloom.

Sandman snapped me out of my reverie with a question. "Do you have a plan?"

"I do," I said. "But I can't tell you what it is, and you need a plan of your own that I can't know either."

"We both need plans. But neither of us can know each other's plan? Why?"

I chuckled softly before explaining. "Zero can read minds, yes? And presumably has perfected using whatever he gained from my DNA by now, yes? So, therefore, he can read our minds, know our plans, and quite possibly kill us without even moving. Not only that, but he has a device that inhibits my ability to kill him with my mind or read his thoughts."

Sandman just stared at me for a moment before punching the wall of the train. "So basically we can't beat him and we are just walking towards imminent death? Great."

I laughed hard at that. I mean really laughed. He probably thought I was utterly insane, like the Joker in the original Batman movie, because I just kept laughing. Tears filled my eyes and my stomach ached. It felt good to laugh. Wiping away the tears and the smile on my face, I allowed myself a somber tone once again.

"We can beat him. We will beat him. But you can't know how I am going to do it. Where did Matt tell us to meet him?"

Sandman pulled out his phone and pulled up a message from a few hours before. *I don't know how much longer I can hold out here. He gets closer every day. I'm hiding in the subway systems under Cincinnati.*

I sat in silence the rest of the way pondering what the most effective scenario might be. More accurately, I stared out the window watching trees and hills blur by while hoping I looked like I was deep in thought.

"Does Matt know I'm alive?"

"No," Sandman said. "He just thinks I am coming to try and help him escape."

"Good. Don't tell him anything. If Zero is catching up to him we need to use Matt as bait. We'll need to meet Matt in a place that will ensure Zero is there when we get there. How do we do that? He is in the subway. Is he just jumping cars all the time? Let's bring up a map of the subway."

Sandman grabs his phone and types away for a while before a concerned look crosses his face. "The subway has been abandoned for years. It is just Matt down there hiding like a rat."

My face must have lit up like a Christmas tree when I heard that. "Even better. All alone, no witnesses, no worries about innocent casualties. How long until we can get there, do you think?"

***

The train came to a gentle stop at the end of its track and we stepped off. As soon as my feet hit the dusty, worn-down platform the train vanished. It didn't speed off in the opposite direction. It simply vanished. I put my hand out and groped around for the door frame I just passed through and my fingers wrapped around the cool metal. Convenient.

Sandman was shaking his head in a way that suggested he should expect such things and not be surprised anymore but can't help it. We exchanged broad grins and walked a few miles before hiring an Uber to take us into the city.

We ate a quick bite at a food truck while we waited for an opening to slip down into the subway entrance that was blocked off. Once no one was paying much attention, we ducked under the boards and made our way down the wide stairs. Graffiti covered the walls leading down and, I assumed, continued on throughout the whole tunnel but light only made it a few feet beyond the last stair.

"Do you get a signal down here?" I asked.

The phone lights up and he nods to me.

"Tell Matt to meet us in this tunnel and to cover you in his goop so you look like one of his creations. Zero won't think to read your mind and, thus, you'll be safe. Once you are covered, just mimic what the others do. Got that?"

Sandman nods again, this time with less conviction.

We head further into the tunnel until we reach a fork with three other main tunnels converging and I hopped down into the track to hide and wait. A faint light lets me know Sandman got a message back and soon he peeks his head over the edge in search of me.

"Matt is on his way and Zero and about twenty Faceless are hot on his trail."

"Perfect, hide up against the wall and wait until you are inked. Try to think of nothing, literally nothing." The fear is evident in his eyes so I give a thumbs up and whisper, "I promise we will be ok."

His head slowly retreats and, a few faint footsteps later, we are immersed in silence. A car horn honks now and again on the streets above. I reach out with my mind and try to implant confidence and strength into Sandman. Soon murmurs and footsteps reach our ears, each noise echoing lightly toward us. Then louder, louder. More steps, more echoes. It sounds like hundreds of people rushing toward us. The footfalls are crashing off of the circular walls now, pounding through me. My heart begins to race, rattle, pound, thump, revolt against me. Then silence.

I hear a whisper, then another. Now a steady march of footfalls echo in unison toward us. Zero.

I make my way cautiously around the curve of the recessed track hoping to end up behind Zero as he faces off with Matt and his black army.

"Tired of running, Patient 315?" It is my voice, with a sneer to it, and slightly deeper.

Instead of responding, I hear a large commotion of motion caused I can only assume by Matt and his minions. I peek up over the edge to gauge the right time. Inches from my face are the heels of Zero! I contemplate grabbing him and pulling him down but the noise above me sends my heart racing once again and I can feel my strength fading. Did Zero just clutch his chest for a moment?

Gathering my strength and courage, I take a step back and leap up behind Zero, my hands grasping firmly to his jaw and forehead and a satisfying snap silences everyone. Faceless turn to me, Matt drops to his knees gasping for breath, Sandman shakes free of the inky gunk covering his body. All at once the Faceless run toward me and drop at my feet. Strength flows from my heart to my fingers and toes.

No one said anything. After all of that, what was there to say? I nodded my head, scooped up Zero and began to walk away.

"Harrison, what are you doing?" cried Sandman.

"Research."

March
—2017—

The Black Library

By Caitlin Spice

There are two things in this world that can surmount any obstacle ever created.

The first of these is love.

Our capacity to love creates in us a drive and purpose that goes beyond survival. We do insane and superhuman things in the name of love, things that would not be possible under any other circumstances. Tiny women lift wrecked cars off their injured husbands. Men carry their wives through ten miles of snow to get them to a hospital. Parents sacrifice their lives for their children.

Such is the power of love.

But there is another force that is just as powerful as love.

Human intelligence.

We will never know who first discovered how to make fire, but that act sparked a revolution. It expanded our minds, giving us the power to shape the world around us. What seemed impossible became possible. Jungles could be turned into fertile farmlands, mountains could be ground down into blocks of stone to build grand towers and high walls. With the power of our intelligence, we conquered diseases, tamed nature, walked on the Moon, and sent our likeness on a golden disk to the edge of our solar system and beyond.

And when love *and* intelligence collide, truly impossible things can happen.

Having an eidetic memory has been a boon for most of my life.

The ability to store and recall anything is the dream of every school child because, with that gift, exams become nothing to fear, largely a mindless exercise in easy recall. It was so simple for me when I hit the age where standardised testing began. For the other children, the concept of 'one hundred percent' seemed some sort of mythic uncertainty; a shibboleth signifying unattainable success. For me it was a constant—a variable as certain as my memory.

They pushed me ahead in school until it became clear that I had both a perfect memory *and* a stupendously high IQ. Then, with very little discussion and even less warning, I was shipped off to university at the tender age of fourteen, where older, wiser students gawped at the child in their midst who still wore pigtails and Rainbow Brite sneakers. I may have been embarrassed by my youth and lack of worldliness, but they were more embarrassed by being academically trounced by someone who still had braces on her teeth and sparkles on her backpack. Eventually, I finished my first degree, then a second, then my third. By the time I was twenty-five I had a post-doctoral fellowship, was lecturing classes under tenure, and had received a special research grant.

But, better than all the academic success in the world, I was in love.

It would do a disservice to my lover to lavish praises on her character and beauty. When you are truly, mindlessly, besotted with someone, a heady haze of your own bias surrounds them, buffing away every flaw until they shine like the most precious stone in existence. Thoughts of her warm, soft skin consumed my mind during the day, and I longed for the nights, to be with her, inhaling the dusky natural perfumes of her body and listening to her chatter about her day at work. Others may have disagreed but, to me, she was the most perfect person in the whole world.

I knew that Tess was depressed—and had been since before we met. In my arrogance, I thought I could cure her, that I could achieve what generations of psychologists and peddlers of pharmaceuticals could not. On the bad nights, she would just sob until she shook with fatigue. She would lie awake for hours, her traitorous mind tormenting her with the kinds of 'what if?' scenarios a normal brain can so easily dismiss. I would hold her and tell her it would all be okay. I'd talk about our bright future and how, eventually, we would just live in the countryside where she could pull weeds and prune rose bushes; activities which soothed her bruised synapses and helped banish the dark thoughts.

When the call eventually came, I knew what had happened as soon at the police officer introduced himself on the phone. Tess was gone.

I tried to process her death as the text books described; denial, anger, bargaining, depression, acceptance. I seemed to flip fluidly between the first and the second stages, angry at myself for not doing enough to stop her suicide, unable to believe that this was the end of her, that she was gone forever. Science could not assuage my grief, regardless of which studies I read, no matter how promising a piece of research seemed at first. And I read everything I could find. I sought for any kind of answer to the question of Tess's death, any way of making myself okay with her abrupt exit from this existence. Every rational, logical, reasonable source of information told me that she was gone; that, while there might be cellular activity on a basic level in the brain for some ten minutes after death, no part of Tess could have survived her suicide.

Hopeless, broken, and lost in self-isolation, I started looking elsewhere.

Religion offered me hope in the form of every flavour of afterlife, but I'd abandoned religion long ago. After all, Tess and I were lesbians; so, if the Christian gospels were true, she now languished in a lake of fire, being eternally tormented for the sin of homosexuality. Still, reading through the various beliefs of other cultures throughout the world bought me a sort of temporary peace. And so I persisted, gathering esoteric tomes from different universities, using my influence as a child prodigy to purloin particular pages from antique anthologies. I began to feel as though I was being led on a sort of academic scavenger hunt, because every time I found a new piece of information, it appeared to provide clues about where to find another. And so, with the desperate need to fill the empty hole left in my life where Tess had been, I pursued those tenuous connections until I reached the end.

The monastery was quiet, as I'd always imagined such a mountain-top retreat would be. But these monks wore robes of black velvet, the sheen of the rich fabric at odds with the tales told about monkish austerity. And the fingers of the monk who led me inside the gray stone walls to meet the librarian were heavy with gold. Clearly, this was no ordinary religious order. The librarian greeted me jovially and asked if I'd like coffee—it was genuine Kopi Luwak, he explained, one of the most rare and expensive types of coffee in the world. When I declined, he simply smiled, busying himself with preparing his brew in the small kitchen to the side of his office.

"We never thought we'd have a *student* come to us, not within our lifetime," he said, as the smell of the aromatic beans filled the room. "So you do us a great honour."

"Why is that so unusual?"

He pointed a manicured nail at my manila folder of scanned and copied pages. "It takes a rare level of genius to decipher the map to this monastery, the sort that is only born once into any generation. And, even then, it takes a particular kind of *motivation* to push such an individual in our direction."

"The library?" I prompted, impatient now.

He placed his coffee down carefully, then indicated the brocade chair in front of his expensive looking desk. I sat down, and he studied me silently for a moment. "What do you know about the library?"

"My research indicates it's a trove of information that survived the burning of Alexandria. Books older than the Dead Sea Scrolls, unaltered and perfectly copied, which have survived the trials of time."

"But you also know it's more than that, don't you?"

I nodded. "There are common themes in the stories I found. Men entering the library, and then leaving it after three years. In those stories, they emerge with knowledge that shouldn't have existed in their time. How to create and fold steel thousands of years before smelting was discovered, how to make gunpowder, or engines, well before even the rudiments of those methods were organically discerned."

"There is a contract," he said, his brown eyes turning serious, "and it is deeply binding. Binding on a level you may not yet comprehend."

"I figured as much, otherwise the rest of the world would already know about this place."

"Will you sign?"

I considered for a moment, then nodded. "I have nothing else to live for."

The stairs wound down into the darkness beneath the monastery cellars, curving out of sight. The librarian left me there, telling me that what I sought was at the bottom. Regarding that shadowed spiral of steps, fear finally thrilled through me. I'd felt quite numb up until that point, perhaps not truly processing that what was happening was real. Was this actually genuine? Was there really a library at the bottom of these stairs? Perhaps these genial, well-appointed, lavish-living monks accumulated their obvious wealth by kidnapping idiot academics with too much free time. That seemed far more likely but, if I left now, I knew I would spend the rest of my life lying awake tormented by genuine 'what-ifs', not just the inflated ghosts that had haunted my Tess.

The darkness closed around me like a blanket as I took another turn down the descending stone stairwell. I kept my hand on the wall; that and the regular height of the slab stairs the only things keeping me from stumbling in the lack of light. I shuffled along like that for a long time. Several times I thought about giving up and going back, but I reasoned that perhaps this was another test, much like the ones that had brought me to the monastery. The faintly luminous hands of my wrist watch told me that two hours had passed, and my ears had popped over an hour before. How deep underground I was, I couldn't fathom, but it was definitely well below sea level.

My mouth was dry. I wished I'd accepted that coffee, or at least had something to eat or drink before I'd begun my descent. It was cold now, cold enough to make me shiver and curse my lack of a decent jacket or coat. When my teeth started chattering uncontrollably, thoughts of returning to the surface became stronger. The darkness was so oppressive, so *cold*. But the thought of climbing back *up* three hours' worth of the steep stone stairs made my stomach lurch with fear and exhaustion. Yet I needed to decide, and soon. The longer I continued my descent, the longer that journey back up would become. Surely there *had* to be an end?

Eventually, the builders of these stairs must have been forced to stop, unable to tunnel any further into the bedrock of the mountain.

And at the very moment I mustered that thought, I found the last step.

My foot dropped into empty air, but I was too tired to even reflexively pull it back. I had been in a trance-like rhythm for hours now, hand on the wall, shuffling the next foot down. Off balance, I scrabbled to grip the smooth wall, trying to dig my nails into the stone.

To no avail.

As I fell into the icy darkness, fear welled up within me, a great ball of gas colder than the cosmos expanding up from my bowels and compressing my lungs. The terror erupted from my lips in a scream that was so loud it ripped through my brain and tore my consciousness away.

***

The cell was dim. A ruddy glow emanated from some sort of dull red quartz set into the ceiling, providing little more light than a bulb in photographic dark room. There was no door, just walls of smooth black stone. The pallet on which I lay appeared hewn from the same stone as the walls. At the foot of the bed were some neatly piled clothes, all deepest black; a robe, gloves, and a pair of slippers. I still wore my own clothes, but it was chilly in the cell, and the dark attire looked soft and warm. Clearly there was a way into the cell, I reasoned, else how did they get me in here? Perhaps one whole wall was a door, the hinges cunningly hidden by the corner of the cell.

Welcome warmth engulfed my hands as I pulled on the gloves. The black slippers would not fit over my sensible shoes, so I removed my own footwear first. Lastly, the robe, which proved wonderfully comfortable as

I pushed my arms through the thick sleeves and pulled the hood up over my head. As if in response to donning the clothes, the light in the room brightened incrementally, and the outline of a door became visible. It swung open, noiselessly, revealing a red-lit corridor. With no other choice available, I stepped out of the cell, and immediately regretted it.

The black robe shrank *tight* around my body, so sudden and constricting I felt instantly unable to breathe. The black collar snapped up over my mouth and nose, and I tore fruitlessly at it in a wave of powerful claustrophobia. I let out an involuntary yelp of panic, but the sound was absorbed completely by the thick black cloth that muffled my face. My breathing was fast—too fast—I was sucking in air in short gasps, and I was becoming light-headed. I needed to calm myself, to use reason, my most powerful and faithful weapon, to get through this situation.

Hunched against the wall, I tried to ignore the oppressive tightness of the black clothes, telling myself that they were not rigid, that I could still breathe. The panic abated, and my panting breaths slowly returned to normal. Straightening up, my gloved hand spread against the smooth stone to steady myself, I once again had the suspicion that I had just passed another test.

As I walked through the black corridor, others emerged from cells apparently identical to my own. Clad in the black robes, only their eyes faintly visible under shadowed brims of their hoods, they all looked the same. As I joined the dark river of bodies that flowed along the corridor, I realised, with an involuntary shiver, that we were also all exactly the same height.

It was as if the robes, gloves and slippers had erased every shred of our individuality. I tried to talk, of course, to ask questions. But every word I spoke vanished into the black muffler over my face, never reaching the ears of the others around me.

The queue of robed figures eventually emptied out into a hall, so large and so dimly lit that I could see neither roof nor walls. As the others stopped and began to spread out in that fathomless space, black desks of stone rose smoothly and noiselessly from the floor. One for each student in the room.

I knew this place. I had read this legend. Were it possible to scream, I would have. I wondered how many of the others *were* screaming under the tight cloth covering their faces. Surely, they had read the same tales as I had during their own research, and must be coming to the same conclusion.

Letters of red fire appeared on the black stone desk before me, and I memorised them reflexively. Instantly, they vanished, and were replaced by new words, describing events recorded in no human history book. If what I had researched was true, then this place, this *classroom*, was housed in no earthly realm. And if I did not memorise all the words presented to me and do so before all of my peers, then, as the last person to leave this room, my soul would be forfeit to Lucifer himself.

Sweating and shaking, I forced my eyes to absorb the page of flickering scarlet letters, then another, then another. Nearby, one of the other students must have realised their predicament, because they tried to tear off their robes. They twisted and turned, pulling and grabbing at the unyielding cloth in a perversely silent and terrible dervish dance. Eventually, they began to smash their head repeatedly into the sharp edges of the obsidian desk, until they collapsed. The other students stared silently, just as I did. As the bloodied desk slid slickly back into the floor, hands emerged from the stone around the fallen student. Corpse gray, long-nailed and covered with pale, shaggy fur, they pulled the body into the ground with the only sound I had heard thus far; a whisper of black cloth on stone and the clicking of claws.

For now, the rest of us might be safe; Hell had already claimed a soul for today.

Every day was the same; we would rise, put on our jet robes and the door would open. Then we would all file into the cavernous classroom, where we would frenetically memorise the words of fire, desperately trying not to be the last one to finish. After we returned to our cells, the door would close and the robes would loosen, allowing us to take them off and regain our individuality. Those same gray hands that had taken the first fallen student would emerge from the wall, clutching dull pewter plates of rich foods and carved goblets of exotic drinks. When I was done eating and drinking, they would emerge once more to take away the plates and cups.

I knew the reason for the robes; I'd figured it out on the second day. Our demonic tutor did not want us to know who the other students were. That gave me a valuable clue towards figuring out another part of the puzzle, because the librarian had told me himself that someone like me was only born once every generation. The classroom *must* exist outside time itself. That was the only way there could be so many students. Initially, I had been confident, being one of the first to finish almost every day. But, as the lessons became more complex and I had to truly *understand* every concept instead of just memorising text, I began to slip several places.

Against whom was I studying? If the classroom was truly outside time, then it could be anyone. The man to my left could be Aristotle, the one on the right Einstein—or even Da Vinci. My former confidence became tainted with fear and it began to affect my concentration. When the frightening day came that the classroom was almost empty when I finished, I knew I had to do something more.

Alone in my cell, unrestricted by the cloying wrap of black fabric, I lay on the stone pallet and wracked my brains for an answer to my predicament. If I was truly up against the very greatest minds of history, then I didn't stand a chance. I knew I was good. My intelligence was leagues beyond anyone I'd known in life, but that meant I was smart enough to realise that with *all* of human history stacked against me, the odds were very bad. As I mulled over all my experiences thus far, my mind kept returning to probe one singular fact: the anonymity of the robes was not complete. I had already picked out certain individuals with particular habits. One of them nervously tugged at their hood periodically, as though worried the others would see their eyes. Another always ensured they took the desk at the far left-hand corner of the room, circling it once before sitting. And both of them always left the room early, but never *first*. That was unusual in itself, since the other students I'd marked by their behaviours fluctuated wildly in their placement. These two were clearly so sure of themselves, so monstrously clever, that they could practically *choose* when they would finish.

But that still didn't tell me who they were. The man in the corner, if he was in fact a man, might be Johann Goethe or Nicola Tesla; or it could be some unknown who never made it into the history books. Even worse, if the classroom was outside of time in every direction, as I suspected, he might be from the distant future, where humanity had perfected itself to a level beyond imagining.

This information was critical in some way, I knew it. Our headmaster, Lucifer, could just as easily have made us study alone, in our cells, doing away with the need to interact with the others at all. He must have *wanted* us to see each other, to be aware of our peers. The obvious reason for this would be to instill fear, to motivate us to study harder—but in a classroom outside the bounds of time, why would that even matter?

There was no one to see my triumphant grin when I realised I had my answer.

You couldn't leave the hall until you had finished the lessons. Oh, you could get up and walk around, but if you approached the door without finishing, the gray hands would catch you and drag you into the black stone, your soul forfeit to our Headmaster. I waited until the lesson was something I wouldn't struggle with too much. It seemed that none of my remaining peers had a memory quite as perfect as mine, since I was always the first to finish those lessons that were comprised of sheer volume of information.

That day, the last page lay in front of me, unread, waiting for me to glance at it and burn the letters into my memory. I kept my eyes purposefully averted. The figure in the corner, whom I'd named Leonardo for the sake of convenience, stood up as the red glow faded from his desk. As he did so, I finished my own work, but waited. He paced through the rows of students, eventually reaching the door—and as he did so, I also stood and made my way out. Along the corridor we walked, me keeping several paces behind him. I knew which room was his because I'd memorised the number of steps. As his door swung open, I took six running strides towards him on my soft, silent slippers, then smashed his head against the obsidian-sharp edge of the door. He dropped immediately, dark blood gouting from his hood. His own slippered feet twitched and spasmed, and one arm flapped in a palsied seizure, slapping noiselessly against the stone. As the gray hands emerged to pull him down into the darkness, I knew I had found my edge.

I would *never* be the last one to leave the classroom.

If the others knew what I'd done, they didn't give any indication of it. I switched up my mannerisms and moved desks regularly, so that if any of the others had been observing me as I had them, they couldn't possibly track me. I always watched the corridor behind me as I left the classroom, to ensure that nobody did to me what I had done to Leonardo.

In the first year, I murdered ten of my peers—the brightest and the best, and therefore my strongest competition. But I monitored myself carefully for any signs of over-confidence. I could never let down my guard, because if *I* had figured out this deadly loophole, then so, too, could another student.

And indeed, when my mental headcount came up short one morning, I felt a strange thrill. It seemed another murderer had joined me in the Devil's classroom. He was careful, very careful. I took me months to unriddle who he was, and, during that time, the paranoia gripped me like one of the giant, shaggy gray hands. Every walk through the black corridors was riddled with fear.

In the end, it turned out his technique was simple; he would simply wait until only he and one other student were left in the cavernous classroom, then he would kill his unsuspecting peer by bashing his head into the desk. It was so crude and uninspired that I laughed to myself in the dim light of my cell, realising that his modus operandi was born of desperation, rather than true cunning.

I had to kill him, of course. He was going about it completely the wrong way; by killing off the worst students, he was only hastening our own demise.

He died on the day I crawled deliberately slowly through my work, ensuring we were the last two left. As he came to bludgeon my face into the sharp stone, I struck his knee with my foot, then threw him sideways into the desk. The struggle was brief; it seemed that with the robes constricting us to the exact same size and shape, my greater experience as a killer won out. There was a chance I was not the greatest mind in this classroom, but I suspected I was now the best murderer.

The others had noticed the declining numbers. Of course they had; none of us were stupid people. Strange, silent alliances had formed, where little groups would sit together, wait for each other, and leave together. With silent hand gestures, I'd been invited into one such group, and I played along—for, if I marked myself as an outsider, they might unriddle my dark secret. The lessons were incredible now; imparting insights far beyond the reaches of ordinary science. The origins of the universe were clearly revealed to me, along with the fundamental laws that bind everything together. If Einstein were present, he must have cursed himself for a fool, as the lessons we learned made him seem like a plodding idiot, woefully out of his league. On the day that one group of students stood mid-lesson and attacked another group outright, the uninvolved students just stared, their eyes shocked in the depths of their hoods. I wanted to tear off my mask and scream at them, to ask them what the *fuck* they thought would eventually happen in a competition plotted by Satan himself? The fight was long and brutal, the only weapons being soft-gloved fists, feet, and the obsidian furniture. Those not involved just watched, knowing that today's quota was more than full. The rest of us could take our time studying.

Counting on that, when the others had left, I stayed behind. There was blood pooled and splattered everywhere, though it was hard to see on the dark floor. Fragments of bone and hair clung to the desks, here a severed finger had been missed by the hands of our ghastly cleaners. But amongst it all I found something wonderful, something game-changing. Along the edge of one desk, the obsidian had fractured, and a razor-sharp shard lay on the floor, nearly invisible. Picking it up, I pushed it carefully into my sleeve.

Now I had what no other student had. A *weapon*.

In game theory, such an advantage instantly marks you out. As soon as you reveal that you have such a thing, others will want to take it off you. An uneasy truce reigned in the classroom now, with no group willing to risk a confrontation, lest the fight lower their numbers. The hand signals became increasingly complex, each group developing a distinct 'language' which the out-groups didn't understand. But with my memory, I could replay the gestures in my mind, and teach myself the dialects, giving my group a vital edge.

I think my group knew I was the original killer, the one who had started it all. They deferred to me and feared me. In my periphery, I saw one refer to me as 'The Ripper', spelling out the letters individually in our crude sign language.

Betrayal happened regularly now that we could communicate. The game became less about the lessons, and more about politics. We still studied, but the learning of forbidden knowledge had taken a distinct back seat to the wheeling and dealing that had become commonplace. After watching one group sacrifice the smartest man they had to ensure their tribe's survival, I knew we had reached a turning point. Soon there would be anarchy.

It started on the walk through the corridor, before we had even divided off into our groups, before we had exchanged the secret handshakes that confirmed our membership of the cliques. Students just started leaping at one another. A man came at me and we struggled, a perfect physical match in our arcane robes. An elbow from another fighter knocked him off balance and I pressed the advantage, knocking him down and head-butting him in the nose. When the madness slowed, then stopped, the gray hands began to claim the dying and seriously injured. With a nod, one of the survivors pointed toward the classroom. Not knowing what else to do, we slipped and skidded through the pools of blood, the hems of our robes leaving dark trails into the classroom. The footprints left by our sopping slippers marked the paths to our sparsely-spread seats. There were only five of us left.

They jumped me on the way out. I finished first, and the other four all rose together, not a hand signal between them. They knew who I was. *Everyone* knew who everyone else was by now. We had spent two full years together in this place.

The first man went down in a tangle of robes. I'd nicknamed him Byron, but unlike his bombastic namesake, he was not a fighter. The other three circled me, glancing at one another, askance, still unsure quite how to handle me now that Byron's limp body was being pulled through the floor. Shakespeare and Curie stood to either side, while Gauss circled, trying to get behind me. With a snarl only heard in my own head, I turned and threw myself upon the figure sidling up to me, the obsidian shard slashing through his collar and deep into his throat. The other two were instantly on top of me, but they hadn't seen the black knife. It licked out vengefully, leaving Shakespeare flailing and already falling, a jet of blood pumping from the stump of his wrist. As Curie and I scrambled to our feet, she simply bowed her head and shrugged, admitting defeat. The shard of obsidian went through her eye and into her brain, killing her instantly.

The shaggy gray paws pulled the dead into the bowels of the earth, and for the first time, I was alone in the vast classroom. The robes loosened their constrictor grip, and I pulled down the muffler with blessed relief, gasping for air.

"Well done," crooned a voice from the darkness.

Black shelves full of books began to rise from the floor.

***

The knowledge in the library is exquisite, and I've barely begun to taste it. There are tomes from so far forward in time that it will take me decades of study even to begin to comprehend them.

But I know that's not why I'm here. That was just the cherry on the sundae, or the cheese in the trap. You see, Lucifer didn't just want someone brilliant. The classroom always has been—and always will be—a ruse. Intellect isn't unique, but intellect combined with raw, animal cunning? That's really special. Almost as special as human intelligence coupled with true love.

And *I* am special.

There is a book, he tells me, that is not in this library. The *only* book that he doesn't own. The book of *Life and Death*, which resides in Heaven. All I need to do to bring Tess back to life, is to wrest that book from its owner and erase her name. Then she will return to me, as if she had never been taken. And with the infinite knowledge of the Black Library, I can fix her.

But that's enough for now; I have work to do—bringing down Heaven is going to take some planning, and I need a new weapon if I'm going to succeed. Fortunately, I'm no longer confined to the Black Library, I can come and go as I please. I can do *anything* I please. And I do know where to find the perfect blacksmith.

Mister Pleasant's House For Broken Children
By Tanja Simone

I knock on the screen door, softly enough not to scare anyone, forcefully enough not to be ignored. Soon the kids run around my ankles like flies on rancid meat. This mobile home makes the term mobile home sound like even more of a euphemism than it already is. The mother's skirt is covered with grease and ketchup stains, her breath stinks of cigarettes and worries. A woman with more kids than teeth, more worries than shits to give. She lights up her Pall Mall 100's, and points to a door in the back, letting me know he's in there.

I kneel down to his race car bed, touching his forehead. His tiny body lies limp, sweaty, and motionless and thin legs and arms, too thin, poke out through the pajamas. He's too small for a 5-year old. Too fragile. Candy wrappers are scattered over the dirty floor.

The mother barely looks up as I hand her the 50 dollar bill, carry the boy out to the car, and put him in the trunk. The neighbors don't honor me with as much as a glance, too stoned or drunk to care or notice.

They call me Mr. Pleasant, for I am a pleasant man. I've been told my demeanor is soft and caring, so I never correct them. I don't mind my moniker. I've been doing this for a long time; this young boy with ratty hair and dirty cheeks is one in a long line of lost boys and girls. Mothers with too many to feed, the ones that fall between the cracks of CPS.

There are always *broken* children. And those children belong to me.

The boy wakes up after we've crossed the state border. I carry his eggshell body from the trunk to the backseat. I can hear his crying over the radio, twangy country punctuated by hiccups and hulks. I pull over at a roadside fast food joint and turn my head to the back of the car where he lays. He's trying to hide on the floor, so small and frail he's almost successful. I gently place my index finger over my lips and give him *that smile*, the smile that earned me the nickname I willingly wear. Sobs and stutters settle, what he sees in my eyes is a playful glimmer, not a threat. They tell me I have the eyes of a child, innocent. He, too, lifts his skinny, sticky finger to his lips. The sound that he makes reminds me of a deflating balloon at a birthday party no one showed up to. Sssssshhhh.... He seems to know he's my secret.

I return with french fries and a hamburger. His eyes grow large and primal, hunger transcends the fear and he snatches the greasy bag from my hands and retreats as far away from me as he can get like a beaten dog. I wonder what will become of this one. I fasten my seatbelt again and steer back out on the highway. I carefully watch the boy in the rearview mirror, he's rubbing the bag on his face. First gently then more and more desperately. Reused frying oil makes his cheeks glisten when the dim lights hit him and the sobbing returns. The paper bag has broken from his careless, eager hands and he tries to force the burger to his mouth. The bun breaks and he looks bloody now. His face and the front of his already dirty pyjama shirt are streaked with ketchup and pieces of meat.

Most of them can't eat normal food anymore, but I've found that at least letting them try makes it easier to accept me and my presence; I buy some peace and friendship in a fast-food currency. I have made the mistake of not at least trying to let them eat before, it's very clever to find out if they can feed. Having an indicator of what they're soon about to turn into can save me a lot of stress. I hate it when it gets violent, when their eyes slowly turn darker and darker and the hunger builds and their tiny bodies become pure force. I call those ones the *Pouncers* or the *Biters* and only quick reflexes and stakes can stop them. The *Pouncers* try to tear you limb from limb and one of them nearly succeeded, many years ago. My left shoulder still dislocates at times and the bright pink scar down my chest itches and aches when it's about to rain. I broke her neck and watched her eyes turn from swirling black shadows to a dimmed gray covering what was once a light blue as the stake broke through her ribs. I cry every time it comes to that. The weaker side, the *pleasant* side of me, still views them as broken children. It's why I wait to name them. The *Biters* mostly go for the Iliac Artery, the hamstring, and sometimes the inner thigh trying to tear through my black suit pants with their baby teeth. The sexual connotations of it make me sick and I have my theories of why they became what they are. The thought makes bile climb up my throat. But the *Biters* are rare. Most of my children are like the boy cowering on the plastic mat in my backseat.

He's crying again, this time silently but I can see his blonde hair shake as he sobs. I turn up the radio and let the country music fill the car to console him.

'I'm not in your town to stay,' said a lady, old and gray, to the warden of the penitentiary.

'I'm not in your town to stay and I'll soon be on my way.

I'm just here to get my baby out of jail, oh, warden;

I'm just here to get my baby out of jail.'

A fitting song. I keep driving until the sun starts setting and find us a motel that takes cash and asks no questions. The boy's going to change tonight and the lack of cars in the parking lot is good; sometimes they scream and their bones crack loudly if they become one of the *Tall*. The fewer neighbors the better. I flip through the pages of my diary until I find my definitions, my short list of what the *broken* children become.

3. Flighter—The Tall are usually made from boys between 3 and 4 years of age. They often come from homes with much older siblings, and the siblings are usually the ones that perpetuate the abuse. After they break and are collected, their bones will elongate, especially their spines. In their final form they can reach up to 6'1 ". Kind and silent, best placed in a separate room with other Talls as they can intimidate the Ghosts. Theory: Subconscious wish to outgrow their abusers but no wish to inflict their accumulated pain on their aggressors.

I have two lists in my diary, one for the broken children who, before they *break*, focus the pain and abuse inwards, blaming themselves and flee. The other list is for the children who aim the hurt the world has laid upon them outwards in rage, kicking and screaming and clawing with hunger for revenge. Flighters and fighters are the subclass; what kind of creature of broken children they become. The boy in the pyjamas, now curled up on the stained carpet under the motel room desk is very clearly a flighter kind of kid and I feel for him. Pain and fear radiate out of him like an aura, almost tangible. I am almost certain that he will become a *Ghost*. I sit on the bed and wait for the inevitable to happen. I anticipate his edges to fade at any time now. I expect to see through more than this paper thin skin and the faint lipstick smear on the nape of his neck, but through his bones and thready muscles. Light blue shadows moving through thin air. I wait for him to almost disappear. Even after they turn into *Ghosts*, their crying is always present, as loud as when they were little boys and girls. It fills my house, Mister Pleasant's House for Broken Children, making it seem haunted. Maybe it is.

But the boy is silent and suddenly a loud snap fills the room. He stops shaking and his edges are as firm and real as ever. This doesn't happen; I've never seen it before. This is a first. I frantically find my lists again and stare at the words. *1. The Ghosts 2. The Shadows 3. The Tall 4. The Biters 5. The Pouncers 6. The Under-the-beds.* I've seen them all change and I have never seen them just freeze. I have heard bones break and souls being ripped from their bodies countless times but never this deafening snap, like the cracking of a whip or a twig being broken. The boy is so still, I should at least see his back shift slightly with what used to be such laboured breaths.

Have I made a horrible mistake?

Then it dawns on me and my body goes numb and cold. Jesus Christ, was this child not *broken*? Every single thing implied that he had *broken* under his mother's poor excuse for care—from starving, from fetal alcohol syndrome, from the bruises on his upper thighs. Then I realize my second mistake; this child wasn't *broken* when I bought him from his mother, collected him. He just *broke* before my eyes.

The bruises on his upper thighs. The lipstick on his neck. How could I not understand what was going on? The poor child, the poor, poor child... My mind flashes with the images of me, a pleasant man, handing his mother the 50 dollar bill and in the memory I glance to the door and meet the eyes of the boy through the crack. I see his thoughts reflected in his dark pupils. His mother selling his body, not to get rid of him, but to a man who, in his experience with adults, would bruise places of his body that must never be touched in that way in motel rooms like this. I've *broken* a child for the first time and I break with him. Not like the children break, but no pleasant facade can keep me from sobbing. The boy still hasn't moved. He seems frozen in time. I must pull myself together and see what has risen from the pieces of this shattered child.

He slides down the wall before I get a chance to touch him, and his lifeless head jerks towards me. I freeze and my eyes are neither innocent, calm nor playful as I witness what lays before me. His button eyes stare back and the grain of the wood follows the shape of his fragile nose.

I wrapped up his—*its*—body in a blanket, carefully avoiding touching it with my bare hands. He's almost weightless. I put him in the backseat of the car and, after I reach the house, my Mister Pleasant's House for Broken Children, I add him to the list in my diary. I didn't know where to put him so I let him, my first, sit in the leather chair in the common room. The *Ghosts* and the *Shadows* avoid him at first but, as the days drag on, they are drawn to him. The more I pull away the more they flock around him, and I do pull away. Seeing him kills me. Yet I let him sit in that chair, always staring at me by my desk. I must never forget what I did. He never moves or responds but they whisper and cry to him. Console him. Every time I leave the room I find him somewhere else when I return. I let one of the *Tall* return him to his throne in front of the fireplace. I mustn't touch him, no adult shall ever put their hands on this broken Doll again. This is the first time in many years, far more years than you can fathom, that I have had to make a new class of creature. Is it fighting or fleeing? Is he hiding in there, his body numb and impervious to the outside world's horrors?

7. Neutral—the Doll. Wooden body similar to the child (visual examination only). Lack enough data to be certain but I advise against any adult handling the Doll, reaction unknown. Neutral status may be changed at later date.

***

There are more lost and broken children than you can imagine and a house can only hold so many souls. There are a finite number of beds that can hold those who are still tangible. I find some satisfaction and relief in the fact that there is only so much I can do without the ability to bend reality to my whims and wishes but it is a regretful satisfaction. But I am just a man and I can't will physics or metaphysics to change to please my needs and the needs of the many. The world isn't utilitarian or kind, it is neutral and I do what I can, what I must. I can't blame the ones who end up trying to tear my aortas into thin slices with sharp teeth or those whose arms and legs grow extra joints. It is not their fault, never their fault. We made this world and, therefore, made them.

6. Fighter—The Under-the-beds are usually made of highly empathic children between 4 and 6 years of age. Many come from backgrounds with domestic violence between parents or caregivers, but are rarely targets—neglect and being exposed to others being hurt is more likely the shape the abuse takes. During change, the distal, middle and proximal phalanges of hand and feet will disjoint and curl out through the skin in the hand palms and soles of the feet into hook shaped, skeletal claws. While keeping the same strength and speed as before the change their sharp teeth and hooks make them difficult to fight once attacked, and the hooks will rip apart muscle and skin without effort. While being a Fighter, I advise caution rather than elimination—they will rarely attack unless the perceive a threat to someone else in the vicinity and will direct their rage towards the aggressor. Protective attacks outnumber pre-emptive or unprovoked ones but avoiding contact is advised. Theory: Incapable of protecting other abused parties in their lives, while still being broken from neglect and the harm of others, aims the rage outwards but in a directed and somewhat controlled manner. Changes give physical advantage to protect and avenge others as well as themselves.

I've read and reread this list innumerable times while retelling my memories in ink. The *Doll*'s vacuous eyes are watching me from the leather chair by the fireplace in this library. I have filled these shelves with notebooks, their contents as dark as the night outside the covered windows. No one ever comes here to peek through the glass, no one can find Mister Pleasant's House for Broken Children, but I keep the heavy curtains closed to keep the world outside. I have yet to decide if what lies beyond the gates of this mansion is the prison and this is their only respite or if I am their jailor and warden. The loose jaw and rose painted, birchwood lips smiling at me from across the room have put doubt in my mind. I awake every night ridden by nightmares echoing like migraines in my head. The constant movements of the *Shadows* on the wall make me feel less alone but a nail of doubt has been hammered into the nape of my neck and the cool taste of steel hasn't left my throat.

The name that was chosen for me is mocking me, but here I sit behind my desk and I read notebook after notebook of the *broken* children —their names, their fate, and their stories—and I know that, despite good or evil, just actions and wrong actions, I am doing what I must do. Shelf after shelf of black books of written memories. I am meticulous about my records, as if the typed words would lift and remove them from the *broken* children and into the paper. The pain that I carry and vapid words don't compare to the wails of the *Ghosts* or the growling escaping from under the beds of this vast house. Experiences cannot be reduced to the confines of language. I straighten my black silk tie and fetch *the* notebook, my first one. Its pages are thumbed and the paper is ripped so I handle it with care. I have soft and tender hands, like care itself lived in my bones and tendons, and I browse the pages until I find what I'm searching for. Something to ground me in my eternal profession.

I felt it like a tug in my spine pulling me, steering me in an unknown direction. Like a homing pigeon, I navigated the street not knowing what I was searching for but taking notes of landmarks, a bloodhound with an unknown scent lingering in the air like a trail but no will to hunt or prey on it. These words echo through time to where I sit today. I have considered myself a caregiver and not a caretaker, and the predatory simile resonates in my recent worries. Its duality is both calming and upsetting. *I placed the blame on the boredom of the long and winding summer days, the hot sun burning my shoulders without school or work to distract or give me direction in life must have sent me on a subconscious journey, I hypothesized. Was there something calling out to me? It was someone. I found myself at a bus stop in the outskirt of town, a suburban haven of well-kept lawns where towering cypresses guarded the gates.*

She sat on the bench waiting, school books bound together by a belt lying on her lap. I never made a decision or even took note of the change within myself, there was just a silent acceptance of what was to come. She had her arms wrapped around her chest, as if trying to reassure herself and tell herself that everything would be ok. There was something hopeful in this gesture of self care. Her hair, the deep color of chestnuts, was carefully braided and framed her face awkwardly. This polished appearance seemed banal. Her eyes were oceans of a dark blue, and their severity and growing fear made the frills and bows appear plastic and fake. When the bus arrived, I could feel her anxiety grow in my bones like it was my own; she hesitated before climbing the steps. The last bus ride back to a home that should never be called a home. Houses where families break children cannot be more than buildings, never homes. Perhaps she scored too poorly on a test or stained her dress—I will never know what justifications that allowed fire to rain on her back. I didn't know this at the time. I just let myself be driven, a passenger in my body, following the scent of sweet jasmine in the humid air. There was a strange sense of urgency, and I hurried along the gravel road. I don't know why I dressed up, but there was a solemnity and expectation of importance itching inside me. I polished my shoes carefully and my tie knot was impeccable; I took great care.

I have maintained this tradition, I consider it a sign of respect and reverence for their struggles and what they have lived through. These pages are filled with memories, and there are some memories that start clawing at the walls of the room I've locked them in—*whispering screams of a pleasant boy and no one ever comes to collect him*—and I'd rather not present them with keys to their door. As I lift my head from the notebook to tend to my duties, I find the *Doll* staring back just inches from my face. I don't dare to move and I hold my breath. I do not know what to expect. His button eyes and their emptiness terrify me but they echo those of every single child I have collected. His back rests against the green lamp, blocking its dim light and even the *Shadows* that usually dance across the wall are frozen. I did not see it move, I never have, and I wonder—is this a threat or forgiveness? I remember who I am, I regain my core. I am Mister Pleasant and the gentle curve of my smile have calmed children more scared than I am now so I smile and my pulse settles slightly.

"I never collected the girl on the bench." My voice is steady and melodic. "I wish I had. I didn't understand the world back then, I didn't know what lurked at the edges of reality, and if had known I would've brought her into the woods and helped her change. What became of her was so much worse, but I was young and I didn't know. She *broke* that night and I heard her scream as her father's belt, not unlike the belt with which she bound her books, whipped through the air but I never knocked on that door and I never helped her. She never had the chance to change. My dear broken *Doll*, the absence of change when change is needed... It's an unstoppable force meeting an immovable object. It didn't leave her untouched yet it didn't tear her apart, just the constant roar of eons of time in her ears, she died yet was more alive than ever. I just stood at the edges of the woods as her back was slashed to pieces by leather and despite feeling her break and the urge that pulled me towards her door for day after day after never-ending day after it happened; I never returned. And—after 13 days—the urge stopped."

The *Doll* isn't moving, just silently listening to the words falling out of me. Words not meant for children's ears but important words nonetheless, and the relief is welcome. I remove my reading glasses and I dare to break eye contact with the boy I *broke*. The room is empty besides us now, the *Shadows* aren't cast along the walls or ceilings and I can hear the nervous shifting of the floorboards in the *Tall*'s rooms above us. The pajama shirt, its sleeve stiffened by dried ketchup, has slid down the skinny wood of his arm. The woodgrain run along them like golden veins. His hands are placed under his chin now, and his yarn hair is covering one of the eyes. I didn't see him move despite sitting right in front of him, no more than inches apart, so very careful not to touch him. The adrenaline hits me like a punch to the gut and I can feel sweat roll down my forehead, beads of ice. His pose suggests intense listening so I continue and hope he doesn't hear my voice tremble like my hands. My heart beats like the fluttering of the wings of butterflies.

"My body didn't will me to her door anymore and, where there was a forceful tug before, another urge resided; an urge to run. What before had sucked and pulled and begged now repelled me, pushed me away. It felt much like magnets when pushed towards sides of similar charge. Do you understand what I am saying?" The world hacks and twitches like reality is a broken record, lightnings of black stroboscope before my eyes and, in between the flashes, I see his pale birch chin tilt up and then down. It last only a moment and I am not sure if it happened or my tired, broken mind is playing malicious tricks on me. When the edges and symmetries of the world return, the *Doll*'s pose hasn't changed.

"I did watch her at the bus stop bench where I had first been led by this cosmic leash of mine, but she no longer wrapped her arms around herself. There was no need to try to hold her pieces together. Just the roar. This is why I collect now, I must always collect," I stutter as I gesture towards my list. "She isn't on there because I do not know what was made. You are there, yet I do not know what was made. But you do not repel nor nauseate and you have a home here. I am sorry. I am so very, very sorry." I blink away the tears that blur my vision and when I look up, the *Doll* again views me from the chair by the fireplace.

I hear the wails of the *Ghosts* from the walls and some wispy figures of light blue smoke again crowd around what I *broke*. My leather shoes softly taps against the carpet and I close the door to the library with my usual care. Some of the guilt that crawled through me like soldier ants has been relieved by my confession about the first child I let down. I feel the tug at my spine and I know that tomorrow is collection day, so I climb the dining stairs of this house to ready the changing device.

I wish to remind you, Dear Reader, that even if there are many *broken* children that I must collect and change—an endless stream of what cannot be mended but maintained—there are even more who never *break*. When my pleasant eyes kindly offer comfort, that comfort comes from the knowledge that the mind is not rigid but flexible and durable, capable of withstanding more than it deserves. And that there is a powerful tide of children that were pushed towards the point of no return but never broke. Even more that never have had to be examined in the trial of fire, walked through the purgatory of childhood. That speaks of immeasurable strength in those who live through it but do not misunderstand me: it is not a testament of weakness or absence of strength in those who *break*. It only attests the cruelty of others.

But I am just a man and there is a finite amount of beds, a finite amount of time at my disposal. I carefully avoid the gap beneath my bed by quickly climbing into bed without letting my bare feet linger by the darkness. The low gnarling from beneath, not unlike that of a sleepy kitten, lulls me into a sleep where dark blue eyes, ocean-like and swirling with violent currents, watch over me without blinking while I try to run through auburn molasses air.

***

I don't know what possessed me to bring the *Doll* on this collection. Perhaps my heart taps out *you're lonely* in Morse. Perhaps what drives me to these journeys, hours and hours of tunnel vision on empty roads, attracts me to him like he attracts the care of the other *broken*. I have viewed my loneliness in this task that has been handed to me a fortunate equilibrium, but what separates *lonely* and *alone* is a blurred line where the subject controls what meaning it carries. Perhaps I am reading too much into this newfound need for companionship. I am begging this camaraderie from a creature I do not know the intentions of and I might simply consider the fact that he has caused me no harm, though I suspect he is fully capable of it, as approval. I allow him to sanction my actions. But then again, I might project approval onto this blank canvas, again allowing the subject define the object. The semantics confuse me and I force my attention back to the road.

5. Fighter—The Pouncers can be made from any age group but are likely to be older than average, 7-9 years old. Many are scrawny and weak before breaking and will have made good targets for the misguided fists of other children. Most of them have been severely bullied. The changing process can, at first, be mistaken for that of a Tall as the bones break and regrow in a similar pattern. I advise trying to feed them after collection. Physical appearance: Arms and legs with three joints below the shoulder and hip, curved backs, will move on all fours. Strength will grow exponentially after change and Pouncers must, sadly, be terminated within minutes. Theory: Wish to overpower their aggressors is made possible with their gained, ferocious strength.

This school could be mistaken for any other school and this town for any other forgotten town just off the highway. They have become uniform through the years, pale carbon prints of each other. The shrill bell rings and tears a hole in the silence, the damp air is cut by children scurrying out of the doors. They look like ants from a distance, scampering out on the school yard. Laughter and fragments of fast-paced conversations echo towards me. I left the *Doll* in the car and I've been waiting on a bench close enough so I can follow the movements of the school, yet far enough not to attract any suspicions of my motivations of lingering around children unconnected to me. Soon the yard is empty, most have been picked up by parents or run off to play at some friend's house, but the pull grows stronger and I head towards the brick building, barely legible graffiti telling me names of teenagers: Ha$ard, lil' DawG. They've marked their territories with spray bottles and permanent markers. I enter the corridors of many children's nightmares or dreams come true.

This bastion of potential knowledge is full of smells; cheap perfume and candy, hormonal sweat and locker room. I let my feet lead the way as the pull grows stronger.

He's sitting on the floor by the lockers, a child that had no friend to bring him over to play and no parents that had remembered to pick him up. There is no doubt in my mind that he is *broken*, the eyes fixed on the chewing gum on the floor in front of him are dead. Perhaps he *broke* because he was forgotten one too many times. No mother or father waited outside the school for him—again—and no teacher raised an eyebrow. No friend who realized someone was left behind again, as many times before. Forgotten. I have seen many children like him, so many of them are *Ghosts*.

It doesn't take physical pain to *break*, you can fracture every bone in your body without *breaking* inside like my children do. It doesn't take unkind words; lack of kind words or any words at all is more than enough. A towering silence around you will steal your voice in the end.

He might be 7 or 8 years old, black hair swooping down across a pale face with high cheek bones. There's something Russian about him, he reminds me of a sombre portrait by Valentin Serov. I offer him my hand and he takes it, his hand is limp and damp and we slowly walk out of the building. As I collect the children, the pull that guides me to them almost vibrates. Not of excitation but some sort of release. It is not a pleasant nor uncomfortable feeling, it just is. But as we step out of the doors into the blue March light of the setting sun, it doesn't vibrate. It pounds and aches. It pushes.

The push goes stronger and, almost by instinct, I push the boy behind my back. He stumbles from my brusque treatment but doesn't fall. The school yard is empty and my now hyper-alert ears only pick up the sound of the breeze rustling through the dry leaves and the creaking of the slowly swaying swings. The push is immense yet I can't identify a threat— my view is anticlimactic in the absence of police, parents, teachers… Anyone. My grip around the boy's hand tightens and I drag him behind me as I rush towards the car. Wrong, everything's wrong and my gut screams for us to get out of here.

She's sitting on the hood of my car, elbows resting on her knees and her hands cradling her face. She looks bored almost. And not a day older than I last saw her; the girl I left behind, she who *broke* and kept on *breaking*. Her hair is still the deep auburn it was as she sat on that bench, and my chest hurts as the deep blue eyes that have haunted my nightmares since I first made the *Doll* pierce into mine. I bend over from the pain that churns, the push is making it hard to breathe. She hums absentmindedly.

> *The bad man came*
> *and the bad man went*
> *but he didn't take me away.*
> *So I tore the bad man*
> *limb from limb*
> *just to make him pay.*

Her voice is clear and her singing beautiful, as if she were singing a nursery rhyme or a lullaby. The grotesque words seem even more terrifying with this sweet girl's light timbre and the vibrato carried by the crisp air. Her movements are unnatural, twitchy and sharp as she climbs down from the hood of my car. The light blue of her dress looks shrill against the rust-colored car and, as she skips towards me, time intervenes. Her movements glitch in midair, speeding up and slowing down rhythmically. I empty the contents of my stomach on the dirty asphalt, yet I smile when I look up at her. The blue of her iris covers her entire eyes now, deep oceans of never-ending pain. I wish I could mend her and my pleasant smile must've conveyed this wish. The way her jaw drops and her sing-songy voice turning into a shrill scream tells a tale of how my lack of fear angers her. She isn't singing the next voice, she shrieks it—an adolescent harpy out of time and synch with reality.

> *I'll save what's broken*
> *that you killed.*

I'll raise them from the dead.
They pounce and bite
and growl and fight
and they're all in your head.

Her wails raise in pitch for every word and I can feel the blood dripping from my nose and down my face. I haven't let go of the *broken* boy's hand. He's curled up into fetal position behind me and I'm gripping him too tightly, his flesh almost white. I let go as the first images hit my head.

I am laying on the ground and the blonde girl, only five. No, not a girl—a Pouncer now—is sitting on my chest. Her limbs are too long and have too many joints and her thin arms are pulling at my left arm with an unnatural strength. I hear my shoulder dislocate with a loud pop and her nails dig into my chest as I manage to get my free hand around her little neck. My hand reaches all the way around it and I try to make it swift. The crunch of her neck breaking punctuates the memory of the stake pushing through her chest, staining her Care Bear T-shirt with black blood, and I am pulled out of my body. *I am in a field at night and the rapid movements of the three-year-old boy remind me of a spider. As he hurls towards me, his teeth grow longer, bigger, his mouth is full of them now—rows and rows of stained white. I have dropped the changing device on the ground; he changed so quickly that I was caught off guard. I am a man of some physical strength but I am not a fighter. However, I am fast and I crouch and roll away before he is upon me. I grab a rock and I am over him now. I keep forcing myself to keep striking him with the rock until hundreds of baby teeth are spread like a halo around his head.* I am again pulled out of the memory as the stake pierces his heart and I keep being pushed into memory after memory of every *Fighter* I've terminated.

I don't know how I manage to pull myself out of her torture. The push she emits is still immobilizing and her screaming is so violent. I am, however, back in the present and kneeling on the ground. Every scar or healed fracture my *Fighters* have done to me continue to ache. I can no longer make out the words or the melody but the rhythm of her song is still there. Suddenly, she's on the hood of my car again and the silence is deafening. Her eyes of all blue are focused on the curled-up figure behind me.

"Make him change," she demands. "I want to see him change." I arise from the ground and brush the dirt off of my suit.

"Make him change!"

What she insists is perverse, allowing someone to see someone change is too intimate and exploitive. There is a level of respect that is demanded. I try to avoid comparing what I do to the work of an undertaker, but the similarities have to be acknowledged. I will not stand for it and I will not allow it.

I fight the push as hard as I can by focusing on the urgent pull that still connects me to the boy. She may torture me but, since I do not know the full extent of what she is capable of, I decide to disregard the threat implied in the fact that she likely is capable of much worse. I lift the boy to my chest, gently cradling him like a baby. He is shaking like a newly hatched bird.

"No." My voice is steady yet gentle and pleasant, always pleasant. I must be.

She glitches across the pavement towards me, her feet take no steps yet she is approaching me rapidly, and again the blue of her eyes are whirlpools on a violent ocean. I must protect the boy in my arms, but I don't know how to. The pull is so strong that I'm unable to let him go, let him fall to the ground to shield him, and the push is so strong that it's numbing. As she moves she's pointing at me, an accusation and a claim—

a claim to the *broken* boy in my arms.

She freezes only feet away from me and her eyes widen, impossibly wide. She doesn't look afraid but surprised. Her outstretched arm moves to the left as she now points to something behind my shoulder and she snarls like an animal. I don't dare to move, so I just stand still, smiling and hoping my arms and hands will shield the child I'm holding.

Time stands still for what feels like minutes but must be only moments. And, as suddenly as it started, she twirls around and skips away from me down the street. Again she is singing.

The evil man
can run and run
but I will always find him.
Ghosts and Tall and
Under-the-Beds
will eat what is inside him.

Before she turns the corner, she turns back to look at me—no, not at me, over my shoulder—she smiles widely and waves happily. When she is gone I dare to turn around.

On the pavement behind me lies the *Doll* who was locked in my car.

The motel room looks like any motel room, just as this highway looks like any highway. They are all the same and blend together in my mind. Only the children differ. This boy, empty eyes staring from a pale face, sits on the floor, holding his knees to his chin. I open the suitcase that I always carry with me on collections and take out the device. The matte metal is, for some reason, always the same temperature as my skin. I've come to regard it an extension of me. Its curves are beautiful. I make sure that the stakes lie ready in the suitcase in case something goes wrong and, as the device touches his skin and I turn the dial, he looks up at me. He looks calm and grateful. I sit down on the bed and wait for him to change, and after only minutes he dissolves into shadowy smoke the color of the sky on a misty summer morning. The *Ghosts* will have a new friend when we return.

I Was Almost Involved In A School Shooting
By D0nutblink

I've been wanting to get something off of my chest for a very long time. The only person who knows the whole story is my wife, and she didn't find out until we were already engaged. I didn't have anyone to talk to about this, because anyone who knows will think ill of me. It's been fifteen years since these events took place, so I finally feel safe enough to talk about them anonymously.

I had a really hard time in high school. Traumatic events in my childhood combining with hormonal changes didn't make me the most easy going guy. I'd consider myself handsome now, but at the time I was 5'4', paler than fresh linen and bone thin. My hobbies were all indoors and solitary in nature and I found it hard to make friends. I was the "lone wolf" that everyone warns you about.

The only friend I had in the world was my creative writing teacher, Mr. Artis. He was an older guy but I think he saw some of himself in me. He let me hide out in his office to avoid the jocks who taunted me daily. We would talk about writing and what we were reading but, most of the time, we just talked about life.

He had talked me down a few times. I was massively depressed, suicidal even. I never went through with my plans because he was always there for me. He talked me through things that I thought no one else would understand. He understood the anger like no one else did. I hated the boys who would bully me, I hated the girls who would giggle at me as I walked by, I hated the teachers who turned a blind eye or the ones, like my gym teacher, who almost encouraged it.

I think if it weren't for Mr. Artis, I wouldn't be here to tell my story. If I hadn't had him to talk to, to confide in, the self-loathing and anger and disgust would have bubbled over a lot sooner than it did. I'm thankful for that.

My Junior year of high school, Mr. Artis got sick. They didn't tell us what he had, but he missed almost a month of classes. Not having anyone to talk to took a toll on me. I wasn't allowed in his office alone, so I lost my hiding place. Being around more often meant that I was an easier target. The assholes who tormented me day in and day out stepped up their game.

Almost every day was torture. The bullying escalated from just taunting me to physically hurting me. I was punched square in the nose one day; another time, they slammed my hands in my locker door and locked it shut.

On top of everything going on at school, my mom and dad had been fighting for a while. The week of the event, my mom left. Neither of my parents understood me, but mom tried. Leaving me alone with my father is something that I still haven't forgiven her for, fifteen years later.

I know what I did was stupid. I know that it was the most drastic solution to something that would change over time. I didn't see it that way, though. My dad kept a gun in the attached garage. It was loaded and tucked away for emergency situations, like going to the shooting range with his buddies.

On Monday, I took the gun to my room. Dad didn't notice that it was missing, because the drawer where it's kept is mostly empty. I posed with it in the mirror, practicing my icy stare. I knew right away what I wanted to do, although the thought of just using it to blow my own brains out crossed my mind a few times. I didn't want to go out like that though, I wanted to leave a lasting impression.

I counted the bullets in the gun seventeen times; there were only three. I didn't know where to find more ammo, so I knew that I would have to make every shot count. One bullet was for John Carter the asshole who filled my locker with piss filled balloons. The second bullet was for Mike Wallace who catfished me for weeks pretending to be a girl in our class, and then stood me up when I asked "her" out. The final bullet was for myself, I didn't want to go to jail, and I sure as hell didn't want to keep living.

On Friday morning I tucked the gun into the waistband of my jeans, wearing a big hoodie to cover the bulge. Everything felt different; entering the school felt like I was dreaming. The school itself almost looked like a set on a TV show, all conversation blurring like background murmurs. I suppose, looking back, that I had detached myself emotionally from the situation.

I was calm and collected as I walked the halls, looking for my victims. I was early and classes hadn't started yet, but I figured John Carter would be in the gym shooting hoops. I made my way down the corridor that lead to the athletics wing with determination.

"Harold!" I heard a familiar voice and stopped. I turned to see Mr. Artis standing at his office door, "Come in, I need to speak with you."

"Hey-ah, it's good to see you," I awkwardly smiled back at him. "Listen, I'm kind of busy right now, can this wait?" I was a man on a mission, I didn't want to lose momentum.

"No, it cannot. Come in." His tone was kind, but the sternness was undeniable. He held open the door to his office and entered behind me.

I asked him why he had wanted to see me, but he simply stated that he wanted to talk. He asked me how things had been while he was away but I didn't want to talk. The answers I gave him were short, cold, nothing like my usual self. I could tell that he knew that something was up, but didn't want to push me.

As I leaned back in the chair, wishing he would just leave me alone, my sweatshirt lifted slightly, the bulge becoming more evident.

"Harold," Mr. Artis whispered. "What on earth is that for?"

My cheeks turned bright red with embarrassment at being caught and my heart started to pound in my ears. I knew it was over then. Mr. Artis was cool, but he was still a teacher. I assumed that the police and my parents would be called, that I would be kicked out of school and possibly sent to prison.

I tried to speak, but I couldn't. Words got caught in the back of my throat, my eyes welling up with tears and I just broke. The weight of the world which I had been carrying finally broke my back and all I could do was sob. Mr. Artis didn't say a word, just waited for me to compose myself. When I finally did, I told him about everything that had been going on. I had never cried in front of him before, and the emotion that flowed out of me was surprisingly relieving.

When the tears stopped and I had run out of things to say, Mr. Artis held his hand out for the gun.

"Are you going to have me arrested?" I asked.

"No. What good would that do?" He asked.

I couldn't stop apologizing, but Mr. Artis's eyes were kind as he told me that everything was going to be ok. He told me that he understood what I wanted to do, but that it was the wrong solution. Comforted by his presence and finally being able to get everything off my chest, I almost agreed with him.

I gave Mr. Artis the gun, which he said that he would dispose of. I knew my dad would be livid that it went missing, but that was a problem for another day. I thanked Mr. Artis for everything and went to class.

I was late to Spanish, but I told the teacher that I was in the nurse's office. Señora Miller didn't question it; my eyes were still red and my nose was runny. The rest of the class was uneventful but, just as the bell was supposed to ring, the principal came over the speaker with an announcement:

"May I please have everyone's attention. Last night, at 8:06 p.m., our school lost a beloved member of our faculty. Mr. Gideon Artis found peace last night, after a lifetime struggling with a hereditary disorder. There will be a service on Tuesday, for anyone who would like to attend, and all counselors will be available all week for any student of faculty member who would like grievance assistance. We will now have five minutes of silence, for Mr. Artis."

There were gasps around the classroom as the announcement played, but Señora Miller quieted us down. We bowed our heads out of respect and sat in silence.

I often ponder what happened that day. I wonder if Mr. Artis was a ghost, but seemed so real. My mental state that day was far from sane, and it's possible that I hallucinated the whole thing; my subconscious finding a way to stop me from making a terrible mistake.

The biggest mystery of all is that of the gun. I know I took it from my dad's drawer, I remember counting the bullets, over and over again. I remember the way it felt, heavy in my waistband, and I know that I handed it over to Mr. Artis. The next weekend my dad went to the shooting range and I was ready for hell when he couldn't find it. Except he did find it; it was right there in the drawer, still loaded with three bullets.

I can't explain the events that took place, but I guess a part of me wonders if Mr. Artis just wanted to look out for me one more time.

The Town I Grew Up In Was Torn Apart By A Serial Killer

By Eve Ben Ezra

February 29. The day that Middlefield changed forever. You probably haven't heard of Middlefield, Oregon because it doesn't exist anymore. It doesn't exist anymore because of Him. And that all started on February 29, 1988 with the disappearance of Carol Grott.

It was raining the day that Carol Grott disappeared. She was fifteen, two years younger than me. Middlefield was pretty small—a few thousand people, and no records of it now. But back then, before Carol went missing, it was a pretty calm little town. Situated near the border of Idaho and Oregon, it's one of those farm towns where everyone knows everyone and nothing ever happens.

At least, nothing ever happened until February 29, all those years ago. That day all of us walked to school, just like any other day. The school was a plain building, six stories with a track and a football field that also doubled as a soccer pitch. Not that we really had many sports, there were only 400 students from kindergarten up. It was impossible not to know everyone, and even more impossible to not know everyone's business.

Carol never showed up. The teachers called her parents, who were concerned but not too concerned. It wasn't unheard of for kids to occasionally play hooky or to sneak off somewhere with someone of the opposite (most of the time) sex. Of course, word got around then. We all knew she wasn't there and it was most of what we talked about on the walk home.

I thought she'd be grounded for a few days. Freddy, my younger brother, said he bet her parents would make her help when their cow birthed its next calf.

Even after all these years, I never got over the disgusting nature of helping birth a calf.

That night, we ate dinner, did our homework, and went to sleep. I remember that my dad was still in the living room, the news blaring into my bedroom. My door was open just the slightest bit, and I fell asleep with the picture dancing over my ceiling, flickering light that seemed to extend beyond the window into our fields beyond.

The next morning I woke up to my mother shaking me. "Laura," she said softly, her hand on my shoulder. "Laura, baby, wake up. Wake up."

Birds were chirping. The sun was streaming in through my window; the rain had stopped. I remember groaning, turning over in bed.

"I don't wanna go to school," I said, like I said every day.

"There's no school today," my mom told me. "Get up, Laura. The police are here."

I feel so guilty, now, for what I was thinking. I remember thinking they'd caught wind of me and Jeremy cow tipping a few weekends ago; they knew about the empty beer bottles we'd buried in the Smith's backyard; they were aware that Charlotte McDonald was no longer a virgin, and she'd been pregnant and had tried to give herself an abortion by throwing herself down the barn stairs.

I got up and changed out of my nightgown, sleep still clinging to the corners of my eyes as I came outside. True to my mother's word, there were three cops sitting at the living room table. Sheriff Williams was there, smack dab in the middle, and that's how I knew I'd fucked up big time.

But, of course, it was about Carol Grott. And, again, I can't forgive myself for being relieved that I wasn't in trouble.

"Laura, have you heard from Carol lately? Any word that maybe she wasn't happy at home?"

I looked from one of my parents to the other. They gave me blank stares in return.

"Carol and I weren't very close… but no. No, I didn't hear anything."

"Well, we know you and the Jenks boy are close." Their words for 'dating.' "His sister is quite close with Carol, and so we wondered if maybe, when you were around the Jenkses' place, you'd ever heard anything, eavesdropped, been privy to any information."

I shook my head. My father was sitting in his chair at the end of the table, a coffee mug between his two palms. His hair was still brown back then. I remember his face, the solemnity of it, like he knew what was coming; the wrinkles between his eyebrows were just starting, the flesh on his cheeks just beginning to sag. He was already preparing for it, he just didn't know it back then.

"Sheriff Williams, is Carol in trouble?"

The Sheriff looked from me to his officers, to my parents. "Carol never came home last night."

Have you ever felt your blood turn to ice in your veins? Like the feeling of getting caught in a really big lie, when your face grows hot and your stomach feels like pure acid driving against your insides, eating away at you? The kind of panic that manifests in shaking and shivering, trembling…

It was like the whole world was filled with water. Everyone was sitting at the table, still and somber and grounded. And I was just trying to find which way was up.

That's when I started hyperventilating. I don't know why it bothered me so much. Like I'd told the sheriff, I didn't know Carol very well. Yes, she was Jeremy's sister's friend but that's a lot of removal. She was two years younger than me. Different class at school. I only knew her as the girl with the long yellow curls, the blue eyes, the cotton dresses she was partial to.

I remember those cotton dresses because she was wearing one in the missing poster. They went up that same day, March 1, all over town. Carol looking down at us, smiling like she'd never been taken.

As for all of us, school was cancelled for quite some time. It was cancelled for a week because all the teachers were in the search party, and half of the seniors and juniors, too. We searched the woods, the fields, neighboring areas. We drove all the way down to Twin Cities and all the way to Salem. We called the highway patrol of five different states: Nevada, California, Oregon, Idaho, Washington...

None of it mattered. Because she showed up on a Tuesday. At least, her body showed up on a Tuesday.

It was found on the side of the highway leading out of town. Right there on the side of the road, laid out with an orchid sitting on her forehead. The rumor was—and all I got were rumors because the adults were worried that we couldn't handle the truth, at least for Carol, at least not until more started disappearing. The rumor was that she'd been found with her eyes wide open. Staring at the sky; blue marbles. The orchid had been arranged so that the long tendrils of roots were planted into her ears and nose and mouth. The stems leading up out of her body, flowers pointed to the sky.

She'd been dressed in white, the rumors went. A white dress, laid out on the side of the road, dead. There were other whispered rumors. Things like *sexual assault* and *rape* were whispered quite a bit. Apparently the ME had thrown up when he looked beneath that white dress. He said it was the bruises, and what was done to her down there.

It was noted, also, that Carol was missing a foot.

As for the official cause of death, we didn't know. The ME had no idea, said there was no sign of strangulation, stabbing, asphyxiation. He said of all things, Carol, 15 year old Carol, had had a heart attack. Post mortem, the orchid had been planted inside of her. Indeed, her brain had been scooped out, severed at the optic nerves. Her skull had been turned into nothing but a pot. But why she had died? The exact method of his killings?

I wish I still didn't know. The truth is, I do know. I know exactly what he did to his victims. I know, because I was his last. And I know how Carol died, because I was there when Freddy died. He took us. He kept us.

I'm the only one who got out alive.

***

We weren't allowed to watch the news for some time after Carol's body was found. There were pictures that showed what had been done to her head. But rumors flew rampant at school back then, and we all knew how the orchid had found its place inside of her: the back of her head, a long slim incision made at the base of her skull. Another, at the base of her jaw. The skin had been peeled up. The tendrils of orchid roots had been snuck inside her nose and ears. Some surgery had been done on the plant, too. It had apparently died within days of Carol's body being found.

The worse rumors said that the Surgeon had carefully planted the orchid within her skull after her death. There were rumors about how she'd died: spontaneous heart attack; injected with a drug that couldn't show up on the screenings; psychologically tortured; raped. The list went on.

The worst rumors said that the Surgeon had carefully planted the orchid before her death. How that was possible, I didn't know. It made me sick to think of it. It made my stomach turn, the acid and bile scrubbing against my insides until I had to excuse myself. That's what I did frequently, those days. Carol hadn't been my friend, but I could still see her. I could see her in the hallways, smiling as she opened her locker. And when I vomited—the bile rushing up out of my stomach and into whatever vehicle I had managed to reach—the image of her pain and suffering almost transferred to me. I knew what she was feeling.

I thought I knew.

Middlefield was under curfew. We had to be home before dark, and it was suggested against leaving the house before first light. Of course most of the farmers didn't listen to this; they had to be out and about before the sun came up. But there was no problem. Middlefield had a small police force but they were pulling all-nighters patrolling the town. More volunteers signed up. City police came down from Eugene to help. There were even some fancy detectives who walked around in ties and carried their badges on their belts, right next to their guns.

One night, three weeks after Carol's body had been discovered, I heard a noise outside the house. My room was on the second floor. My brother and I shared a wall, with our parents' bedroom down a small hallway and separated by a bathroom. Freddy and I both had windows that pointed outside to the street, though his window was partially obscured by the branches of an old oak that grew on our property.

I thought at first the noise was a patrol. It sounded like rustling. Someone going through our garbage. Then I thought that maybe it was raccoons there looking for food. The rustling was loud, a clanging of glass on tin and footsteps. I swear I could hear grunts. I could hear someone making an effort, really going through their paces.

My heart was pounding. Trying to be quiet, I grasped around in my nightstand for the flashlight, rolling out of bed and going to the window. There were more grunts and crashes, and then a quiet curse. My heart skipped a beat, the blood in my veins turning to ice as I slowly pushed the window up and held out the flashlight. *Turn it on,* I thought to myself. *It's just a policeman. It's nothing. It's Dad trying to do some late night work. He threw out something he didn't mean to.*

I took a deep, shuddering breath. Still holding the flashlight aloft but unlit, I said out into the night, "Hello?"

The rustling stopped. There was the snap of a twig, the sound of footsteps.

"Hello?" I said again, more loudly. "Dad? Sheriff Williams?"

There was silence on the other end. I waited, my heart pounding. I was scared to turn on the flashlight. I didn't know what I would see if I did.

I held my breath and clicked on the flashlight, sweeping it over the yard. There was a scuffling near the base of the house, by the trunk of the oak tree. I hitched the window up more, leaning out of it and sweeping the light over the grass. But there was no one there.

Slowly, I clicked the flashlight off and closed the window. I latched it, staring outside at the road for a long time. I half expected someone to come out of the dark or yell, "Boo!" But there was no one there. No one came.

I went back to bed. I dreamed of rustling noises, of orchids, of screeching laughter.

The next morning our neighbors, the McDonalds, found a severed foot on their porch. Their daughter, Charlotte, had been taken from her bed.

But she wasn't the only one. My boyfriend Jeremy was gone, too.

***

Before Carol Grott, there weren't any murders in Middlefield's history. Sure, sometimes cowhands got into fights when they'd had one too many beers at The Bar, and that ended with Sheriff Williams carting them off to the one cell jailhouse so they could *work some stuff out*. But there was never really any serious crime. Cow tipping, underage drinking, and sex were part of growing up.

Of course, just because there aren't murders don't mean there aren't deaths. The old church down the road from the Jenkses' place joked that they hosted as many wakes as they did sermons, since Sunday morning was a day to sleep in after a hard week's work. Mr. Tom White doubled as a pastor and the county veterinarian, specializing in equine births or something of the like, so he was often tired, too, and more than happy to hold off a sermon in return for another few hours of sleep.

Life didn't take a break in Middlefield, is what I'm saying. Babies were occasionally born, old folks died. There were tragedies on occasion, as well. Ten years before I was born, a boy belonging to the Millers had drowned when he went up to Lake Owyhee on his own. His body had never been found. When I was five, a young boy hung himself in his parent's barn for reasons my dad would never speak of. There were rumors, of course, but nothing ever came of them. Similarly, just two years before Carol Grott disappeared, one of my friends had died going into labor. She was twenty and married, so no scandal there, but it was sad to say the least.

The thing about the Surgeon is he never really gave us time to have peace. He wasn't, of course, officially a serial killer until Jeremy and Charlotte's bodies turned up, but that wasn't until June. In the meantime, I'd turned 18. The search never really wound down. We were always on the edges of our seats, just waiting for the two to turn up. The detectives, two white 30-somethings who had driven down all the way from Portland, seemed at a loss. The extra police from Eugene would get in their cars to drive home only to come back again, claiming they couldn't bear it if another kid was taken and they had just given up.

But we were all losing hope toward the end of May. School was back in session, then finished. Freddy had a summer vacation and I had the rest of my life. Of course I hadn't applied to college; my family didn't have the money and what good would it do me to have a college education if I was just going to work on a farm my whole life? Once upon a time, Jeremy and I had talked about getting married and moving to Bend or Eugene or Salem, starting up our own family or a little farm or maybe even a bookstore or a restaurant. We didn't have any set-in-stone goals, we only wanted something exciting and new.

June 5, 1988 was the day of my graduation ceremony from high school. I got to put on the cap and gown with my small class of seniors, and we were to sit on fold-out chairs on the football field in the blazing sun while Mayor Radcliffe gave some speech about education. Then we'd all go home and have barbecue or else play a friendly game of soccer or football, and the next day some of us were planning to truck up to Lake Owyhee and go swimming.

But those things never happened, I'm sure you could guess, because June 5 was the day that Jeremy came back into my life.

I was the one who found Jeremy. I think it must have been planned that way. I think, during his imprisonment with the Surgeon, Jeremy must have told all about Middlefield. Maybe even all about me. I found Jeremy from my bedroom window, looking out at the road and watching the dawn on the day that I was supposed to get my diploma. I knew what it was before I even really *knew* what it was. That doesn't make sense, I know. But I ran down the stairs and out into the front yard without thinking about it, and there he was.

His hair had been trimmed, and he didn't have a beard. His eyes, brown and empty and staring up at the lightening sky, obscured only by the large purple petals of the orchid that had been planted on his face. His mouth was opened wide, and the long tentacle roots had been somehow planted through his nose and were emerging again through his mouth, snaking their way down his chin. It looked like he was vomiting roots, his mouth hinged open with those green snakelike veins coming out. Stem and leaves and even a bit of root were coming from his nose, reaching to the sky.

I was sick, of course. I can't remember much but that image. Someone must have found me, because I heard screaming. I leaned down and tried to put him in my arms. He was dressed in white: a white shirt that had been starched so stiff it felt like cardboard under my hands, and white slacks, and white shoes. All white, as I held him the screaming got louder, like there were more people joining, and I heard my dad calling my name and then he was yelling too. There were lights. Blue and red, flashing. Screaming, screaming, screaming. It hurt my ears, it hurt my head. And it was only when Sheriff Williams squatted down beside me and put his hand on my shoulder that I realized the screaming was coming from me.

That's all I remember. What I've heard since is that my dad carried me up the stairs and put me in my bed and the doctor came around and gave me a sedative, and I slept for almost a week straight, drugged and dreaming of nothing and remembering nothing and coming around only to learn from Freddy that Charlotte's body had turned up too, and that Tom White Jr. and Olivia Frank and Sandy Green had been taken, and there had been a foot on the Franks' porch and also on the Whites' porch but not the Greens', and that the detectives figured the Surgeon was trying to figure out how much damage he could do and how many he could take all at once.

I stopped going out. I just wanted to stay in bed. The doctor came, and Freddy came and sat by my bed, and even a specialist from Eugene came to talk to me about trauma and grief. There were different pills to take, and most of them make those next few weeks before the latest three turned up fuzzy.

That's how I learned the details then, in a state of half consciousness. So I hope you'll forgive me if I don't get them all right. The ME had found that Jeremy's death was as inexplicable as Carol's. Charlotte's death, though, had been by strangulation. There was nothing forensically left on the body that would have been useful. Apparently there had been some hope when seminal fluid had been found on Charlotte. But then the DNA matched for Jeremy. Both of them had bruises and scars and lacerations beneath their white clothing. Jeremy, post mortem, had been castrated.

Charlotte had been found with an orchid just as Jeremy had.

I didn't want to hear any more. I wanted to block out the world. Freddy was my only source of sanity in that time. He used to get in bed with me and hold me while I cried for hours. He hauled up the old TV and VCR and took Dad's car and drove all the way to Boise and back (4 hours round trip) to get brand new movies and cold cheeseburgers that we could heat up and eat. It was comforting, even though the buns were chewy and the fries were soggy. It was comforting to the extent that anything can be comforting when you see how your boyfriend has been murdered and turned into a pot for a plant.

It was the middle of July when the three latest bodies turned up. I was still in bed, though I'd been taking small walks in the afternoon. Freddy had even convinced me to get on a horse one day and I'd gripped the reins until my knuckles went white while Freddy spoke soothingly to the mare so she wouldn't buck. Then, after about ten minutes, I got off and Freddy took my hand and we walked back home where I got back into bed. The morning after I'd gotten back on the horse (heh), the bodies turned up.

I'll spare you the details, except to tell you it was more of the same. Orchids, rape, and torture. One body with no identifiable cause of death, while the other two had been strangled. The ME guessed they'd all been killed at the same time, all kept for a day or two before their bodies were planted back at home.

None of the funerals had taken place. All of the bodies were being kept in cold refrigeration units until the investigators decided there was nothing else of use. Of course, it wasn't those two detectives from Portland anymore. They'd been replaced by feds in black SUVs.

People were leaving by then. In some cases, leaving was making them go broke. Several families I knew had just picked up and left in the middle of the night, spooked, saying they were going to stay with family in Eugene or Bend or Boise. Others sold off all their farm animals and tried to move ship and sell their land. No one wanted to buy, not in a town where children kept going missing. So they ended up losing most of what they had but got to keep their children. In the two weeks between the end of July and when the Surgeon took his next victims in August, the town became a shell of itself.

I woke up from a nightmare on August 10, 1988. In it, I'd been making love to Jeremy when suddenly roots sprouted from his mouth and ears and nose. He started gurgling and choking and then fell dead on top of me. Even though I was screaming, the roots took hold of me, winding their way into my ears and nose and mouth, forcing their way down my throat. I woke up gasping.

I hate to say it. I do. I hate what I'm about to tell you, because I think it makes me a terrible person. But part of me wishes I hadn't woken up that night. Part of me wishes I'd taken some drugs to go back to sleep. Then I never would have had to go through it.

But I did. I didn't sleep through it. I did wake up and hear the rustling outside the window again, just like the night before Jeremy went missing. I did reach into my nightstand with my heart pounding and grasp my flashlight. I did go to the window. I did see a figure.

Two figures. A black vehicle of some sort. There was a figure, tall and large and shadowy, dragging another across the grass of my front yard.

It was Freddy. I knew it was Freddy. And without even thinking—without even doing anything remotely smart like you'd think I'd have done—I ran down the stairs without my shoes and out onto the front porch. I ran into something strange and soft and cold, and across the grass toward the figure. And I started yelling at that point, telling Him to get away from my brother. The lights went on in my house, I think, because the shadows got worse.

I was on him, then. He hit me hard across the face, then in the stomach. He picked me up like a rag doll and threw me in the back of a box truck. The metal sheet was rolled down, and the world was black. I felt around with my hands, desperately reaching around for something to use to get out, but the only thing my fingers found were two sets of legs. I could hear yelling outside. There was banging on the back of the door, and I was screaming for my mom, my dad, for help. Then we were moving. It was pitch black in the back, and all I could do was feel around on my hands and knees. There were two other bodies back there, and one at a time I felt until I could identify their chests and pressed my ear to them, listening for a heartbeat. I kicked against the side of the vehicle where the driver would be. I slammed my fists on the metal.

My heart was pounding. I told myself it was another dream, as we drove further and further away. I screamed until my throat went numb, even though I knew it wouldn't do any good. I banged on the metal. I tried to open the back hitch.

Finally, the car slowed. I started to cry. I knew I was going to die. I knew Freddy was going to die. Whoever else was in that trunk with us was going to die. And we were all going to die after something truly horrible was done to us. Then we would be dressed in white and orchids would be planted in our skulls, and we would be deposited back at home.

We were going to die.

The hitch slid open. I lunged, scraping and kicking and screaming for all it was worth. I got a hand to the throat, a quick dart that sent me breathless and gasping for air.

There was a hissing sound, and the sound of metal tumbling in the back of the van. I'd lost my voice and my air. I was going to die. I was going to die. I was going to die.

It hurt. The gas. I looked for new air, but couldn't. The air I gulped down was anything but pure and clean. It burned the inside of my throat, my nose, my eyes. I tried to scream, but couldn't. I choked, sucked in more air to try and compensate, choked. The world got fuzzy. My stomach contracted and I vomited. I felt wetness on my thigh and thought I'd peed myself. I coughed, sucked up air, choked. I could feel myself suffocating, could feel my brain trying to get oxygen.

That's all I remember until I woke up in the Surgeon's Room.

***

When I woke up, I was on a bed. The room was bright and white.

Floodlights, that's what they call them. There were floodlights glaring down at us so that, when I closed my eyes, there was still this red fire. My entire body hurt. My lungs burned and when I coughed it sounded like it does when you have a cold that lingers far too long. My eyes hurt, stung, felt too dry. The exact feeling is hard to describe. Like every part of my body had been dried out. I would have done anything for some water.

Freddy was on a bed, too. It was bright, but there's always a degree to which your eyes adjust. I remember lifting my head up to look at him, but my head throbbed so badly I had to put it back down. I turned my head enough to see that his chest was rising and falling. That was enough for that moment.

The other room was taken up by a girl. Her face was turned away from me, but I thought I recognized her hair. I'll just tell you: her name was Madeline Davis. She was my friend.

I don't know how much time I spent on that cot when I first woke up. I remember turning over, trying to get my bearings. Shoving my head into the pillow to try and block out the light.

Eventually, Freddy and Madeline came too, as well. But we were in cells made of something—plastic, I think. We could put our hands up against the plastic, but we couldn't touch each other. Against the wall, out of our reach, were three orchids with long, hanging roots.

A reminder of what would happen to us, eventually.

I can't tell you how many hours I spent in that bed at first wondering who had been there before me. I wondered if Jeremy had been on my cot. I was afraid, yes. I was terrified of what would happen, but I also still ached for him. Part of me, a really fucked up and small part, wanted to see him again. I wondered what would happen when I died.

The Surgeon kept us there for what I think was an eternity before we saw him. There was no food and no water. I passed the time by turning on my side and counting as high as I could before I lost track. The floodlights never turned off. My eyes ached for sleep but, every time I felt myself drifting, a loud, high pitched siren sounded that threatened to burst my eardrums. All three of us would scream, covering our ears from the noise until it abated. By that time we had been yanked from sleep.

And so it went.

Finally, we saw him. I wish I could say that the Surgeon was gruesome or terrible. But he looked like any other adult. He had glasses and wore slacks, held his hands behind his back when he walked. He had a cruel half-smile that was always on his face as he tortured me. He was in his thirties, maybe forties. A grown man.

The first time we saw him, he offered us bottles of water. He slid them through little slots in the plastic cells. I drank mine greedily.

He left us. He didn't say a word.

And so it began.

The floodlights were so bright. So incredibly bright, that I almost didn't notice when the drugs started to change them. They tightened into thin streams of light, staring down at me. Then they turned to fire, burning my skin. Holding up my hands I could see the flesh melting off, and I began to scream. The floor of my cell was covered in the roots of orchids, and they reached for me with long waggling fingers. The very air itself was deadly. I could see that it had been changed from air to poison, and the few shadows that weren't eliminated by the floodlights turned to demons that watched me with piercing eyes.

I tried to look for Freddy. In the cell over, he was curled up on his side with his knees to his chest. I watched as his flesh ate at itself. His clothes and skin were dying before my eyes, curling into black ash and dribbling down on his bed. Madeline's hair was made of snakes, their eyes staring at me as they opened their mouth to hiss. But my own hair was made of snakes, too. I pulled at it, tried to yank it out. I scratched at my skin until blood ran from it. I screamed until my throat went numb.

This was the schedule: We were not allowed to sleep. The Surgeon would enter, give us drugged water, and leave. We were caught, then, between being drugged or going thirsty. My head hurt constantly. A corner of my cell—humiliating, horrible, I know—turned into my toilet. I pissed the bed when I was on the drugs. Eventually, I had sores along my legs. Watching Freddy and Madeline scream was almost worse than taking the drugs myself. There were times, after the effects had abated, that I thought of not drinking the water and letting myself die of thirst. I didn't know how long it would take. I knew it wouldn't be pleasant.

I didn't notice when the Surgeon came for Madeline the first time. Or when he came for Freddy. I was in the middle of a hallucination about the floodlights—those terrible fucking lights. I wanted to sleep. I wanted to cry. My entire body hurt. On the drugs, I could feel parts of myself that had no nerves—my hair hurt, my nails hurt, my eyelashes hurt. Every part of me on fire, itching, sweaty, smelly.

He came for me, eventually. It was always while we were on drugs. Eventually, we just went with him. It was better than being punched and kicked and dragged through our own shit to get there.

He would take us into a separate room and strap us to a table. There would be bands on our heads, our wrists, our ankles. That's where he would rape me, if he so saw fit. He would ask us questions about Middlefield and our parents and our friends. He never told us his name, or anything about him. But he said that it was the town's fault that this was happening to us.

I won't tell you everything he did to me, because it would take too long and be far too exhausting. I can tell you that he tortured us. He had tools, an entire array of them that he would spread out on a table before approaching us. He said he liked to watch us scream.

I don't know how much time passed. We were rarely allowed to sleep, and the drugs kept us confused. Sometimes it seemed like years went by. Other times, it felt like it had barely been a second between one visit to that table and the next.

I remember my last time. I was crying. I was so tired. I was in so much pain. He told me it would be over soon. The human body could only take so much, he said.

He would always tell us what he was going to do to us. "I'm going to collapse your lung now," he would tell me. "It will be uncomfortable. You will feel like you can't breathe."

He was always right, too. He asked me about Jeremy. He asked me about how we had sex and what it was like. He asked me about the town. He broke my finger when I didn't talk.

Drugs. Torture. Seeing the orchids on the wall. It formed a new time. A new era.

In what I have to think was the day before Freddy died, the Surgeon gave us a rare respite. We were all on our cots with the floodlights on. I mouthed the words to Bob Dylan songs to Freddy through the plastic barrier. Our full water bottles sat on the floor near our beds. It was a brief moment of lucidity. Freddy was crying. On the other side of me, Madeline had curled up and hugged her knees to her chest.

None of us had been able to speak to each other since we had been taken. None of us had felt the touch of another person on us. None of us were allowed to sleep.

Freddy died first. He was there and then he just… wasn't. The Surgeon took him and, when he brought Freddy back, Freddy was dead. The Surgeon dumped him on the floor of the plastic cell, in the midst of Freddy's own waste. My brother's head was turned toward me, and his eyes were open.

I was almost glad, because it meant that he wasn't going to suffer anymore. None of us were going to suffer anymore. It was time.

I'd given up by then. I didn't care. It was going to hurt, it was going to be unbearable. It was going to be torture. At one point I had refused to drink the drugged water he gave us. In return, the Surgeon had drugged my food. The living nightmares returned. I drank the water. What was the point of trying to resist?

He strangled Madeline in front of me. But he didn't strangle me.

Instead he picked up both the bodies—Madeline and my brother—and dumped them in my cell.

I cradled Freddy's head in my lap. I ran my fingers through his hair. No more water came, no more food. The Surgeon did not come and collect me to torture me after that. I was alone.

They tell me it was three days. Three days that I sat with my dead brother's head in my lap, cradling him and rocking back and forth, unable to sleep. "Soon we'll all be together," I would whisper to him. I sang songs to him. There were no drugs, but still sometimes I would look down at him and see his skin melting from his face. I would see his jaw turn into a gaping hole before my eyes. When I blinked, it was over.

What I'm told is that, because of the commotion I made, they were able to see the kind of car the Surgeon drove. They found clues, the G-Men in their black SUVs and tinted shades. The Surgeon went out after killing Freddy and Madeline and dumping them in my cell, got cornered, and had killed himself rather than given himself up.

But they found me. I don't remember what it was like, being found. There are many memories, fragmented and smashed to bits. Did I think they were angels? Did I think I was dead? It's hard to say now.

I stopped talking. For six months, they put me in a special hospital and I didn't talk. I developed severe agoraphobia. I would hide under my bed, clutching my knees to my chest and shaking. I had incessant nightmares where I would wake up clawing at the air, screaming, thrashing. Naturally, there were no orchids in that wing of the hospital.

The police tried to question me. They wanted to know everything that had happened to me. Every sordid detail. I would tell them, eventually, but not then. I had to be sedated again. I was told that I went far away. My parents thought that whatever the Surgeon had done to me had ripped the soul right out of me.

His name was Jonathan Miller. He was 46. When he was 18—ten years before I was born—his mother had found the remains of animals he had killed as a child buried in their yard. His father, William Miller, had driven him up to Lake Owyhee under the guise of a graduation present, knocked him unconscious, and thrown him in the lake to drown. Then they'd claimed he went up by himself, that it had been an accident. The town had mourned Jonathan Miller, and then moved on. The doctors told me this while I was still mute, staring at the ceiling of the hospital room. The Millers had been arrested.

I didn't go to Freddy's funeral. I didn't go to any of them. Eventually, I spoke again. I drank water without fear. I took a step outside, and then another. I let my father hug me.

My parents sold the farm. Everyone did. No one wanted to live in that town anymore. The government came through and bought all the land and turned it into some sort of factory.

We moved to California. The warm part. My room had blackout curtains so that, whenever the light became too much, I could close them and experience the dark. I never *got over* it, I guess you could say; I healed. The scars on my body disgusted me less and less. I met a man who lets me sleep with a gun in the nightstand drawer and who holds me when I wake up screaming.

I wish I could say something else came from it—I wish I could say Freddy's death meant something. 8 children died at the hands of Jonathan Miller. It destroyed my life. I can't tell you the number of times I've thought about killing myself. But the thing that keeps me from doing it is Freddy. I got to live, and he didn't. He died. Madeline died. I sat with their dead bodies for three days before they found me.

So I stay alive for Freddy. Because he didn't get a choice. For better or for worse, I do.

About The Creators

Ha-Yong Bak

Ha-Yong Bak is an editor for a conference organizing company, an author, and a person that likes to get demolished at basketball. He does seem to say a lot of random things throughout the day, but it's all in the name of research. His vivid imagination will either help him become a successful writer or fall into a pit of absolute lunacy.

J.M. Flynn

My nom de plume is J.M. Flynn and I write from creaky old farmhouse in a remote corner of Ireland. Hobbies include an unhealthy interest in lycanthropy and swimming. You can read more of my work at https://www.reddit.com/user/Clarimonde/submitted/.

Conor Murray

Conor is a stand-up comedian and game designer who lives in Dublin, Ireland. He mostly does his surreal stand-up act in Ireland and the UK. He also created a small narrative driven VR game called "Sanctuary VR" for Oculus Rift, which is available for free on steam, go check it out. Recently he has taken to writing horror stories and he is still surprised people actually like to read them. You can see his stand-up on his YouTube channel: https://www.youtube.com/watch?v=4XAgDv06gBw&t=83s and play his free game on steam: http://store.steampowered.com/app/565730/Sanctuary_VR/.

D.J. Creamer

D J Creamer is an up and coming reddit author who won the February 2017 monthly contest. You can find more of his work at reddit.com/u/opinionson.

Preston Yates

Just some guy who likes writing stuff. I'm working on being an author someday but, until I have that going on, you can find some of my work on Reddit under u/TheCrystalGem.

Aaron Hilgen

My name is Aaron Hilgen, or Ahilgen to those on Reddit. I'm married with a beautiful red-haired demon spawn, er... daughter. During the day I maintain and repair hospital equipment to save lives while killing them off in story form by night. You can see more of his work at reddit.com/r/AHilgenWrites.

Caitlin Spice

Caitlin Spice is a Wellingtonian author with a complicated relationship with writing. Primarily a short story enthusiast, she has some 300+ original works posted online on various Reddit writing forums, but has also recently published a collection of thematic works in a book titled 'The Silver Path', which also features artwork from some talented local and international artists. You can read more of her work at facebook.com/CMScandreth/ and https://www.reddit.com/r/HallowdineLibrary/.

Tanja Simone

Tanja Simone is a horror writer based out of Norway and Sweden. Her style of writing focuses on descriptions and atmosphere while trying to connect to the darkness and madness we all carry within us. She finds inspiration in music, Lovecraft and roleplaying games. You can see more of her work at https://www.facebook.com/tanjasimonehorror and www.reddit.com/u/tanjasimone.

D0nutblink

D0nutblink is surprisingly not a baked good but rather a short horror fiction author. She spends her spare time singing, crafting and dreaming up horrible nightmares. She has a great heart . . . although I'm not sure whose it is. You can see more of D0nutblink's work at www.facebook.com/d0nutblink and www.reddit.com/d0nutblink.

Eve Ben Ezra

Eve Ben Ezra is an aspiring author, human rights activist, and educator. She lives with her cat.

Kristopher J. Patten

Kristopher is usually an author, except when he's wearing his editor's hat. In addition to running the monthly contests on NoSleep, he pulled a double duty and edited this issue. Any mistakes found within should have been caught by his watchful eye. Direct all complaints to him. You can find his fiction on https://kristopherjpatten.wordpress.com/.

Ashley Franz Holzmann

Ashley is usually a writer, but continues to be sucked into the other duties of helping his fellow authors. He did the cover for this issue and the internal formatting. He's a writer, though. He swears! You can check out his creative endeavors at asforclass.com.

www.ingramcontent.com/pod-product-compliance
Lightning Source LLC
Chambersburg PA
CBHW022147170626
46807CB00005B/2112